The Kryfanga[...] [...] [...]seback. They'd got the [...] [...]ver costume and had picked up t[...] [...] not far from the riverbank. Keeping close to the shadows, they had the longing for blood again – as if the flesh from the four thousand Scots hadn't abated their appetite. Their faces were concealed, sunk deep into their hooded cloaks, although one of the Kryfangan was revealed by the stark moonlight as its horse strayed momentarily off course. Two pip-like eyes lurked in the depths of the dark, vacant sockets. They glowed red. Puritan red. Jagged, thin teeth, like those of a rat, overlaid its withered lower lip.

It pulled on the reins harshly, almost snapping the horse's neck. The beast duly obeyed and cantered back onto the concealed path.

The Kryfangan hissed, foul breath misting in the pale moonlight.

An Abaddon Books™ Publication

www.abaddonbooks.com

abaddon@rebellion.co.uk

First published in 2007 by Abaddon Books™, Rebellion Intellectual
Property Limited, The Studio, Brewer Street, Oxford, OX1 1QN, UK.

Distributed in the US and Canada by SCB Distributors,15608 South
Century New Drive, Gardena, CA 90248, USA.

10 9 8 7 6 5 4 3 2 1

Editor: Jonathan Oliver

Cover: Mark Harrison

Design: Simon Parr & Luke Preece

Marketing and PR: Keith Richardson

Creative Director and CEO: Jason Kingsley

Chief Technical Officer: Chris Kingsley

ISBN: 978-1-905437-41-2

Printed in the UK by CPI Bookmarque, Croydon, CRO 4TD

TOMES OF THE DEAD

THE DEVIL'S PLAGUE

Mark Beynon

Abaddon
Books

WWW.ABADDONBOOKS.COM

PROLOGUE

The Gobi Desert - Mongolia
1204

The unrelenting sun baked the blood red sand of the battlefield, forming a burgundy coloured mirage that seemed to shimmer across the wasteland. Dismembered bodies were scattered across its boiling grains as far as the eye could see, no one was left standing or moving, although the occasional spasm would shoot through a corpse as a final act of existence – in this lifetime at least.

Genghis Khan had watched the proceedings from the comfort of his saddle on the built-up rocky precipice that was looming high above the battlefield. He had seen his army tear the Naimans limb from limb, finally defeating the last of the tribes who stood in the way of the unification of Mongolia. Although he was a hardened mercenary, Khan was seldom accustomed to such barbaric savagery, and as he ran a tired hand down his long greying beard, his thoughts turned to his old friend Jamuqa, the traitor, deserter and conspirator. Jamuqa had somehow managed to flee the battlefield and the swords of Khan's Subutai. Khan was loath to allow him to escape and join another clan of rogue Merkits, although he sought comfort in the fact that he couldn't possibly have got far in the blazing heat. And the Subutai would have been hard on his heels, their dark steeds somehow immune to the searing temperatures of the Mongolian desert.

He tugged on the reins of his sandy brown stallion, encouraging it into a trot along the dusty path and down onto the blistering Gobi sand.

The Gobi Desert seemed a most fitting place to have such a beleaguered battle. According to local legend it was created when a Mongolian chief, highly skilful in the art of black magic, was forced to flee his village with the Chinese army in close pursuit. As he left, he muttered 'black words' and the land dried up and died behind him, leaving nothing for the Chinese but a moribund and arid wasteland.

Khan's horse ambled its way back towards the camp on the outskirts of the steppe, its dark brown grassland scorched by the swollen sun. Well aware of the legend of the Gobi and with it in mind, Khan remembered his peculiar meeting in the busy marketplace with the man named Cipher, not one week prior to the battle. Market folk didn't take kindly to outsiders, and his appearance had certainly been different – his pale, ashen countenance, bereft of any hair, was not befitting the archetypal Mongolian. Yet amidst the clamour of market day, no one seemed to notice him, and Khan was left with the strangest feeling that he was the only person to observe him at all. Still, Cipher was fluent in Mongolian and had been true to his word, promising Khan a fearsome army to help him defeat the Naimans. Khan had decided to call them his Subutai, fearing their original name to be heretical.

Indeed, in Mongolian the word Kryfangan was roughly translated as 'dark warriors'. And Khan was still unsure of what he had to offer as payment for such an army.

He couldn't sleep. The heat was too much for Khan to bear, and he found himself tossing and turning in his rough-hewn bed on top of a straw mattress. On the few occasions he had found himself drifting off, he was suddenly struck by the image of Cipher's harrowing face sunk deep in his brown cloak; his ghostly white features and dark, rheumy eyes projecting a deranged, terrifying stare as they looked directly back at him. It jolted him into waking, almost as if his heart had skipped a beat. He attempted to reason with himself, angry that this strange man had forged some sort of demonic hold over him.

His large, expansive tent felt empty, and he soon found himself longing for some companionship to take his mind off the delirium. The slightest noise or rustle from the wilderness outside would make him jump; fearing the vast number of darkened pools that surrounded the tent had something untoward lurking within them. He soon came to the rational conclusion that it was nothing more than a rattlesnake or a jerboa creeping through the sand outside.

Khan sat upright and threw some water from the stone basin by his bedside over his face. He wasn't surprised to find that even the water was hot, and he quickly dried his face with a discarded robe. The slender moonlight shafted into the tent, and Khan could see the trail of blood that he had left on the robe. He ran his hand over his nose and was surprised to find droplets of blood falling from his nostrils. Another nosebleed, just like the one he had on the night he met Cipher. As he held the robe to his face and lay back down, he could hear another rustle of sand by his ear, his mattress having been pressed hard against the pigskin of the tent. The rustling soon turned into irregular footsteps. Khan sprang from his mattress, placed his fur robe over his muscular body and unsheathed his jagged sword. Ever so gently, he lifted the flap of the tent and eased his way into the warm night. A light rain was beginning to fall from the sky as he shuffled along the width of the pigskin. Strange, he thought to himself, it hasn't rained in months. The moon illuminated a set of uneven footprints in the sand and Khan knew full well that they didn't belong to him.

He clutched the ivory handle of his sword with both hands and inched his way round the corner of the tent, the vast desert opening up before him. There was a sudden, frantic panting and Khan peered into the shadows as a solitary figure slowly emerged.

Khan could scarcely believe his eyes. "Jamuqa?"

Jamuqa collapsed in a heap by Khan's feet; his eyes wide with fear. Beads of sweat ran down his bald head and settled in his beard. He tried to speak, but the words broke apart.

Khan appreciated just how terrified Jamuqa must be for him to seek refuge in his camp, yet at the same time he knew he should kill the traitor. But he could see from his eyes that he was palpitating with fear, and he felt it best he heard Jamuqa's explanation before deciding his fate. He shook him roughly by the shoulder, hoping that it would propel some sense into him. Jamuqa pointed, trembling, into the gloom and passed out.

Khan peered into the darkness. He couldn't see or hear a thing, not even the sound of wildlife that would usually grace the Gobi night with their chorus of noises. Conscious that his generals and the Subutai were camped on the other side of the rocky steppe, he tapped his sword down onto the remnants of the campfire, the fading orange embers jumping into the air and lighting up the immediate vicinity. He had always requested his privacy, although tonight he wished that the others were close at hand.

In the meagre light of the campfire, Khan was able to discern what appeared to be the outline of a cluster of figures against the sands, not far from the camp. It wasn't until he heard the coarse moaning that resonated from their dead mouths that he felt the prickling of fear creep down his spine. As he looked closely, he was struck with an image that left him as frightened as the shaken man by his feet. He blinked and looked again. His eyes confirmed the very worst of his fears. As the figures became visible, not less than ten yards away, he could see that they were the Naimans, the same army who had been slain in front of him hours earlier. Their improper lurching struck the deepest of fears into the heart of the Khan, and for the first time in his life, he turned to run.

As he clambered up the steppe and passed over its wispy grassland, he knew in his heart that this fearsome horde was Cipher's doing. He looked back over his shoulder and could see the Naimans tearing clumps of flesh from Jamuqa before ransacking his tent. He was unaware that they had already scented him and hungered for his flesh as well.

He was left with the strangest sensation, almost as if a voice in the back of his mind was desperately trying to warn him of something.

Cipher has your soul, he could have sworn he heard it say.

CHAPTER ONE

The Battle of Worcester
3rd September, 1651

The battlefield was stained a dark reddish brown and the once green meadows were littered with corpses. Blood coursed through the Rivers Severn and Teme, whilst the aptly named Red Hill was just that.

Oliver Cromwell surveyed the carnage before him with a wry smile. It was whispered from the narrowest street in London to the vastest field in Edinburgh that Cromwell was the anti-Christ. Closer inspection of the battlefield would only add credence to such rumour mongering. None of those lying dead and decapitated wore red. The Puritans' colour. Cromwell's colour. Instead, almost four thousand Royalist Scots lay lifeless, eight hundred of which came from the Clan MacLeod.

One would have been forgiven for believing that Cromwell had single-handedly slain his enemy as none of his soldiers were in sight, just a handful of his Generals, who had the unenviable task of sifting through the dead in search of one man.

"Have you found him?" Cromwell yelled in the direction of Thomas Harrison, a runtish Major General, aiding those sorting through the nearby body parts.

"No sign of him yet, sir." Harrison hadn't the

heart to tell him that those lying dead were so badly mutilated they were virtually indistinguishable from one another.

"Have your men help you."

"My men are sleeping, sir. I fear the scent and sight of blood would set them off again." Harrison spoke with a faint sign of trepidation in his voice.

"Quite right, Harrison," replied Cromwell, reassuringly.

Even though his pact with the Devil had cost him his friendship with his dear friend, Thomas Fairfax, Cromwell's leadership and authority were no longer in question. He was a far cry from the once obscure and inexperienced Cambridgeshire MP – he was now one of the main power brokers in Parliament. Cromwell had played a decisive role in the revolution during the winter of 1649, which saw the trial and execution of King Charles I and the abolition of the Monarchy and the House of Lords.

The rumours circulating in the taverns would hold Cromwell's decision to execute the King as proof of his diabolism. As a result, so they said, the Devil has covered Cromwell's face in hideous warts.

Those drunken sots would never know how right they were.

"I've found him!" Harrison could barely contain his excitement. He stood triumphantly over a bloodied heap, seemingly identical to thousands of other bloodied heaps. Cromwell flicked the reins of his horse, prompting it to a smart gallop. He marvelled at the thought of being the man responsible for the deaths of two Kings, father and son.

That will send those Royalist bastards back to Edinburgh without a Monarch!

As he dismounted, he examined the evidence – the Royal coat of arms engraved on the man's chest plate. This had to be Charles. The arms of England and France were placed in the first and fourth quarters, the arms of Scotland were placed in the second quarter and the arms of Ireland in the third. The same coat of arms that had belonged to his father, Cromwell noted.

"Well done, Harrison. Well done indeed. We have our man. Send word to the committee that Charles Stuart is dead and the war is over."

However, Cromwell had underestimated his adversary. Little did he know that prior to the battle Charles had switched his armour with a decoy. He had fought side by side with the common man, not leading from the front as a King would. And little did Cromwell know that hiding up in the branches of a nearby oak tree, with the Scottish soldier John Middleton, was none other than Charles Stuart, King of Scotland and rightful heir to the throne of England.

By the time the last of Cromwell's Generals had left the battlefield, a deep hole had been dug and the dead bodies hurled into the dark pit. A vulgar burial not befitting a pauper. The sun was setting in the red sky, mirroring the earth below. It would take months, maybe years for the stains of battle to be washed away.

In the deepest part of the grave, something moved.

A twitch at first, the merest of spasms. The dead soldier with his four thousand comrades piled high around him. In him seemed to linger a vivid spark of vitality, some faint sign of consciousness. And then he blinked.

And so did his dead comrade next to him.

CHAPTER TWO

The Mug House, Bewdley

Cave Underhill shivered as the biting Autumnal wind gripped his young bones. He rubbed his hands together furiously in a vain attempt to generate some warmth as the brisk wind blew his thick tousled hair into his eyes. Although only twelve years of age, Underhill's demeanour suggested he was a good deal older.

He could hear the performance from within; several inaudible lines of dialogue followed by a groan of audience disapproval. They were performing Salmacida Spolia tonight, one of William Davenant's own poems, notoriously despised by audiences of rich and poor alike.

Underhill took comfort in the fact that one day he'd be an actor and some other poor bastard could freeze to death as sentry. Yet he knew his place and he owed his life to Davenant for sparing him the ignominy of returning to the Fleet Street poorhouse. As an orphan, Davenant was the closest thing to a father he'd ever had. He never knew his parents, although he later discovered that he had a sister. Underhill had come to the poorhouse a weak and helpless two year old and was forced to work as soon as he could walk.

He smiled contently; it might have been bitterly cold, but keeping watch outside the tavern was paradise in comparison to his previous job. As a Saltpetre Boy he had had to break into premises or dig up latrines to collect as much urine as possible for the manufacture of saltpetre, which in turn was used to make gunpowder. The Saltpetre Company's slogan – 'We're taking the piss' – caused much hilarity amongst the actors, but it was breaking into Davenant's house that had changed Underhill's life. Davenant had found him trying to escape through his loft, took pity on the poor wretch and offered him a job within his troupe of players. He had to endure frequent jibes and keeping guard wasn't much of a job, but he had found a family, and while Cromwell and his Puritan hordes insisted on banning theatre, someone had to keep a look out.

It was ironic, he thought. Why would a man like Cromwell, a man rumoured to have a close affiliation with the Devil himself, want to close down the theatre, which had long been known as Satan's Chapel? He admired the fine architecture of the building overlooking him: a smart tavern which dominated the narrow street. The theatre might have been abolished, but these buildings left a proud legacy. Intricate carvings depicting bear baiting and cock fighting were embossed in the wooden spandrels. Cromwell had dispensed with those frivolities too, along with 'lewd and heathen' maypole dancing. And Christmas! From the perspective of a child, there was no greater sin. A real killjoy, he thought.

"The rich make full of avarice as pride."

William Davenant stood upon a crudely built stage within the tavern's dingy cellar. The willowy flames of a rough torch hung in an iron bracket revealed the grime and residue clinging to the two-hundred year old stone. The stench of rank ale and sweat was almost too much for Davenant to bear, yet he continued to perform with admirable vigour. His ruggedly handsome quality was well hidden underneath his vulgar, ill-fitted costume and ludicrously garish make-up.

"Like graves, or swallowing seas, unsatisfied." He gestured flamboyantly much to the ridicule of his audience, comprised solely of drunken revellers huddled together in a darkened corner.

"Call yourself an actor? You're bloody 'opeless," bellowed one of the revellers.

Davenant ignored the goading and carried on. "From poor men's fortunes, never from their own."

"We want Shakespeare!" The outspoken reveller had pushed his way to the front, swaying drunkenly from side to side. His taunt drew one or two sniggers from his fellow dwellers.

"Well you can't have him," hissed Davenant, breaking temporarily out of character. He turned pleadingly to Thomas Betterton, a fellow actor stood at the side of the stage. Betterton was young, brash and carried himself with an air of complacency. He shrugged his shoulders nonchalantly, much to Davenant's annoyance.

Davenant had discovered Betterton's precocious talent on the London stage. He was playing Claudio in his company's underground presentation of *Much Ado About Nothing*. The show was abysmal, but Davenant had seen sufficient potential in Betterton's performance to offer him a place within the players. When the majority of Betterton's company were conveniently arrested and imprisoned in the Tower after Cromwell's men had received a tip-off from a vagrant, he leapt at the chance of working with

Davenant, a real name on the circuit. However, Davenant's insistence on performing his own plays and poems coupled with the ensuing heckling had begun to take its toll on Betterton. He wanted Shakespeare too! And he wasn't afraid to let Davenant know it.

Underhill blew warm air into his freezing hands. He could hear muffled bickering emanating from the cellar. He was used to such an occurrence. The previous week in Ipswich, Davenant had called the landlord of some boisterous watering hole a "toothless simpleton". It had sparked a small riot in which Davenant and his fellow players were forced to escape through a small priest hole hidden within the chimney. He ignored the quarrelling and proceeded to sit on his hands. He'd rather they were numb than icy cold.

A faint pounding resonated along the narrow street. Underhill got to his feet gingerly. He craned his neck to peer into the darkness. Five or six mounted shadows moved furtively, yet rapidly towards him. As the shadows drew closer, the noise became louder – a distinct pounding of hooves clattering along the stones, followed by a high-pitched hissing between razor-sharp teeth. Cromwell's men.

The Kryfangan!

Davenant had always told Underhill that the play was not to be disturbed unless it was "of the utmost importance". Well this was of the utmost importance. The Kryfangan had been trailing Davenant for months and Cromwell had even gone so far as to offer a reward for his capture. Underhill could imagine numerous members of tonight's audience willing to make themselves a fast shilling.

He wasted no time in bounding inside the tavern and descending the rickety wooden steps that led down into the cellar. He could see that the play was in disarray. Davenant was appealing for calm whilst Betterton was seemingly egging the revellers on.

"Cromwell's men! They're outside!" Underhill was surprised to find his shrill appeal generating such silence, as he was far more used to being ignored completely. In an instant, every man within the cellar had turned to face him, unsure of their next move. "Well don't just stand there! They're coming!"

En masse, the revellers pushed past Underhill. Davenant and Betterton hurriedly gathered together their belongings, although in the confusion, a solitary silver costume was clumsily left behind. Once in the tavern, Davenant slammed down the cellar hatch, dislodging dust and grime as it bounced off the timber floor.

Rushing outside, they darted along the cobblestones and into the pool of darkness that enveloped the end of the street. Davenant looked back only once. Once was enough. He could just make out the dull red eyes belonging to the Kryfangan as they mercilessly smashed open the tavern door.

Charles Fleetwood, Cromwell's Major General, strode inside. Fleetwood was in his thirties, tall, imposing. His cropped red hair complemented his notoriously fiery temperament. His fellow Generals,

Lambert and Desborough, followed closely behind. Giving the distinct impression of being the hired help, they stood menacingly either side of Fleetwood. All three men were dressed head to toe in black Puritan robes, hats, jerkins and boots – a look that had become synonymous with evil.

Fleetwood scowled as he inspected the ageing tavern. The Kryfangan had already torn it to pieces. Broken glass and furniture littered the floor.

"Actors! The stench of vanity is overwhelming." Fleetwood's eyes wandered around the room until they fell on the hatch in the corner. "The cellar!"

He marched over to the hatch, shards of glass crunching beneath his heavy boots, and flung open the door. He clambered down the rickety staircase, a cascade of moonlight pursuing him. Desborough followed, handing Fleetwood a lantern which he duly held aloft, illuminating the makeshift stage.

Fleetwood turned sharply to Lambert, who was half way down the staircase. "Have your men scour the area. They can't have got far."

Lambert nodded in acknowledgement before hauling himself back up. Fleetwood and Desborough paced onto the stage. The silver costume glistened in the lantern light, catching Fleetwood's attention immediately. He knelt down to pick it up before thrusting it in Desborough's direction, a half-smile crossing his lips.

"Davenant!"

Davenant, Betterton and Underhill emerged from the end of a narrow alleyway, fighting their way through the thick withes and strands of ivy that covered the entrance like a giant spider's web.

Davenant, still dressed in his ridiculous costume, panted from the exertion. "I've had it with these tavern dwellers," he said, in between breaths.

"Well, if you gave them what they wanted," replied Betterton, typically antagonistic.

Davenant stopped dead in his tracks. He turned to Betterton, wearing a face like thunder. "I've told you a thousand times! We will not perform Shakespeare in my company."

Betterton sneered at the remark. It was hard to take a man seriously when he's dressed up like a workhouse whore. "What about us? Don't we at least have a say in the matter?"

"You forget it is I who pays your wage and you'll do as I say. Now, if we're done arguing?" Davenant strode off, Underhill following close behind.

"We'd perform Shakespeare with Killigrew!"

Davenant stopped and faced Betterton once more. This time he'd really struck a chord. "That is because Killigrew is a fat, illiterate windbag. You're far better off performing my plays and learning your craft with me." Davenant was incandescent, even behind the thick layer of white stage make-up. "Besides, Killigrew couldn't write a lurid limerick if his life depended on it!"

Betterton shot Underhill a glance. They both grinned.

Davenant hated Thomas Killigrew more than he hated the lowly tavern dwellers. During the reign of Charles, Davenant and Killigrew had vied for the King's patronage. After much mudslinging and bad-tempered poetry, Davenant was rewarded with the office of poet-laureate and was subsequently knighted by the King. And then the Civil War broke out, ruining the aspirations of playwrights and actors across the country.

A despondent mule, attached to a rickety old cart, sat conspicuously at the side of a woodland path, whilst a stout, middle-aged man kept guard.

"Over here! Mister Davenant, Sir!" The man, George Turnbull, was Davenant's trusted manservant. Davenant put his finger to his lips, appealing for silence. Turnbull was a simpleton and his behaviour somewhat childlike; a stark contrast to his formidable bulk.

It was a marvel he hadn't caught the pox in his hedonistic days. Davenant had found him loitering outside a house of ill repute. On this occasion, he'd got himself into trouble with money, so Davenant generously settled his bill. In return, Turnbull pledged his allegiance and remained his dogsbody a decade later. Davenant knew only too well what happened when someone crossed Turnbull, with many an unruly theatregoer having paid the price for heckling. On more than one occasion he'd had to haul Turnbull off a drunkard before he beat him to death. Shame he hadn't been in The Mug House, Davenant thought. There would have been no heckling tonight.

Turnbull proceeded to wave his arms in the air in an effort to catch Davenant's attention.

"Yes, I can see you, you great lump," said Davenant under his breath. He turned to Betterton and Underhill who were ambling behind him. "Not a word of our narrow escape to the others."

As they reached the mule and cart, a striking young girl emerged from the darkness. Her long auburn hair ran all the way to the base of her spine. Her legs were as long as paradise and her bosom the prize for having made the voyage. She had a kind, caring face coupled with a sumptuous beauty.

"So? How did it go?" asked Elizabeth, Davenant's only daughter.

"As well as could be expected. The Mug House is hardly the Globe," replied Davenant, trying to loosen his costume.

"You should have given them Shakespeare," said Elizabeth innocently. Betterton let out a sly cackle.

"Elizabeth, my dear, could you pass me my clothes?"

"Either give them Shakespeare, or let us girls on the stage." Elizabeth handed Davenant his doublet. It was a shabby item of apparel; the elbows faded to a matt sheen where they had rested on the tables in so many inns.

"The last thing we need is the fairer sex treading the boards," replied Davenant, disappearing behind a nearby tree to get changed.

Betterton waited until Davenant was out of sight before sidling up to Elizabeth. "I missed you tonight," he said, running his hand gently down the silk of her skirt.

"Not here. Not now." She pushed him away, conscious of her father's gaze. Davenant had caught them together before in a deserted barn on the outskirts of Lowestoft. On that occasion Elizabeth had to plead with him not to fire Betterton, yet she could understand her father's controlling nature. Davenant's wife had died shortly after giving birth to Elizabeth and, although he had resented her at first, he soon became the devoted father, not least because of her startling resemblance to her mother.

Although he rated Betterton as a young actor, the thought of him courting Elizabeth made him feel sick to his stomach. She was far too pretty, far too perfect for a young upstart like him. In Davenant's eyes, she belonged to a Prince – or someone with vast sums of money to keep him in his dotage.

The Kryfangan approached stealthily on horseback. They'd got the scent from the silver costume and had picked up the trail not far from the riverbank. Keeping close to the shadows, they had the longing for blood again – as if the flesh from the four thousand Scots hadn't abated their appetite. Their faces were concealed, sunk deep into their hooded cloaks, although one of the Kryfangan was revealed by the stark moonlight as its horse strayed momentarily off course. Two little pip-like eyes lurked in the depths of the dark, vacant sockets. They glowed red. Puritan red. Jagged, thin teeth, like those of a rat, overlaid its withered lower lip.

It pulled on the reins harshly, almost snapping the horse's neck. The beast duly obeyed and cantered back onto the concealed path.

The Kryfangan hissed, foul breath misting in the pale moonlight.

It began to rain. Davenant wanted to get back on the road and as far away from Bewdley as possible. He could have sworn he heard a shrill hissing when he was getting changed behind the tree and was mindful that Cromwell's men were on the lookout for him.

"Let's move out," he commanded.

Turnbull sprang into action, gathering together the few belongings scattered across the path: a lantern, Davenant's gaudy costume, several wooden platters and a spare jerkin. Underhill urinated into a nearby bush. He had been needing that for hours.

Suddenly, a branch snapped close by.

Davenant snatched the lantern from Turnbull and waved it around, lighting up the immediate vicinity. There was nothing.

Elizabeth sought refuge in the unsteady wooden cart. Betterton followed. Underhill didn't move a muscle. They'd rehearsed a drill to prepare themselves for times like these. Underhill cursed his luck – the drill didn't involve him pissing into close at hand foliage.

Another branch snapped. This time Davenant was able to pinpoint its location – it came from above. He reluctantly shone the lantern upwards, half terrified of what he'd find prowling in the treetops.

To his surprise, he found two men staring back at him. One of them was a King.

CHAPTER THREE

The Sun Inn, Long Marston
July 1st, 1644

The crowded inn fell silent as Cromwell stepped through the warped doorway. He glared at a group of his soldiers who were daring enough to partake in a session of ale the night before the most significant battle of their lives. They would incur his wrath later, for right now he was in dire need of a drink himself. As he left them grimacing with embarrassment, he slipped into a private room where he could be assured of some peace and quiet. The timid server, little more than a boy, trembled as he poured rank ale from a decaying cask into a rusty tankard.

There was a time when Cromwell would have thrown the ale, which bore a remarkable similarity to cat's piss, back in the server's face. But not tonight, tonight he received it gratefully and took a hearty swig.

"No one's going to steal it, my dear man."

The guttural voice was unfamiliar to Cromwell, but the tone and choice of words lead him to the conclusion that he was either a brave, foolish man, or that he was unaware of who he was talking to. Either way, Cromwell turned to chastise him for rudely interrupting his respite. He got as far as pointing an angry finger at the crooked man sat in front of him before becoming lost in the dark eyes that prowled deep within the hooded cloak.

"Do I know you?" Cromwell whispered.

"No," the creature chuckled. "But I know you."

CHAPTER FOUR

Bewdley Woods
6th September, 1651

"Good evening, gentlemen." The voice carried a peculiar accent, a strange marriage of French, Scottish and Flemish. Davenant could just about make out a dishevelled mop of dark hair which fell around his ears and a thin moustache which lined his lip.

"Who are you?" Davenant held the lantern aloft and was conscious that a nervous tremble had crept into his arm, jerking the light ever so slightly.

"That is not how you address a King," replied the dark haired man.

Davenant stood, open-mouthed. "You will forgive my ignorance then," he said, finally. "But who exactly are you the King of?"

The dark haired man smiled warmly, seemingly unoffended by Davenant's blunt retort. "My name is Charles Stuart, son of a murdered King and rightful heir to the thrones of England, Scotland and Ireland. And I would very much appreciate it if you could help us down."

It was Davenant's turn to smile. "Charles Stuart, you say?" There was a hint of cynicism in his tone that didn't go unnoticed.

"Yes and this gentleman alongside me is John Middleton, a commander in my army."

Davenant caught his first glimpse of the other man – a tall, sturdy type with a huge florid moustache that ran the width of his face. "So, if you are who you say you are, how do you know that we are not officers in

Cromwell's army? You are taking an almighty risk in drawing attention to yourselves, are you not?"

"Well," replied Charles, "you are wearing stage make-up. I am well aware that the quality of Cromwell's army has dropped as of late, but I am sure that even he would draw the line at drafting up men with a penchant for cross-dressing. Or is that your new uniform?"

Betterton and Elizabeth emerged cautiously from the cart, sensing that any potential danger had passed. Underhill, who had watched the entire episode from his nearby pissing position, was trying his damnedest not to laugh. Charles had rendered Davenant speechless, which was quite an accomplishment.

"Should we not help them down, Sir?" It was Turnbull who eventually broke the silence. Davenant grudgingly nodded, still unable to find his tongue.

"May I know the name of our saviour?" Charles began his descent.

"My name is William Davenant and this hulk is my manservant, George Turnbull." Charles, who was in the process of clambering down from the tree, checked himself. He peered down at Davenant with an incredulous look. "William Davenant? Sir William Davenant?"

"You know of me? I *am* an actor of some repute."

"Of course I know of you. After all, it was my father who knighted you." Charles jumped the rest of the way down, and stumbled as he hit the ground. "I can't thank you enough," he said wearily, as Davenant helped him to his feet. "I had almost forgotten what it was like to stand on solid ground. We've been sheltering in that tree for far too long."

Turnbull turned his attention to Middleton who

had started to vacate his position in the branches. Davenant shone his lantern in Charles' direction, wanting to take a closer look at the self-proclaimed King standing before him. To his astonishment he recognised the eyes almost immediately. They were piercingly dark and surrounded by the familiar hooded eyelids that made them appear to be half closed.

Davenant was immediately contrite, dropping to one knee. "Sir, you have my most humble apologies. Your likeness to your father is startling."

Charles grinned as he pulled him to his feet. "You have no reason to kneel before me, Sir William. I am led to believe that you were one of my father's closest allies. And he didn't have a great many of them towards the end." He extended his hand to Davenant, who received it warmly. "Perhaps, later on, you will indulge me with some stories of my father," he continued. "The tales I have heard hardly paint him in the greatest light."

"I would be delighted to share them with you, my Lord, but not here and not now. We must leave these woods immediately. I fear Cromwell's troops are not far behind us."

Charles nodded solemnly. "What do you suggest we do? I must return to France and we are far from Portsmouth."

There was a loud thud as Middleton and Turnbull came crashing to the ground. The two colossal men picked themselves up gingerly and brushed themselves down.

"So, what have you done to incur the wrath of Cromwell? It seems we share more than just a mutual respect for my father," said Charles.

"We are a troupe of actors, a company of players, my Lord. That does not fit in with Cromwell's miserable regime. Not to mention that I ran several missions for your father during the early years of the war that earned me some time in the Tower. But I digress, my Lord. We must make haste."

"Then we must leave with you."

"Is that wise, my Lord? Surely it would do neither of us any good should we be discovered together." The thought of being found harbouring England's most wanted man filled Davenant with dread. There would be no prison sentence this time around, he thought. He'd surely lose his head.

"We can help each other. Middleton and I can perform with you, undercover of course. In return, you can provide us with safe passage to Portsmouth."

"You can act?" Davenant was genuinely taken aback.

"I can." It was Middleton who replied, much to everyone's surprise. He carried a broad Scottish accent. "Don't seem so surprised," he continued. "I have performed in *The Tempest*, *Hamlet* and *Othello* back home."

"You see," said Charles, "we have plenty of experience between us!"

"We don't do Shakespeare," replied Betterton, piping up.

"That is irrelevant because we cannot take you with us." Davenant was becoming increasingly frustrated. "It's just too great a risk."

"If you won't do this for me, then do it for my father," pleaded Charles. "We need your help, Sir William. You know these roads far better than we. Your assistance at this difficult time will not be forgotten when I return to claim the throne, I promise."

Davenant considered his words for a moment. "Very well," he finally said. "Now let's go!"

The sun was beginning to rise and the sound of birdsong had started to emanate from the woodland they had just left behind. Davenant was relieved to have escaped it unscathed – it had filled him with dread and a dark sense of foreboding from the moment he had set foot in it. And those dark red eyes were still weighing heavily on his raddled mind. Keen to put as much distance between themselves and Bewdley as possible, Davenant's group trudged wearily onwards. No one had spoken for hours, as if in some way speech would sap whatever energy they had left in their somnolent bodies.

It was Underhill's legs that buckled first.

"We need to rest now," said Charles.

"Where are we?" Davenant turned to Turnbull, who handed him a rough map scrawled upon a tattered piece of parchment, before tending to Underhill. "We're here, on the outskirts of Ombersley." He said, answering his own question.

"My sister lives in Ombersley." Underhill piped up. "She can put us up for a while."

"I wouldn't wish to impose," replied Davenant. "And I doubt that she will have room for all of us."

"I'm sure we can squeeze in. If not, there's a perfectly good tavern in town that will put us up."

Davenant noted the blatant desperation in his

tone that longed for rest. "Very well," he said. "Ombersley it is."

As the group joined the narrow thoroughfare which ran through the heart of Ombersley, they witnessed the working day creak into action. The noise and bustle began to grow into an incessant din with every passing cart, wagon, coach and opening shutter. Merchants and tradesmen spilled from dilapidated hovels to take their places on the street. All kinds of trades were on offer – butchers, bakers, barbers and blacksmiths. Within an hour, Ombersley was thrumming. A gaggle of nearby whores had cleverly set up shop adjacent to the Kings Arms, an imposing building that dominated the narrow street, its steep-pitched roof almost touching its opposite neighbours'. The whores, who were flaunting their wares in full view of mothers and children, waited patiently for the drunkards, the husbands, brothers and fathers of Ombersley, to fall out of the pub and take advantage of the services on offer. Their entrepreneurial skills seemed to know no end – a tariff was even etched onto a nearby wall to avoid any confusion or drunken bartering.

Underhill could barely take his eyes off them.

"Maybe some day, wee man," Middleton smirked, as he brought Underhill out of his trance. "Although let me give you a piece of advice. Avoid the red heads like the plague. Unless you want a dose of the pox."

Davenant wandered idly down the street, grateful for the respite Ombersley offered his companions. As he weaved through the commotion a poster, crudely attached to a weathered old beam, caught his eye.

EXOD. 22.18.
Thou shalt not suffer a witch to live.

BY ORDER OF PARLIAMENT

The trials of Mary Cavendish, Faith Howard and Anne Underhill on the charge of Witchcraft.

And how they bewitched Men, Women, Children, and Cattle to death: with many other strange things, the like was never heard of before.

7th September, St Andrew's Church, Ombersley

As Davenant processed the information before him, his heart seemed to drop in his chest. The name Underhill had registered immediately...

CHAPTER FIVE

The Sun Inn, Long Marston
July 1ˢᵗ, 1644

"Of course you know who I am," spat Cromwell. "I am the Lieutenant General, not some grubby cannon fodder. And if you would be as kind as to answer my question, do I know you?"

The strange man didn't answer immediately. For the briefest of seconds, as he stared into the stranger's eyes, Cromwell could have sworn he noticed a glint of red in his black, hollow pupils.

"I am a friend, my Lord, a friend who comes with a proposition. Charles Stuart is a man of blood. I see you as Gideon, the Jewish farmer, summoned to lead the army of the Israelites to kill their Kings." Under any other circumstance, Cromwell would have had his men arrest the stranger. But the malevolence in his eyes and the tone of his voice held him in their thrall. "You're about to partake in the most important battle of the war. But your men are drunkards and your tactics unsound. Should you win, however, you will gain the North."

Cromwell looked through the smeared window into the adjacent room. Many of his men were staggering drunkenly, others had passed out, and some had fallen asleep in puddles of their own piss. The stranger was right – his army were a shambles.

"And what is your proposition?" replied Cromwell.

"I propose an exchange, my Lord," the stranger whispered. "For a small token, a meagre payment, I can give you an unbeatable army, a formidable force with which your victory is assured."

"What is the payment?"

The pause seemed to last forever.

"Your soul, my Lord."

CHAPTER SIX

Ombersley, Worcestershire
7ᵗʰ September, 1651

Davenant turned hurriedly and forced his way back
up the street. He could feel his heart thumping in
his chest and his pulse almost bursting through his
skin. His eyes darted around, desperately trying to
locate a familiar face amongst the sea of strangers.
As he tried to squeeze between a peasant and a stout
fruit vendor, he caught his heel on a loose stone and
tripped, knocking the vendor's cart over and sending
his rank produce rolling across the path. Davenant
heard the man crying out behind him and then felt
a heavy hand grab the back of his jerkin. Just as
the vendor's grip tightened, Davenant managed to
wriggle free, losing his garment in the struggle.

In the near distance he spied Betterton loitering
outside the Kings Arms.

He'd never been so pleased to see him.

"Betterton!"

Half of Ombersley turned to face Davenant.
Betterton was markedly embarrassed and turned
quickly to face the other way.

"Betterton! Where's Underhill?"

This time Betterton picked up on the urgency
in Davenant's voice, sensing that something was
dreadfully wrong. "He's in the Kings Arms with the
other three," he stuttered in reply.

"Find Elizabeth and wait here," said Davenant
as he burst into the tavern, the nauseating stench
hitting him immediately. The Kings Arms was a shit

hole, a boisterous gathering place where many of the conversations were in monosyllabic grunts, where men came to become riotously pissed in the shortest possible time and where shady deals were struck in dark corners. Occasionally a flicker of light from one of those dark corners would reveal a gem or a bracelet being secretly shown, before being packed back into the malodorous cloth in which it was wrapped – most likely by the landlord, more often than not involved in all manner of nefarious activities.

Davenant spied Middleton and Turnbull's vast frames amidst the pungent, opaque haze that enveloped the room. As he scurried over to them, almost tripping over a stray stool as he did so, Turnbull stood aside to reveal Underhill, tankard in hand, enjoying his first alcoholic beverage and blissfully unaware of the news that awaited him.

"Underhill! We need to leave, now!" Davenant struggled to catch his breath.

"Why? The Kings Arms seems a most fitting tavern, and no one will recognise me through this smog," whispered Charles in reply, as he leant back gracefully in a magnificent oak armchair which seemed to occupy much of the intimate tavern.

"It's your sister, Underhill. She's being tried for witchcraft!"

The roaring tavern fell silent at the mere mention of the word and the intoxicated locals at the bar turned sluggishly to face Davenant. Turnbull sensed trouble, as did Middleton, who was clearly of the same breed. They edged forward, both men feeling instinctively for their cudgels.

"Witchcraft?" Underhill bolted to his feet and shot out of the door.

Davenant resigned himself to the fact that their well-earned rest would have to wait.

A large crowd had convened outside St Andrew's Church, waiting patiently in hushed anticipation for death and dismemberment. Although the days of the Witchfinder General were at an end, Parliament still granted warrants to several Puritan clergymen to perform witchcraft trials – even though they had become something of an embarrassment amongst the more civilised communities. Nevertheless, the Ombersley mob had come flocking in their droves, aided somewhat by the balmy morning weather.

A makeshift stage had been erected in front of the vast church doors, complete with stocks, a gibbet, a crude rack and a colossal axe and chopping block. It was enough to reduce even the most stoic of men to whimpering wrecks.

Suddenly, the church doors were flung open and a group of people appeared from within. Davenant, who had joined the back of the crowd, could just about make out three frightened women, a tall, sturdy clergyman, suitably dressed in his Puritan robes, and five guards.

The crowd erupted as the collective made their way onto the rickety stage. Underhill reached out and clutched Davenant's arm, drawing him closer. Davenant frequently had to remind himself that he was just a boy and had to deal with all of life's traumas as such. He placed a caring arm around his bony shoulders, much like a father would a son.

"I am Reverend Henry Kane and I shall perform the

trial this morning," said the clergyman in a grating voice.

The crowd let out a rapturous ovation. They knew full well that Kane was the harbinger of pain, who frequently ignored the traditional modus operandi set out by Parliament to ensure he delivered the maximum amount of suffering. To have him perform at Ombersley was an honour indeed for the community.

Kane tugged open a scroll and began to read aloud. "Mary Cavendish, Faith Howard and Anne Underhill stand before you charged with witchcraft," he bellowed, revealing a mouthful of broken and blackened teeth. Davenant had a clearer view of him now. He had a vile, emaciated face, despite his stout physique, and strange, repellent eyes that were so pale in colour they seemed almost white.

Several cries of "Satan's whores", and "Burn in Hell," rang out across the crowd.

"To begin with we shall perform the pricking," yelled Kane with abhorrent glee.

'Pricking' was first implemented by Matthew Hopkins as a way of extracting a confession from the victim. It was an excruciatingly painful ordeal to endure and involved the use of evil looking pins, needles and bodkins to pierce the skin, looking for insensitive spots that didn't bleed. If any were found, they would be interpreted as a mark of the Devil. If none were found, the victim would have to suffer the infamous ordeal of 'Swimming' until a confession was obtained.

Kane opened an ornate wooden box and proudly held aloft the first needle, which twinkled in the morning sun. "Step forward Mary Cavendish and let

God decide your fate," he commanded.

Mary Cavendish cut a forlorn, diminutive figure as she was forced forward by a guard. She was middle-aged yet due to the torment she had already suffered, she appeared to be a good deal older.

"Kneel before me, witch!" Mary reluctantly knelt down in front of Kane, mumbling an incoherent prayer as she did so. "Pray to your God, the good it will do you!"

Kane tore Mary's rag-like shawl from her neck, revealing her naked shoulders which were already bruised and scarred. Without flinching, he plunged the needle in between the top of her shoulder blade and her spine. As she let out an agonising scream, the crowd gasped collectively.

Kane drew no blood.

"Your fate is sealed," he cried, with a telling look of surprise on his face which suggested that he'd never seen that happen before. The two hulking brutes stood either side of him wrestled with Mary until they had the noose fastened around her slender neck. They would wait until the others had been tried before sending her to Hell.

Tears glistened in Cave Underhill's eyes. Not tears of self-pity or sorrow, but tears of hatred. "We must save them," he whispered.

Davenant could just about make out his muted plea in spite of the raucous bellowing echoing in his ears. "I'm thinking," he replied, tugging on Underhill's arm to stay put.

"Step forward Faith Howard and let God decide your fate." A tall, proud and confident woman took a defiant stride forward. "Kneel before me, witch!"

She made a concerted effort to maintain eye contact

with Kane as she was forced to her knees. One of his assistants handed him the wooden box from which he produced a second needle, a more vicious looking version of the first. Kane paraded around the stage, his long dark robes billowing in the wind, as he held aloft the needle to a chorus of cheering and clapping. Dignified to the last, Faith Howard held her head high, resilient in the face of adversity. Davenant was overwhelmed by her fortitude. She let out the faintest whimper as Kane pierced her skin with dagger-like precision – she would be damned to give him any satisfaction from his cowardly antics. The crowd roared with approval as he pushed the needle in as far as it would go, only stopping when it came in contact with bone. As he withdrew it purposefully slowly, blood seeped from the small hole that had opened up between her shoulder and ribs.

"Your fate is yet to be sealed," howled Kane.

The crowd erupted once again, knowing full well that 'Swimming' awaited her.

Davenant turned to Charles who was lingering nearby; similarly disgusted by the actions on stage. The two men exchanged a nod which, although brief, constituted an entire conversation.

Faith Howard was bundled to the side of the stage, a trail of blood following in her wake.

"Step forward Anne Underhill and let God decide your fate." Kane withdrew a third needle from the box, which was longer, thinner and more striking than the first two. Underhill turned his back as his sister was dragged forward by the brutish thugs. She was far younger than Mary Cavendish and Faith Howard, and seemed entirely out of place. Davenant turned to Charles again, desperately seeking a plan or a hint of an instruction before it was too late. Charles gave a slight hand gesture which motioned him to calm down and stay put. Davenant, like a veteran soldier, didn't question his orders.

"Don't worry, we'll save her. But we have to wait for the right moment." He whispered to Underhill.

Davenant could see the gratitude in Underhill's eyes. Another ovation from the crowd made Davenant jump. As he turned back to face the stage, Kane thrust his third needle through Anne Underhill's skin.

She screamed as a wave of the most agonising, searing pain shot through her slight body. "You bastard," she cried as Kane withdrew his bloodied needle.

He slapped her hard across the face, sending her crashing to the floor of the stage. "Your fate is yet to be sealed," he cried, sending the crowd into jubilant rapture once more. They would get to see not one, but two women suffer the most appalling agony. Entertainment didn't come much better than this. Davenant could just make out Mary Cavendish being watched over by a solitary guard, primed and ready to send her to her death as some sort of grim finale, as Faith Howard and Anne Underhill were dragged by their hair from the stage and towards the waiting River Severn. The crowd barged and pushed their way in pursuit, wanting to get the best possible view of the impending torment.

Charles used the commotion as an opportunity to liaise with Davenant. "Wait for my signal," he whispered. "You and Turnbull take out the guards, Middleton and I shall deal with the priest."

Davenant could see from the maniacal look in Charles' eyes that he relished a scrap. Kane had settled on an elevated spot by the riverbank "If you will not be tried by pricking, then swimming shall seal your fate!" The crowd exploded once more, lapping up his every word and lurid gesture. "The accused shall be bound and thrown into the water. If they sink they shall be deemed innocent and assured a chair at Christ's table. Yet if they float, they shall be deemed guilty and their souls shall rot in eternal damnation."

"Nothing like a fair trial," said Davenant under his breath.

The public spectacle of 'Swimming' was based on the belief that as a witch rejected the water of baptism, so the element of water would reject them in turn, and they would float in an unnatural manner.

Davenant sensed that simply throwing the women into the river wasn't in Kane's style and wouldn't satisfy his sense of spectacle and brutality. He spied Kane's thuggish assistants finishing the intricate binding of the victims. Faith Howard and Anne Underhill were bent double with their arms crossed between their legs and their thumbs tied to their big toes. They had lost the colour from their faces.

At this rate, they won't make the water, Davenant thought.

As the women were lowered into the water, Underhill let out an agonised cry. Davenant winced, praying that it had gone unnoticed. To his horror, he noticed a nearby family shake their heads in contempt as their patriarch eagerly pushed his way through the hordes to alert Kane to the witch sympathisers amidst the crowd.

They'd been exposed. They had to move now!

"Go!" Davenant grabbed Turnbull and pushed

him through the mob, towards the river. Turnbull instinctively withdrew his cudgel and waved it above his head like a deranged lunatic, the crowd dispersing quickly before him.

As Davenant glanced back, he was relieved to see that Betterton and Elizabeth had ushered Underhill to safety.

As they forced their way through the last of the crowd and onto the riverbank, they could see that Kane and his thugs had already prepared their counter attack. Middleton looked on in terror as Kane wielded a chain flail made up of razor-sharp, flat oval links – presumably another device used in his illicit games. Middleton ducked as the flail brushed the top of his head, taking with it a hank of hair.

From the hill by the gallows, Underhill spied the guards on the riverbank drop their ropes and rush to join the skirmish. To his shock, he could see Faith and Anne, still gagged and bound, disappear under the water. Without a moment's hesitation, he bounded downhill and dived into the freezing river. He groped for a hand, a foot or even a length of hair to which he could cling. To his great relief, his hand alighted on his sister's back and then he found Faith's arm. Groaning with the effort, he hauled the two women upwards. As they broke the surface, Faith and Anne gasped for air, coughing up river water mixed with blood.

Having emerged at the riverbank a second behind Underhill, Betterton and Elizabeth waded into the shallows to assist him in heaving the two women ashore. As Elizabeth looked back, she could see her father, not known for his fighting prowess, flanked by two assailants, both wielding colossal swords. She cried out to warn him.

Davenant, who had somehow ended up with a sword of his own, engaged the guard on his right. He was the closest, the most present threat. Yet the man closing down on him from the left was only a heartbeat behind. As Davenant faced his two assailants, his sword began to feel as heavy as a blacksmith's anvil, and his arm jolted painfully every time their metal met his own.

Suddenly, a hole opened up in the forehead of the guard on his right. An axe was embedded there between the bushy eyebrows. Somehow Turnbull had decapitated his own foe and, in a continuing fluid motion, had swung around and flung the axe in the direction of Davenant's assailant. He was lucky it had paid off. How easily the axe could have ended up embedded in Davenant's own skull!

Davenant managed a sardonic smile. "In the nick of time, my dear old chap," he said, as he drove his blade into the stomach of the remaining guard.

Kane, who was still engaged in a frantic battle with Middleton, was unaware that Charles had crept up behind him. It wasn't really the etiquette of a military leader, or that of a King, to attack a man from the rear, but Charles felt that it was appropriate that he make an exception for this tyrant.

Charles waited for the right moment to attack. Then his chance came, and he swung his sword with all his might. Suddenly, Kane's hand was no longer attached to his arm – the severed member, with the chain flail still clenched in it, dropped to the floor while a jet of blood spurted from the stump. Kane dropped to his knees in agony.

Middleton, clearly not in the forgiving mood either,

duly severed his head with one clean swipe of his blade. "You can go to hell, you God-fearing bastard," he growled, as Kane's head rolled down the riverbank and ungraciously plopped into the water.

The last of Kane's thugs looked down at the stump of their leader's neck, fountaining blood over the ferocious form of Middleton and, without uttering a word, they turned and ran.

Charles turned to survey the carnage. To his surprise, he found his compatriots had survived relatively unscathed. The crowd, who had been treated to the show of their lives, had all but dispersed. Many headed eagerly for the tavern to brag to their drunkard friends about the spectacle to end all spectacles.

As the group reconvened by the riverbank, Davenant and Charles hastily tore strips of cloth from their jerkins and bound Faith and Anne's wounds.

"They need to see a physician now," said Charles.

Davenant nodded. "But not here. I daresay Cromwell's men are already on their way."

"Where is Mary?" Faith Howard's voice was weak and barely audible.

"Mary?" Davenant came to the conclusion that she must be delirious. And then it hit him – the third woman from the trial. Mary Cavendish. As one, the group turned reluctantly to face the gallows, half expecting to see a middle-aged woman hanging from the noose.

To their surprise, it was the hulking guard who had been assigned to keep watch over her swaying in the gentle breeze. Mary Cavendish was nowhere to be seen.

CHAPTER SEVEN

The Kings Head Inn, Aylesbury

Oliver Cromwell reclined in his armchair within the Solar Room of the Kings Head Inn. He was weary after his journey from Worcester, the subsequent meeting with Parliament and the procession through the Market Square which celebrated his victory over the Royalists. He yawned as he brought his chair closer to the blazing hearth, the old stone of the building kept a chill which could bite into bones.

The light from the roaring fire flickered off the old portraits hung crudely from the cedar panelling, giving the room an air of dark conspiracy.

Cromwell could imagine the illicit meetings that had taken place here throughout the years. Both Henry VI and Margaret of Anjou, and Henry VIII and Anne Boleyn were rumoured to have spent nights within these same crooked walls. Cromwell hoped that he would enjoy a better run of fortune than poor old Anne.

Indeed ever since that fateful day at Marston Moor it seemed to Cromwell that fortune favoured him. He frequently found himself reminiscing about past battles – Naseby, York, Langport – but it was always Marston Moor that featured most heavily in his musings. His meeting at the inn beforehand with the strange, crooked man had seemed like a dream, until the following morning when he discovered that his army had all but deserted him. He had resigned himself to an embarrassing defeat and an even more humiliating arrest. But the strange man had been true to his word. As Prince Rupert of the Rhine and his army attacked under the cover of a rainstorm, the ragged horsemen appeared as if from nowhere. Shrouded by a darkness of their own making they had counter-attacked with devastating results.

Cromwell remembered the blood-curdling screams and witnessing the aftermath of this most awesome and ferocious display of aggression. The Royalists had been torn limb from limb, their remains strewn across the saturated battlefield. Within an hour, four thousand men had lost their lives and the dark riders had vanished into the night. With his men soundly defeated, Prince Rupert was forced to hide in a nearby bean field. His stiff corpse had been found the following morning. There was not a mark upon his body, but his face displayed an awful expression of absolute fear.

There was a knock at the door, an apologetic tapping.

"Come in, Fleetwood," said Cromwell.

"Thank you, my Lord," replied Fleetwood, shuffling anxiously as he closed the door behind him.

"And what can I do for you at this hour?"

Fleetwood took a sharp intake of breath. "We have a problem, my Lord."

The gentle light from the fire flickered across Cromwell's face, revealing it for the battleground it was. Two or three huge warts dominated his forehead. Fleetwood couldn't help but stare at them. They seem to get worse by the day, he thought. His eyes then met Cromwell's and all thoughts of the disfigurement disappeared from his mind.

"And what appears to be the problem?" Cromwell asked. His voice, although calm and assured, carried a threatening undertone.

"We have received reports of William Davenant's troupe of players in Ombersley, my Lord," replied Fleetwood.

"Surely that is good news, Fleetwood?"

"But it is who they are travelling with, my Lord, Charles Stuart and a Scottish soldier of his."

Cromwell rose menacingly from his chair. "Charles Stuart? But that is impossible, he died at Worcester. We saw his corpse with our very own eyes."

"It would appear not, my Lord," replied Fleetwood. "We have several accounts from reputable sources."

Cromwell took a moment to process the information. He ambled over to the window and eased it open, taking in a deep breath of the cool air.

"That is not all, my Lord."

Cromwell turned slowly to face Fleetwood, who was standing pathetically hunched on the hearthrug "We have also received reports that Davenant and Charles rescued a group of women standing trial for witchcraft, and then murdered the clergyman and his assistants presiding over the trial."

"Well now, that is a pretty little problem, isn't it?"

Fleetwood nodded. "Yes, my Lord."

"I suggest you do something about it, and quickly. I want it to remain strictly confidential of course. Kill your informants before they get a chance to spread the news to their drunken friends in the tavern. In fact, burn the whole fucking tavern down, just to be sure. The last thing we need is some god awful revolt."

"Yes, my Lord."

"Be gone, Fleetwood. And the next time I see you, I want some good news."

Fleetwood nodded and bowed his head in some sort of diffident salute. He scurried out of the room.

Cromwell sat back down by the fire and ran a tired hand across his face. As he leant back, he noticed it. A line of blood smeared across his wrist, across the palm of his hand and down his sleeve. And then the drops of blood fell upon the hearthrug.

He was having another nosebleed. Just like the one that had started on that fateful night at Marston Moor.

CHAPTER EIGHT

Bewdley Woods

The soldiers lurched through the undergrowth. Some were more disfigured than others. One man had what seemed to be a superficial stab wound whereas another dragged himself along with his entrails trailing wetly behind him.

The lights of Bewdley acted like a homing beacon. As the first of the soldiers stumbled into a clearing, the cobblestone high-street was but a few hundred yards away. The sign from a nearby tavern swung gently in the faint breeze. It featured a crudely painted tankard on a jagged piece of timber. Underneath it the words 'The Mug House' were painted in red.

Within minutes, the long, narrow street was bustling with walking corpses, not only attracted by the light pouring from the fleapits, but by the sounds of singing and laughing radiating from the tavern.

The noise of the revellers was soon masked by the sound of a sepulchral groaning and the buzzing of flies.

CHAPTER NINE

Tiddesley Wood, Pershore

He'd had enough of sinister woodlands. But as they left Worcester under the cover of nightfall and entered Tiddesley Wood, with its tall, imposing oak trees, Davenant appreciated that this was the quickest route to Pershore and the legendary Dr Walter Tyrell – an amateur astrologer and a highly decorated and respected man of medicine with Royalist sympathies. Davenant could scarcely believe their luck when Charles said that he knew him well and would guide them to his abode, although what Tyrell thought of witches remained to be seen.

When the slapdash physician in Worcester, a Dr Christopher Sharp, eventually concluded that the women's puncture wounds were the consequence of 'Pricking', he demanded they leave his practice immediately, no doubt fearing that collusion with witches would see him swing. However, a little 'gentle persuasion' from Turnbull and Middleton lead to Sharp reluctantly agreeing to at least dress their wounds. He didn't do a particularly good job, but Davenant expected nothing less from a drunken charlatan.

Davenant was in no doubt that Faith Howard and Anne Underhill still needed proper medical attention. Their temporary dressings had probably given them a day's reprieve, but they were now in the grip of delirium, not aided by the frost that had suddenly appeared. Davenant prayed that the shaky cart would withstand another five miles of overloading, although the creaking that had started to reverberate from the wheels didn't exactly fill him with optimism. He cursed the blacksmith who had sold him the damn thing in the first place.

Cave Underhill had remained by Anne's side since they left Ombersley. As he ambled alongside the cart, he regaled another childhood anecdote to her in a vain attempt to lift her spirits.

Davenant shook his head ruefully, wishing he were able to alleviate their suffering in some way. "So tell me more of this Tyrell," he said, turning to Charles.

"Well, for as long as I've known of him he's been courted by the rich and poor alike for his medical knowledge. Cromwell always had him down as a quack and an evil magician. Admittedly his methods are somewhat... out of the ordinary."

"Out of the ordinary?" said Underhill, eavesdropping on their conversation and clearly puzzled by Charles' ambiguity.

"Anything that doesn't conform to Cromwell's way of thinking is beyond the pale with him. Tyrell is a self-proclaimed doctor, astrologer and dealer in secrets and his ideology is so very far detached from Cromwell's. But that does not make his methods any less effective, just different."

Underhill, satisfied with the answer, nodded apologetically and returned to his anecdote. As he peered down into the cart at his sister, he noticed that her eyes were open, projecting some kind of deranged stare.

"Anne?" Underhill shook her roughly by the shoulder, praying it would prompt her into waking. It didn't, and she remained rigid. "Anne!"

Turnbull tugged on the reins and then rushed round

the side of the cart to tend to the crisis. Davenant and Charles hurried forwards. Underhill was pawing at Anne's throat, desperately trying to locate a pulse. Charles dragged him to one side as Davenant and Turnbull lifted Anne from the cart and placed her gently down on the grassy bank. Middleton held the lantern aloft to provide them with suitable lighting. He heard a faint scrabbling noise in the near distance – a hasty breath and a footfall – and felt compelled to draw the light away from the crisis and towards the eerie noise that seemed to summon him.

"Middleton! The light!" Charles' command seemed to fall on deaf ears. As Middleton squinted into the darkness, he could just about make out a faint, almost ghostly silhouette against a cluster of bushes. "Over there!"

Even as he cried out, the silhouette had lessened its distance by ten yards and was rapidly closing upon him.

And then it emerged from the shadows and into the light. He might have been a hardened soldier, but Middleton couldn't help but let out a faint whimper as Mary Cavendish moved past him and towards Anne Underhill's prone form.

Middleton reluctantly followed her, with the lantern swinging violently in his trembling hand. "What are you doing here?" he cried, as Mary knelt down beside Anne and began to tend to her wound with spindly fingers.

"For the love of God, man, what does it matter?" replied Charles, making way for Mary, who seemed intent on helping. She applied a strange flower to Anne's wound, which had started to seep a mixture of pus and blood.

"What is that?" asked Underhill, his voice wavering with emotion as he pointed at the peculiar, elongated leaf in Mary's hand. She ignored him and proceeded to mutter several indistinct words under her breath.

"Do you think we can get her to Pershore and Dr Tyrell?" Charles was loath to interrupt, but felt the question had to be asked.

Mary froze – the name Tyrell clearly striking a chord. After a fleeting pause, she proceeded to rub the leaf onto Anne's open wound, and within a minute, Anne jolted and vomited all over the grassy bank. A strange odour drifted from her wound.

Davenant shook his head in disbelief. "Well, I don't know what you've done, but it seems to have done the trick."

"She still needs to see a doctor," replied Mary, her voice faint and ethereal. "They both do."

Faith was delirious, but at least she was still breathing. Turnbull picked up Anne with deft tenderness for such a ham-fisted ruffian, and placed her gently back in the cart. Underhill managed a grateful smile and picked up his anecdote from where he had left it. Mary pondered her next move, and after careful consideration, decided to follow Davenant and Charles at the back of the cart. The two men shared an inquisitive glance and a shrug of the shoulders. After all, she did seem quite useful to have around.

CHAPTER TEN

Westminster Hall, London
19ᵗʰ January, 1649

Beams of light poured through the skylights at either end of the long, narrow Hall and bounced off the cold marble floor, giving the chamber an almost ethereal glow. The intricate hammerbeam roof hung low, diminishing the space within the Hall and contributing to the eager atmosphere.

The stage had been set for the following day; the trial of King Charles I. Judge Bradshaw's crimson velvet chair had been placed in the centre of the podium behind a desk on which a red cushion bore the parliamentary mace. His fellow judges would sit behind him on benches hung with scarlet. The chair in which Charles would sit was directly in front of them.

The Hall had played host to several significant trials throughout history, not least that of Thomas More and the Gunpowder Plot conspirators. But none were as important as the trial of a King, and the anticipation was understandably palpable.

A troubled Thomas Fairfax – a General, a Commander-in-Chief and close friend of Oliver Cromwell's – sat alone by the pulpit. He was tall, dark and dashingly handsome; his smoulderingly regal quality accentuated by his long parliamentary gown.

The doors burst open at the far end of the Hall and Fairfax turned. Cromwell marched towards him. "Oliver, you received my note?" he said, standing to greet him.

"Yes. I received it," spat Cromwell, his voice resounding around the Hall.

Fairfax could make out the disgusted expression on his face as he continued to stride up the aisle towards the stage. "And you couldn't meet in the Abbey? We have not prayed together for quite some time now."

It was a loaded question, and Cromwell knew it.

"I do not wish to pray," he replied.

"You do not approve of the contents of my note?"

"No, I do not, my Lord. And I would venture that your wife has put you up to it." Cromwell reached the pulpit and circled Fairfax furiously, adrenalin coursing through his veins.

"No, Oliver. Anne had nothing to do with this. It is my conscience that pricks at me. I cannot preside over the trial of our King that will sign his death warrant, the same King appointed by God," said Fairfax, his voice calm and rational.

"And yet you did not flinch when you killed the King's soldiers. Were they not appointed by God too?"

"But we were fighting a cause and our cause was won. You follow your own agenda now, my dear friend." Fairfax attempted to place a reasoning hand on Cromwell's shoulder. Cromwell shrugged it off and continued to pace up and down.

"No friend of mine would abandon me on the eve of the most important trial this country has ever seen. I tell you we will cut off his head with the crown upon it!" snarled Cromwell defiantly. "And you still insist on wearing your hair long when you know that we are protesting against the decadence of the court. One of your wife's little fancies, I presume?"

"You presume correctly. Yet I fail to see how the length of my hair is of any consequence."

"Or perhaps you wear your locks out of respect for the King? You have many qualities, Thomas, but perhaps political aptitude is not one of them."

"I daresay you're right. But it is not only politics that drives a wedge between us," replied Fairfax. "My men are growing increasingly concerned that they have not been paid in months. You refuse their services and turn to others to fight your battles for you. There are all sorts of rumours circulating, Oliver."

"Such as?"

"That you're dabbling in the occult and that you employ dark agents to execute your orders. And you do not look well."

"And what do you believe?"

"It has been a while since we last fought together. So I have little evidence of my own from which to form an opinion. But I can hardly ignore the opinions of those who I hold in high regard."

"You used to hold my opinion in high regard, Thomas. Have you not forgotten our accusation?" replied Cromwell, opening a small papyrus-bound manuscript which was tucked carefully under his arm. He began to read its contents. " 'That our so called King, out of a wicked design to erect an unlimited and tyrannical power, traitorously and maliciously levied war against the present Parliament and the people they represented.' "

"I have not forgotten."

"Then you will know that there is no sacrifice too great for my country. I once believed you felt the same way."

Fairfax looked him dead in the eye. "I would not sacrifice my soul."

As Cromwell brushed past Fairfax, both men acknowledged that their conversation within the vast auditorium of Westminster Hall would be the last time they would ever speak.

Fairfax also couldn't help but notice that amidst the beams of sunlight flooding the vast hall, Oliver Cromwell cast no shadow.

CHAPTER ELEVEN

Pershore Abbey
9th September, 1651

As they entered the sleepy town of Pershore, Davenant took a moment to enjoy the sight of the Abbey. Although parts of it had been demolished during the dissolution of the monasteries, much of the beautifully gothic exterior remained intact, and it now resembled some strange place of Druid worship, especially when bathed in the stark, silver moonlight. A shiver went down Davenant's spine as he imagined the monks getting burned alive for resisting the reformation. As the chief minister to Henry VIII, it was Thomas Cromwell, the great grand-uncle of Oliver, who was responsible for much of the bloodshed. *A family of evil, vindictive bastards*, Davenant thought.

As they passed into the grounds of the Abbey, he turned to observe Mary's progress. To avoid the consecrated land filled with gravestones and monuments, she had split from the back of the group and had taken a well-concealed pathway through the surrounding woodland.

"Quick, look," whispered Davenant, pointing discreetly in her direction.

Charles could see Mary fighting through the thick withes, slipping and sliding her way through the dense undergrowth. "Well, she seems happy enough."

"Do you not find her... peculiar?"

"Sir William, I've been rescued from an oak tree by a group of actors, saved three witches from the hands of a demented priest, and am being hunted by the very man who wishes to hang you. Watching some deranged old woman fight her way through the bushes is spectacularly normal in comparison."

"Yes, a fair point," replied Davenant, grinning for the first time in days.

Charles landed several blows onto the ageing oak door belonging to the strange little hovel, far detached from the well-appointed buildings that formed the remainder of the narrow lane. The door seemed to crack and creak under each bang of his huge fist. The lantern light moved from an upstairs room and quickly reappeared, spilling out from beneath the warped wood of the doorway.

An unusual coarse voice bellowed out from within. "What is this furore? Mind you don't bend the house timber!"

There was a loud clunk as the bolt was pulled across followed by a creaking as the door swung slowly open. In the doorway stood a curious looking gentleman clad in a shabby nightgown and holding aloft an oil lamp. He was tall, thin and bespectacled with a sporadically patchy beard that only served to give the impression that he was diseased in some way.

He recognised Charles immediately and dropped down onto one knee. "My Lord, if I had known it was you, I would have arranged a hearty supper. And a thousand apologies for my appearance," he said, almost dropping the oil lamp in his embarrassment. His bumbling charm was infectious and Davenant felt the collective spirit of his downcast troupe lift noticeably.

"Please, Dr Tyrell, it is I who should apologise for my intrusion at this late hour, but I must ask a favour of you. I have two women in my care who are desperately ill and in urgent need of medical attention," replied Charles, helping Dr Tyrell to his feet.

"I should be delighted to help, as always, although I fear my abode isn't big enough to house you all."

"We shall remain outside," said Davenant, gesturing to Betterton, Elizabeth, Turnbull, Middleton and Mary. Dr Tyrell caught his first glimpse of Mary, purposefully skulking behind the nearby cart as if to avoid detection. His eyes widened with recognition and Davenant vigilantly picked up on his telling glance.

"Very well. Underhill and I shall assist you in any way we can," said Charles in agreement.

"In which case, I shall get my wife to prepare us all some food whilst you explain to me exactly what has happened. Do come in."

Charles and Underhill adroitly lifted Faith and Anne from the cart as Dr Tyrell ushered them further into the confines of his house. He carefully closed the battered old door behind him, fearing any further hardship would see it fall off its hinges.

Betterton and Elizabeth meandered down the narrow lane for some privacy.

"Don't go too far," called Davenant, as they disappeared into a pool of shadows swamping the end of the path.

"Don't worry, Mister Davenant, Sir," said Turnbull compassionately. "I'm sure they'll be all right."

"Thank you, Turnbull."

"If it's all right, sir, would it be totally inappropriate if we went for a drink?" he replied, gesturing towards Middleton who was loitering next to him – the hollering from the nearby tavern catching their attention.

"Of course not, I think you've earned one," said Davenant, mindful that he was duty-bound to keep his troops happy.

"Aye, thank you Mister Davenant, sir," slurred Middleton in his thick Glaswegian drawl. The two men nodded their appreciation before bounding round the corner to join the noisy revelry. Davenant grinned; the innkeeper had no idea what was in store for him.

He rested his back against a wall and let out a weary sigh. He had waited patiently for this respite, and he smiled thankfully. It had been a tiring three days to say the least and recent events played heavily on his mind.

The low-pitched murmuring from nearby made him jump out of his skin. As he staggered forward, he saw Mary, obscured by the cart, kneeling in prayer. She turned to face him and rose slowly to her feet.

"I'm sorry if I interrupted you," said Davenant, his voice wavering ever so slightly.

"You must pray with me." Mary's eyes seemed to shine bright in the darkness.

"I am not a religious man, Mary."

"Neither am I, but they're coming, and we must pray."

"Who are coming? And how do you know Dr Tyrell?"

"We are of the same... ilk."

"What do you mean?"

"You will find out soon enough."

Dr Tyrell had brushed everything from his vast dining table – which seemed to double as an operating slab when deemed necessary – onto the surrounding floor. He had sent his wife, a rather plump and jolly old woman, to prepare a meal for his guests. She obliged quite happily.

Tyrell turned to Charles. "I received word that you were killed in battle," he said. "And now this?" He gestured towards Faith and Anne who writhed in agony as they were lowered gently onto the table next to one another. Underhill ran his hand affectionately over Anne's hair and wiped the tear away from her porcelain white cheek.

"I shall tell you all when this is done, I promise," replied Charles. "But there are more pressing matters at hand."

Dr Tyrell nodded. "I understand," he said, as he tore open the bloodstained blouse belonging to Faith Howard, revealing her lean shoulders and the infected wound. "I think it might be best if you leave this to me. The methods I use are somewhat... delicate. You might wish to send the woman who travels with you inside. She may be of use. I would have invited her in earlier, but she is not sound in the head."

"You know her?" Underhill asked.

"Yes I do. After all, it was I who taught her all she knows," the doctor replied.

"I don't believe you," cried Davenant. "That is heresy, downright heresy. We should have left you to hang!"

"I can prove it," replied Mary, her monotonous voice not fluctuating in the slightest.

"How?"

"I know your secret."

As Davenant stood open mouthed, he could have sworn he felt his heart stop beating. He was only brought back to life when he heard the clattering of footsteps rapidly approaching.

"Father, look at this!"

Davenant turned to see Elizabeth and Betterton scampering up the lane. Elizabeth was clutching a parchment which she thrust into his hands. It was a poster of some description and he squinted as he tried to make out the words scribbled upon it. He fumbled for the lantern on the floor, picked it up and reduced its outpouring to a mere silver of light, just enough to read what was written before him.

WANTED

For crimes against the country, including the Murders of an Ordained Minister and Public Officials, Assault, Theft, Performance of Illegal Theatre and Harbouring Witches

WILLIAM DAVENANT, CHARLES STUART & their band of players.

Reward of one double crown for their whereabouts or proof of their demise

"Well, that's fairly damning," said Davenant. Betterton snatched the poster back and proceeded to devour its contents with eager fascination.

"Have we interrupted anything?" asked Elizabeth, looking at Mary, who was stood with her gaze fixed upon Davenant.

"No, no, Elizabeth. We were just talking about Dr Tyrell."

The door opened to Tyrell's house and Charles and Underhill emerged wearily from within. "Mary, Dr Tyrell requires your assistance," said Charles, picking up on the patent tension. "My, my, what have we missed?"

"There will be a battle, an almighty conflict," replied Mary, after a drawn-out pause. "Two armies of the dead shall wage war with one another. The apocalypse is nigh."

"On second thoughts, Mary, perhaps it is best if you stay out here."

"I can prove it," she replied, pointing triumphantly at Davenant. "I know his secret. I know everything."

"What secret, father?" Elizabeth was understandably anxious as she reached for Davenant's hand.

"It's nothing, Elizabeth. She's just trying to frighten you."

"What's going on?" asked Dr Tyrell, appearing in the doorway.

Mary took a step forward and stared unflinchingly at Davenant, glaring up at him through dark eyes that were made darker by the shadows that encircled them. "He is the bastard son of William Shakespeare!"

CHAPTER TWELVE

The Palace of Whitehall, London
30th January, 1649

The bustling throng had amassed around the execution scaffold which had been erected in front of the Banqueting House – the scene of the gaudy triumph of the Stuart court – with many jostling and elbowing to get a better view of the imminent beheading. Indeed, hundreds of the spectators had even taken to lining the rooftops of the buildings nearby. Several skirmishes had broken out but were quickly interrupted by the countless mounted officials.

Cromwell had taken up his vantage point to the left of the scaffold from where he could oversee the proceedings. He had an excellent view of the multitude and had noted their division – half were chanting Royalist mantras, the other half were Regicidal disciples. It was bitterly cold, and Cromwell was already worn out. He had spent much of the day trying to locate an executioner after Richard Brandon, the common Hangman of London, had refused to do the deed, fearing his actions would incite an assassination attempt by Royalist sympathisers. Eventually Cromwell agreed to pay the princely sum of one hundred pounds to a drunken Irishman by the name of Gunning, after he was found bragging of his prowess with an axe in a nearby inn. Cromwell hoped he was as useless as he appeared and that it took several agonising blows to sever the King's head from his shoulders. He had agreed to let the executioner wear a mask so that his identity would be hidden, although Cromwell concluded that it was necessary not least because of his unsightly features, which included pockmarks and several gigantic boils that encrusted his nose.

As the bells belonging to the nearby church tolled two, the emaciated figure of Charles was led out onto the scaffold, and a deathly hush descended upon the crowd. His grim countenance was not as they remembered. Indeed, his sallow features, which cast the heavy bones of his face into sharp relief, were in stark contrast to his once proud and regal handsomeness.

One of Cromwell's soldiers tugged opened a parchment scroll and stood to address the crowd. "Charles Stuart, you are charged with high treason in levying war against Parliament and the Kingdom of England in order to gain unlimited power. Do you have any final words?"

"I am the Martyr of the People!" Charles bellowed, much to the awe of his audience.

Cromwell, dismissing his passionate declaration, took a moment to remember the lengthy trial and the swift resolution that followed. It had taken what seemed an age to get the trial up and running following Charles' refusal to acknowledge the authority of the court. From signing his death warrant in the ironically named Old King's Head in Windsor, to transporting him as a prisoner from Carisbrooke Castle on the Isle of Wight to Hurst Castle in the New Forest, and then through Farnham before finally reaching London, Cromwell had begun to speculate whether the trial would ever take place at all. It had also been gruelling without his friend Fairfax to support him, but he eventually achieved what he had set out to achieve, and was duly proud of his accomplishment. It saddened him to see both sets of followers standing shoulder to shoulder; almost as if the enormity of the event dwarfed whatever futile belief they held.

Charles, dressed in white, was wearing two shirts to prevent the cold January weather causing any noticeable shivers that the crowd may have mistaken for fear or weakness. Cromwell cursed whoever had allowed that; he would have been far happier to see the King piss his pants.

Charles knelt defiantly by the chopping block, his long hank of black hair caressing either side of the cold, hard slab. "I have delivered to my conscience; I pray God you do take those courses that are best for the good of the kingdom and your own salvation," he whispered under his breath.

He looked up pleadingly to Gunning, who was savouring his time in the limelight as some sort of tawdry pantomime villain. His performance was not going down well with the baying mob, as he strutted over to the chopping block, holding aloft the enormous axe which almost dwarfed his hulking body.

"I shall say but very short prayers and then thrust out my hands. Strike a clean blow, I beg of you," said Charles desperately, as he nestled his chin onto the smooth grooves carved into the dense block. He whispered several indistinct words under his breath before flinging out his arms. There was a collective gasp as Gunning swung his axe back and landed it with pinpoint precision onto the back of Charles' neck, severing his head cleanly in one perfect stroke.

The gasp from the crowd turned into a groan as Charles' head dropped into the waiting basket, lined with velvet, a spurt of blood covering those standing in the first few rows.

"Behold the head of a traitor," shouted Gunning in a thick, slurred Irish accent.

Cromwell looked on in dismay as the nearby horde of ghoulish spectators barged their way towards the front in an effort to dip their handkerchiefs in Charles' blood, his heart sinking at the thought of him becoming a martyred King. And then he felt compelled to study the crowd again, his eyes running over the hundreds of men, women and children gathered together.

And there he was, huddled in the mass, a crooked figure in a hooded cloak with a pale, wasted face staring right back at him.

CHAPTER THIRTEEN

The Tower of London
3rd June, 1642

Damnation. This was terrible, truly terrible.

The chill of the Tower pierced into his bones as Davenant peered out of the narrow window and over the Thames. His hand trembled, not with fear or trepidation, but with exhaustion, as he carved another mark into the grimy wall, its wetness glistening and sparkling in the willowy lantern light. As his eyes glanced over his many carvings, Davenant estimated that it had been almost two months since his arrest in Faversham and the subsequent journey to London. He chastised himself, not the first time, for being such a fool. Trying to persuade an army loyal to Parliament to overthrow the Commons was suicidal, and as he stood accused before the Long Parliament, Davenant spared a thought for his darling Elizabeth. How would she cope, a helpless infant without her father? The thought of leaving a six year old girl in Turnbull's care filled him with dread, but he had been left with no alternative. As he leant sluggishly against his cell wall, he muttered a prayer for her wellbeing.

Looking out of the barred window again, he could just make out a riverboat being rowed under the rattling portcullis, past the lichen-covered drawbridge and into Traitors' Gate. He didn't envy the poor bastards onboard – for that short journey through the cold, dark, stinking water was a journey through a gallery of true horror. The decapitated heads of the prisoners, crudely stuck on the sharp spikes, acted as a sign of the impending torment for those entering into the belly of the Tower. By the time the prisoners had come this far, many of them would be wishing they were already dead.

Davenant's cell within the White Tower stank, although much of that was due to his cellmate, a ruddy faced man by the name of Bray. He hadn't uttered a word in the two months that Davenant had been incarcerated with him, although the guards took great pleasure in telling Davenant that he was arrested for being a sodomite.

There was a loud thud as the lock sprang open and the cell door was opened. Two imposing Yeomen Warders, carrying wooden platters and goblets, lurched across the slippery stone floor, unceremoniously dropping the meagre meals before each prisoner, before lumbering back out, locking the door behind them.

Davenant picked up his platter and examined its contents – a stodgy muck of oats and water. Several weevils provided the seasoning for this foul porridge. The contents of the goblet were just as poor and had a slight tang of the sewer. However, none of this seemed to put off Bray who was happily devouring his supper.

Davenant offered his plate to his cell-mate. "Would you care for mine as well? I couldn't possibly."

"No, thank you." Davenant was shocked. He wasn't expecting a reply, let alone one in the tones of what sounded like a reasonably educated man. "I daresay the food they give you isn't of the same quality as mine."

"You have a different meal?" Davenant was

understandably dumbfounded.

"But of course. I couldn't abide the filth they serve you. You see, I have a 'special arrangement' with our friends, the guards. In return for some 'services rendered', they provide me with sufficient sustenance."

Davenant could barely believe what he was hearing. Two months of eating the foulest, most putrid tasting, stomach churning shit on offer, and all it would have taken was a small bribe to ensure some edible food?

"How do you pay them?" he said, as he got to his feet eagerly.

Bray shook his head and a condescending grin stretched the width of his grubby face. "Oh, I don't pay them in money, my good man. Life gets lonely as a prison warder and I provide them with... well, a spot of much needed company shall we say? When they drag me roughly from the cell they aren't taking me to the rack. Do you get my drift?"

Davenant sat back down despondently, acknowledging that he had been priced out of the market.

"Of course, my position has various other advantages beyond a decent meal," said Bray.

"Such as?"

"Such as allowing me to purloin a bunch of keys from the discarded breeches of one particularly 'distracted' guard." Bray produced the set from within the folds of his grubby rags and grinned widely.

"My God! If they catch you with those you'll be for the chop!"

"That is why, as soon as I have finished my meal, we will be leaving. I know more about this place than most of the prisoners here due to my liaisons."

"What if they catch us?"

"They won't. Now come on, old man, buck up, you can't think like that. We'll be out of here in no time!"

Davenant couldn't quite believe his luck and he spared a whimsical thought for Cromwell and what his reaction would be when he discovered what was responsible for the escape of one of his most despised enemies. The thought of his wart-ravaged face boiling with fury warmed his heart as they fled the damp chill of the cell.

CHAPTER FOURTEEN

The Palace of Whitehall Lodgings, London
11ᵗʰ September, 1651

Richard Cromwell was delighted to have his father home from the battle unscathed. However, as he ambled into the beautiful vine-covered courtyard directly adjacent to the old Palace of Whitehall, he reflected on the strange, repellent warts that had started to infest his father's face. Cromwell had never been particularly struck by vanity, but the cause of these unsightly blemishes must have weighed heavily on his mind, Richard thought. And his behaviour was becoming increasingly unpredictable.

Richard plucked a sprig of thyme from the well-kept garden as the rain began to trickle down. The weather had taken a dramatic turn for the worse since his father's return and the temperature had dropped markedly. As Richard looked up at the imposing Palace which loomed above their modest lodgings, he took a moment to appreciate the irony of his family living in the quarters that had once belonged to his father's adversary. He caught a glimpse of his father through the tall, mullioned windows, pacing restlessly in the kitchen. He noted his eyes, not just the bags that surrounded them, but their colour. They were much darker than he remembered them. As Richard pushed open the door that led into the orderly kitchen, he placed the sprig of thyme on the nearby table.

"Is it raining, Richard?" His father said, looking up.

Richard turned to see his mother, Elizabeth, emerge from the larder. She had short hair and a dour face that was accentuated by her thin, pointed nose and drooping eyelids. "It's getting worse now," he replied, and was suddenly startled by his father's reflection in the darkening window. For the briefest of moments, it didn't look like his father at all. Instead, he could have sworn he saw a terrible wizened visage. The hairs on the back of his neck shot up, but he looked again and it was his father's warty face once more.

"Your father and I were just discussing my birthday celebrations," said Elizabeth, breaking Richard out of his nightmarish daydream.

"Good. That's good," he said. "And what it is that you have decided to do?"

"Your mother has insisted on having a play performed for her! I was hoping you would be able to persuade her to enjoy some other frightful frivolity. She knows how I feel about the damned theatre," replied Cromwell, disparagingly.

Richard had always hated being stuck in the middle of his parents' disputes and could never fathom how they found the time to quarrel so often. However, his uneasiness was short-lived, and he breathed a sigh of relief as Bates, their manservant, appeared in the doorway. Bates was a short, rotund man with rosy cheeks and a mild manner.

"Excuse me, Sir, I'm sorry to interrupt, but there is a gentleman here to see you."

"His name?"

"It is a Mr Fleetwood sir," replied Bates. "He's waiting for you in the study."

Cromwell's study gleamed, rich with the shine and smell of polish on mahogany, his colossal desk littered with papers and leather bound volumes, none of which had been disturbed in the months that he had been away.

"Good evening, Sir. I come with important news," said Fleetwood, rising to his feet in greeting.

Cromwell closed the door gently behind him as he stepped into the room. "It had better be. I wouldn't appreciate the first night I've spent with my family in months being interrupted by irrelevance."

"A member of Davenant's group has supplied us with information concerning their movements. He will want paying of course."

Cromwell's eyes lit up. "Yes, yes, in good time. Now, where can we find these theatrical brigands?"

"They're in Pershore and heading south. And it gets better, Sir, because Charles Stuart himself is still with them!"

CHAPTER FIFTEEN

Evesham Abbey

Another war-scarred abbey and another night in the woods. Davenant was beginning to get the feeling that he was reliving the same day over and over again. His group had set up their camp under the remains of the old abbey – its Bell Tower cut a forlorn figure as it overlooked the camp and the rest of the sparse woodland. After much effort the group had finally managed to get a fire going. They cheered as the flames illuminated the old limestone of the tower. Davenant had decided not to help them, not because he didn't want to, but because of the recriminating looks and the whispered conversations that he had been the recipient of since their swift departure from Pershore. He felt sick to the pit of his stomach, much like he had been ostracised by his own family, the same family he cared and provided for. It had been a strange two days, he thought. He was glad that Faith and Anne were on the mend, but was equally distraught that Mary, the devilish bitch that she was, had bared his secret for all to hear. Elizabeth had refused to listen to his explanation, or even to speak to him, and yet despite Betterton revelling in the irony of his misfortune, Davenant was far more distraught by his daughter's reaction than any others.

It was none of their damned business, he stubbornly concluded. Besides, they didn't know the half of it, and if they did, perhaps they wouldn't have been so quick to judge. As he sat alone on a threadbare rug watching Elizabeth, Underhill, Middleton and Turnbull playfully skimming stones on the nearby river, he decided that he would wait for them to come to him. At least that way he could maintain some form of pride.

"Are you still sulking?"

Davenant jumped at the sound of the voice and he turned to see Charles, his face half masked by the night.

"Yes."

"Do you want to talk about it?"

"How long have you got?" Davenant said, shuffling across the rug to make room for Charles to sit. "If I'm honest, I thought I'd carry my secret to the grave. To have it shouted out in front of a group of strangers was nothing less than galling."

"We're hardly strangers, Sir William. Talk to me." Charles said, settling himself beside the actor.

Davenant struggled to understand why Charles was suddenly being so compassionate, but he didn't care. He was just happy for the company. "Where do I begin?" he said.

"With wine," replied Charles, thrusting a goblet into Davenant's hand.

Davenant drained half the cup and then sighed. "My parents were the proprietors of a humble inn by the name of the Crown Tavern in Oxford. My father was frequently away from home on business. As Oxford was en route to Shakespeare's home in Stratford, the playwright would often spend the night when away from London and the Globe. It was obviously on one of these nights that Shakespeare and my mother decided to embark on a physical relationship of which I was the product. There were all sorts of rumours flying around, but my father, being the proud, foolish man that he was, decided to bury his head in the sand. After all, William Shakespeare was quite the icon. Christ, they even named me after him and asked him to be my godfather! I myself didn't discover the truth until after my father had passed away. It was purely by chance, but when someone remarked to me that I had a 'wit with the very same spirit of Shakespeare', I decided to confront him about it. We even shared a striking resemblance. At the time I was serving as his apprentice. We were in the middle of rehearsing Romeo and Juliet when I walked up and asked him face to face whether there was any truth to the rumours. I was ready for him to say no, but when he confirmed my fears, I felt sick, sick that I had been deceived and sick for the lie my false father had been living. What made it worse was that the man I had known as my father for all these years knew all along and that it didn't trouble him in the slightest. So I left Shakespeare's apprenticeship under a cloud of mistrust and he set me up on my own. After all, it was the very least he could do. But to this day, I refuse to put on any of his plays."

"Did you grieve for him, Will?"

Davenant thought long and hard about his reply. "Yes," he said, eventually. "I didn't find out that he had died until a good three weeks after, and yes I still felt anger towards him. But I did grieve."

"It is a terrible thing to lose a father, but to lose two must have been doubly hard to bear," replied Charles.

"I can count myself fortunate at least that my 'father', John Davenant, died peacefully. What they did to your father, the King, was beyond the pale. I was heartbroken, really I was."

"I know you were," said Charles softly. "And to have seen it with my own eyes as a young boy..."

"You were at your father's execution?" Davenant exclaimed.

Charles took a moment to collect his thoughts, no doubt the retelling of such a distressing anecdote was still hard to bear even years later. "I was hiding underneath the scaffold and watched... watched it through a crack in the wood. I saw the drunken executioner parading around the stage, lapping up every jeer and taunt, before cutting my father's head off with one blow of his axe. I can vividly remember it dropping into the basket not ten feet away from me."

"With Cromwell looking on with jubilant glee, I daresay." There was vitriol in Davenant's voice now.

"Still, we have found solace in our mutual ire, have we not?" replied Charles.

Their heart-to-heart was cut short by a sudden, blood-curdling scream that tore through the night. The two men stumbled to their feet and darted across the slippery grass towards the tent from which the chilling scream had issued.

"It's Faith and Anne," gasped Charles, as the two men ran through the cool darkness. Davenant pulled the flap of the tent to one side and poked his head reluctantly inside, terrified of what he'd find. To his relief, he found both women alive and well, attempting to kill a spider that had crept its way inside.

"Can we help you?" said Faith, holding a slipper in her hand.

Davenant noticed that the colour had returned to her cheeks and her blue eyes seemed to glisten as a cascade of moonlight flooded the tent. He paused, as he contemplated her natural beauty. Dr Tyrell's medicine had patently done the trick.

"No, no. We heard a scream and came over to see if you were all right," he replied.

"You came rushing over on our account? You've done enough for us already, Sir William."

"You know my name?"

"But of course. We've heard all about you." Faith glanced over at Anne who was grinning wickedly.

"From Mary, no doubt," spat Davenant, almost losing his cool.

"No, Sir William, from your daughter. She was telling us what a kind, considerate father you are."

"Where is Mary?" he asked.

"She's gone for a walk."

"Fine, I shall catch up with her later. How are you ladies bearing up?"

"A little better, thank you."

"Perhaps when you are quite yourselves, you might explain why you were being tried for witchcraft?"

"And perhaps you might explain why you chose to risk your lives to save us?" Faith replied.

Davenant suddenly became aware of hurried footsteps approaching the tent.

"Father, it's Betterton, he's gone!" shrieked Elizabeth, her voice penetrating through the canvas.

Davenant staggered back outside, almost colliding with Elizabeth and Underhill as he did so. "What do you mean, gone?" he spluttered.

Elizabeth grimaced; her face was raddled with worry. "I hadn't seen him for about an hour, so I went to his tent to see if he was all right. There's no sign of him and all his belongings are gone."

Davenant let out a weary sigh. "Do you have any idea where he could have gone?"

But he didn't need to satisfy himself with an answer. He knew full well where Betterton was going.

CHAPTER SIXTEEN

Kempsey, Worcestershire

Thomas Betterton trekked through the tiresomely persistent undergrowth that seemed to greet his every step with a vice-like grip of sodden earth on leather boot. As he spied the cluster of lights belonging to the dwellings of Kempsey, he spared a thought for Elizabeth and what her reaction would be when she discovered his betrayal. He had managed to convince himself that in spite of his affection for her, no relationship was worth one double crown, no matter how beautiful she was. It must have been his parents mutual hatred for one another that had left him a shallow, loveless son-of-a-bitch, he mused. Either that or he was just, in fact, a covetous bastard. Davenant weighed heavily on his mind also, and as he waded through the mire, he almost felt a tinge of sorrow for him.

Still, no time for regret when there's a reward to collect.

He hauled himself from the shallow ditch that was clinging to his ankles and onto the cobbled pathway that led into the scenic hamlet, its smattering of lodgings full of character with their whitewashed walls bedecked with flowers. He searched for an inn from where he might get directions back to Bewdley. He couldn't have been that far away, he thought to himself, as he spied the local hostelry, comprised of a row of cottages. As he ambled along the walled tavern garden, fragrantly planted with roses and honeysuckle, he cast his mind back to what the soldier had told him in Pershore. As Davenant was being interrogated following Mary's declaration on his parentage, Betterton had skulked into the nearby inn, armed with the wanted poster, and had spied the Parliamentarian soldier in the corner. He was a peculiar man by the name of Danes, a robust, full-bodied type, which made his effeminate nature seem all the more bizarre. He had told Betterton to return to Bewdley and that he would make arrangements for someone to meet him there. Betterton began to lament that it would have been far more prudent to wait for the money to arrive before divulging his information. But there was little point in worrying about that now, he concluded. What was done was done.

There was something strangely amiss in Kempsey and it bothered Betterton that he couldn't quite put his finger on what it was. Was it the rich smell of the nearby clematis, or perhaps the sprawling, disjointed layout of the buildings? As he mulled it over it suddenly dawned on him – there was no one in sight, no sound of conversation or drunken singing. Betterton warily approached the tavern. He was surprised to find the door ajar, gently swinging on its hinges in the cool breeze.

"Hello," he called out as he peered inside.

Inside the tavern was empty; lanterns blazing and tankards untouched. Betterton decided that his next best option would be to try one of the nearby dwellings, see if he could find out where everybody had disappeared to.

He held aloft a lantern that he'd liberated from the tavern as he made his way back down the dusty street. He felt a rush of relief as he saw a young girl shuffling towards him.

Thank God, he thought to himself.

As he approached the girl he was suddenly struck by a chilling realisation. He fearfully held the lantern up to reveal the cavernous wound – a wound so deep that her head was barely attached to her neck. As the girl staggered onwards, blood poured from the gash saturating her yellow petticoat. Betterton dropped his lantern and ran to her assistance.

As he reached out to the girl, she collapsed limply into his waiting arms. "God in heaven!" he exclaimed, easing her to the ground and wiping the blood from her neck. He soon realised that his effort was futile, as another wave of blood poured from her. Betterton began to sob as the girl's eyes rolled back into her head, but before he could make any sense of the horrendous situation he had found himself in, a noise of dragging feet caught his attention. As he looked up, he could see the silhouettes of a group of seven or eight men against the moonlight, lurching their way up the lane, not with the step of normal healthy men, but with some kind of ungodly stagger. Long, dry moans emanated from coarse throats that didn't have the capacity for speech.

Betterton didn't wait to try and piece together what deranged situation he'd stumbled upon and got hastily to his feet to make his escape. As he turned to run, he found to his surprise that the young girl was back on her feet and reaching out towards him.

"Come with me!" he said, grabbing her hand. "We must go, now!"

It didn't occur to Betterton that he was trying to help a girl who had died in his arms seconds earlier. Instead, his only thought was of getting her to a doctor and away from the strange group staggering their way. She resisted his tug and when Betterton tried a second time to move her, she reciprocated by crushing his hand in a vice-like grip. Betterton let out an agonised yell as his knuckles cracked and popped. The girl's face was hideous, a feral snarl marring her features. What had once been a pretty little girl was now a monster. Crying out, Betterton swung his fist and struck her hard across the face. The force of the blow severed her head completely and she dropped.

Betterton allowed himself a glance over his shoulder as he fled. He was horrified to find that the group of men had gained on him and he could smell their stale breath on the icy wind. As they shuffled into the light he saw their wounds and knew that they were dead. Yet they walked!

Right at that moment, there was only one place in the world Betterton wanted to be and one group of people he wanted to be with. He sprinted back onto the country lane that led to Evesham Abbey.

CHAPTER SEVENTEEN

Onboard the Algernon, the Solent
20th June, 1642

They hadn't long left Portsmouth and Davenant
was already feeling seasick. He leant over the side
and took several deep breaths in a hopeless attempt
to stop himself from vomiting, but the rolling of
the vessel and the sight of the monotonous waves
caused him to lose his lunch. This resulted in much
hilarity amongst the crew, a mixture of jovial sailors,
smugglers and pirates of all ages, races and religions.
A regular melting pot.

He ignored their jibes, many of which he couldn't
even comprehend, and took in the view of the ocean
as he wiped the mixture of spittle and bile from
his lip. Theirs was the only craft in view on the
vast expanse of water. The sun was shining in the
cloudless sky and a fair wind licked over the surface
of the sea. After taking deep breaths, Davenant rolled
onto his back, squinting as the sun disappeared and
reappeared behind the sail. The rigging garlanded
the sky, scoring it with the dark lines. He noted the
hordes of sweating men heaving the barrels of brandy,
beer and gunpowder along the deck and fastening
them in place with thick rope. What a journey those
barrels must have had, Davenant thought. Through
secret tunnels and onto covert carriages before being
hauled onboard the Algernon.

"What do you think of my boat?" Bray said, as he
took a hearty swig of whatever putrid liquor filled
his carafe.

"Your boat?"

"Yes, William, my boat. These men are working for me. What do you think got me imprisoned in the Tower in the first place?" Davenant cast his mind back to what the guards had told him and smirked. "You haven't answered my question, William. What do you think of my boat?"

"It's very grand," replied Davenant.

"Have you always been a terrible liar?"

He was right, Davenant thought. He was lying. The boat was a pockmarked ageing bark, barely held together by pitch and rope; the weathered timber could have sprung a leak and drowned them all at any moment. And the stink was almost unbearable. At least he could console himself that he would be in France within days, free from the threat of Cromwell's men and the judgemental eyes of Bray's comrades. That aside, Davenant was grateful for Bray's assistance in helping him escape the grim confines of the Tower and they had even managed to strike up a peculiar friendship in the two months that they had been on the run. Their journey down from London to Portsmouth had been a perilous affair. They had almost been caught on two separate occasions by Parliamentarian soldiers, and Davenant had felt a heady blend of relief and gratitude when he had seen the glittering coast for the first time. However, his contentment was not without a tinge of sadness, and the thought of Elizabeth's welfare continued to occupy his thoughts and even his dreams. He had managed to send word to Turnbull of his plans to stay in France until he could secure military stores for the Royalists' battle with Parliament.

"I wonder what our friend Cromwell makes of

all this?" said Bray, as he removed his jerkin and stretched out on the deck.

"I hope he chokes on his own venom and vitriol," replied Davenant, allowing a rare glimpse of his rancorous side.

"What do you plan to do when we reach France? You know, I could use a good man like you, a man lacking in moral fibre, a man willing to fuck the hierarchy. And who knows, maybe you might end up making some money from it? Enough to buy your own boat, perhaps?"

Davenant smiled. "Is that a veiled complement?"

Bray shrugged. "In truth, although I appreciate your kind offer, I have my own agenda. There are several people I need to see in France."

"To help you pursue your incessant tryst with Cromwell, no doubt."

Maybe he was right, Davenant thought. Maybe he should settle down and find something else to do rather than gallivanting around the country catering to the whims of Royalists. It would certainly mean that he would see more of Elizabeth and less of the dank cell walls belonging to the Tower. But then, in a moment of lucidity, he regained his perspective. He'd be damned if he was going to let Parliament and Cromwell ruin his country.

"Cromwell is the man who threatens our freedoms, our daily lives and the man who threatens to take away my first love."

"Bellyaching?"

Davenant let out a wicked cackle. "No, my dear old chap. The theatre."

"In which case, I shall wish you the very best in your endeavours."

There was genuine warmth in Bray's voice and Davenant truly felt as though he had made a friend for life.

CHAPTER EIGHTEEN

Evesham Abbey
12th September, 1651

It was becoming increasingly likely that Betterton had sold them out to Cromwell's mob and so Davenant began the task of organising his troupe. They had to leave before the wrath of Parliament caught up with them.

As Davenant snuck into Middleton's tent to wake him, Middleton mistook him for an intruder and grabbed him in a vice-like headlock, much to Charles' amusement. In spite of his embarrassment and evident discomfort, Davenant recognised the need for Middleton's prowess. The man was a thuggish brute, he thought, but was equally glad that he was on his side. And he was immediately apologetic – although that was the least he could do, Davenant pondered. The man had almost broken his neck.

After gathering their possessions, the men crossed the dewy grass to join their companions.

Davenant was still cagey around Elizabeth and her discontent towards his secretive past. He resigned himself to the fact that he would have to remedy this problem before they could function again as father and daughter. Davenant understood her feelings for Betterton and had attempted to convey his disappointment in the boy to her as reasonably as possible. In the end he had managed to stop short of threatening to kill the bastard, which was about as reasonable as she could have possibly expected. And then there was Mary – he hadn't quite made up his mind whether to leave her in Evesham, or to utilise her bizarre ability. He was in no doubt that the answer to his quandary would present itself at the right time. He was presently more troubled by his feelings for Faith and had tried to put his attraction to her to the back of his mind. This was no time for lust, he kept on telling himself. Yet the more he spoke to her, the more he felt beset by her beauty. He cast his eyes over her companions and was shocked, although not totally surprised, to find Mary staring at him intently.

"Good morning, Mary," said Davenant, as politely as he possibly could. He noted that the others were beginning to stir.

"Good morning, Master Shakespeare."

Davenant could feel his blood rising, and just as he was about to launch into a foul-mouthed tirade, he saw Faith smiling at him as she let out a restrained yawn. It calmed him immediately.

"I'm so sorry to have disturbed you," he said. "But we have to leave as soon as possible."

"Why?"

"We have a traitor in our midst."

"A traitor? But who would do such a thing?" replied Faith, as she gathered her belongings.

Davenant steadied himself – he was fully aware that what he was about to say would hurt young Underhill, as Betterton's closest friend, the most. "I have reason to believe that our so called friend, Thomas Betterton, has informed Cromwell's troops of our whereabouts."

Underhill was now fully awake. "How can you be sure? Have you any proof, other than the fact that he's gone?"

"After he left without telling anyone where he was going, it was brought to my attention that he had kept hold of the wanted poster he had found in Pershore."

"That's not proof! Has it occurred to you that perhaps Thomas wanted to leave because of your choice of plays?"

"Enough, Cave!" interrupted Anne, barking at her brother to keep quiet. "Have some respect."

A stony silence descended

"Please, Cave. You must believe me." Davenant said.

"Very well," replied Underhill, cagily. He grabbed his belongings together rather petulantly and stuffed them into his sack.

Elizabeth sat alone on a rock by the Bell Tower and Davenant sauntered nervously up to her, half expecting her to stand and stride off at any moment.

"I'm so very sorry, Elizabeth," stuttered Davenant, as he knelt down beside her. He was surprised that she'd given him the chance to apologise, although she still looked glumly down at the damp undergrowth.

He decided to seize the opportunity to patch things up as best he could. "I'm sorry that I was never honest with you, and I'm sorry for what has happened these past two days. I wish to God I could go back and make it all up to you."

"I'm sorry too, father," she replied. She allowed her beautiful emerald eyes to meet his. "I know you have all of our best interests at heart. But from now on, I want you to be honest with me."

Davenant nodded firmly. "Of course I will, I promise."

"And I want you to tell me all your stories about Will Shakespeare."

"Some other time," replied Davenant, smiling tenderly.

Suddenly, he was struck by a figure running madly across the adjoining field and straight towards them.

"Unless I'm very much mistaken," he said, "that is young Master Betterton heading this way."

Elizabeth bolted to her feet and waved her arms to catch his attention. Davenant glanced over to Turnbull, Middleton and Charles who were all alive to the situation. He could see that the three men were caressing their weapons, tucked conspicuously in their belts. He almost felt sorry for the young scamp, for the brutal interrogation he was about to receive.

As Betterton moved rapidly closer, his shouted words became audible upon the wind. "The dead are coming!"

"What did he say?" said Davenant, looking in Charles' direction.

Underhill's face lit up when he spied Betterton galloping towards them. "It's Thomas! He's come back!"

Davenant sidled up to Middleton. "What do you think we should do with him?"

"Let's see what the wee shite has to say first, shall we?"

Betterton was only a couple of hundred yards away now and Davenant could clearly make out the lines of fear etched upon his face. "This doesn't look good," he whispered under his breath.

And then it came again. "The dead are coming!"

This time everyone heard his declaration. As the

group all turned to one another in bewilderment, Betterton followed his latest yell with a series of deranged hand signals which made no sense to anyone whatsoever – apart from to Mary.

She turned mockingly to Davenant. "I told you they were coming, didn't I?"

Davenant decided to ignore her and focused his attention on Betterton, who had pulled up, fatigued and exhausted. He leant against a tree as he gasped for air.

"Have you alerted Cromwell's men to our whereabouts?" Davenant snapped.

Betterton looked up fearfully. He gave a sad little nod of his head as his eyes filled.

As Davenant stepped forward to pass Betterton his water skin, Middleton thumped him hard across the face, sending him tumbling to the floor. Elizabeth screamed out in anguish as Underhill struggled to restrain her.

"Consider yourself lucky you didn't receive a worse punishment." Middleton spat at him.

Betterton ran his hand over his swollen cheek and bloodied nose. All from one punch, Davenant noted.

"I am truly sorry for my actions, but there is no time for that now," Betterton said. "You must listen to me, all of you. I have been in grip of the Devil. Look at my hands! They're covered in blood."

"No sob story will get you out of this! Do you have any idea what you've done?" barked Charles, his eyes wild with rage.

"No, no, I – I don't. But I'm telling the truth. I've seen the..."

"I say we hang the bastard!" Charles interrupted.

Davenant felt as though he was in some kind of

deranged, surreal daydream. He could hear Elizabeth sobbing uncontrollably behind him. "Perhaps we should hear him out? He looks like he's telling us the truth."

"He's an actor. You're as good as lying when you're on the stage!" spat Charles.

As Davenant listened to the flood of accusations, Mary took a hesitant step forward and knelt down beside Betterton. "He is telling the truth. The dead walk, I've seen them too."

Just as Davenant was about to open his mouth to deride her, several mounted soldiers surged forward into their camp. They quickly encircled the group with a ferocious clatter of hooves – their vast horses with their immaculate coats just as intimidating as the length of their swords.

"William Davenant and Charles Stuart?" asked the General, a tubby, red-faced man with a speech impediment.

"I am Sir William Davenant," he said, as he took a defiant stride forward.

"And I am Charles Stuart," said Charles, matching Davenant's fortitude. "Take us, by all means, but you need not harm our companions. They have done you no wrong."

"I am bidden by Parliament to arrest you all and to take you to the Tower. You may leave your belongings where they are."

Davenant could bear the Tower – he knew what it took to stomach it and survive – but the thought of Elizabeth suffering at the hands of the Guards made him feel sick with worry.

The soldiers leapt from their horses and seized the group forcefully, hurling them into a waiting carriage. Middleton and Turnbull didn't go without a struggle, but were overwhelmed by the sheer number of armed men.

As their carriage slowly pulled away, Davenant noticed a group of men lurkng aimlessly in the nearby field. Strange, he thought, they weren't there a moment ago.

CHAPTER NINETEEN

The Siege of Gloucester
5th September, 1643

William Davenant was dog-tired. Having seen his hard earned military supplies from France go to waste on a siege that could have and should have succeeded, he believed that he had as much right as any to feel more than a little aggrieved. The King had ordered their retreat from the ancient Roman walls of Gloucester little more than five hours ago and Davenant now found himself encamped in a forest on the outskirts of Cirencester. The mood amongst his compatriots was understandably glum, not surprising considering what they were up against. A twenty-three year old governor by the name of Colonel Massey who had only one-thousand five-hundred regular troops under his command – surely not enough to fend off the Royalist insurgence that had just reclaimed Bristol so convincingly?

If only Charles had ordered an all-out attack, Davenant lamented. Although he later acknowledged Charles' compassion – his choice to order a formal siege so as to avoid a repetition of the heavy casualties sustained at the storming of Bristol probably saved the lives of many civilians, even if it did result in their retreat. He also cursed their run of bad luck. Had it not been for the terrible weather, they would have been able to fire the mine before it became flooded. Not that any of this mattered now, Davenant thought. He was glad to be alive, even if he felt a little disgruntled that his endeavours in France hadn't even earned him so much as a 'thank you' from His Majesty. He concluded that Charles must have been in another fit of depression, as he hadn't emerged from his tent all evening. Davenant could see a lonely shadow pacing awkwardly up and down the canvas, occasionally stopping by the entrance, no doubt wondering whether or not to come out and face the barrage of questioning. He was surprised when a smaller, almost dwarf-like figure emerged grudgingly from the tent and headed in his direction. It was Hugo Stanger, Charles' aide, a vile little cretin and sycophant. Just the type Davenant despised. Like a venomous snake, he slipped his way past the group of soldiers stretched out by the campfire and crept up to Davenant.

"Yes, Hugo, what is it?"

"It's His Majesty, he is greatly troubled. He wishes to have a moment alone with you to seek your counsel."

"Now?" asked Davenant, surprised by this summons, but equally aware of Stanger's Machiavellian qualities.

"Yes, William, now. He even suggested that he speaks with you alone."

Davenant allowed himself a smug little grin, knowing full well how much that would have hurt Stanger as he strode briskly to the King's tent. As he gently pulled the entrance flap to one side, his mind was racing with possible reasons for his summons.

The King was sat on a fabulously ornate armchair which took up much of the tent. A pungent pall of smoke, wafting from a strange china device, filled the room with the scent of dried herbs and spices. Davenant gasped in the close confines of the tent.

"It's balsamic resin from the sacred plant of the priests, William. It is supposed to be relaxing."

Relaxing? Not when you can barely breathe!

"You wanted to see me, Your Majesty?"

"Yes, William. It dawned on me earlier that I have yet to thank you for your good grace and valour..." *You're damned right!* "... so I thought it was about time I addressed that."

"What did you have in mind, Your Majesty?" Through the haze, Davenant could just about make out Charles removing his mighty sword from its scabbard.

"On your knees, William," said Charles, his voice calm and measured.

"Please, spare me Your Majesty! I am your most humble servant and I do you no wrong! I have only ever sought to serve your best intentions and I do not deserve to lose my head."

Charles laughed. "You fool, William! Why, I should dress you up as my court jester."

Davenant was totally dumfounded. Was he to be executed in such bizarre circumstances? As he dropped to his knees for forgiveness, he appreciated that for the first time in his life he was at the mercy of a complete and utter madman who had lost control of his senses. He wondered what heaven would be like and Davenant muttered a small prayer as he felt the cold steel of Charles' sword as it touched either shoulder. And then the words came that he would remember forever.

"Arise, Sir William."

CHAPTER TWENTY

Bishop's Cleeve, Gloucestershire
13th September, 1651

The weather had changed overnight, bringing
with it an incessant wind, ominous skies and a
modicum of rain. The air was bitterly cold and
had managed to penetrate right through into the
carriage. A small crack in the roof let in tiny drips
that had dampened the seats, smudging the leather
and leaving it clammy to touch. The wind came in
gusts, shaking the carriage as it trundled round the
sharp bends of sunken country lanes, or over high
ground in exposed places of barren wilderness. The
wheels of the carriage squealed as they sank into the
many furrows and potholes that littered the badly
kept roads.

The group huddled together for warmth. Davenant,
looking out of the filthy mud-streaked window, could
just about make out a convoy of mounted soldiers
galloping alongside. They had passed through
countless villages and towns where the locals had
braved the adverse conditions to greet the party as
they travelled through. Word would reach the next
village before they did, and more peasants would line
the roads to see if the rumours of a carriage carrying
Charles Stuart were true. Charles was evidently
touched to see many of the crowds saluting, and as
they passed through the village of Bishop's Cleeve,
several of the well-wishers had draped their rag-like
blankets over the numerous puddles in respect for
their King. Others had dared to throw stones and rotten

vegetables in the direction of the soldiers, which had filled Charles with a smug glee and the sense that the battles and hardships had been worthwhile.

The driver of the carriage, a hulk of a man with no neck, had lost the feeling in his hands hours ago and could barely clasp the whip which hung limply in his left hand. The horses had thus found themselves at a temporary reprieve and could travel as fast or as slow as they wished without fear of reprisal. It meant that the soldiers had expunged much of their energy in trying to keep up with the carriage and subsequently failed to deal with the few unruly villagers.

The group let out a collective groan as the carriage jolted over another deep rut, the shock of which sent them tumbling into one another. To his embarrassment, Davenant found himself nestled head first in Faith's bosom.

"I'm sorry," he mumbled as he felt himself turning red in the face.

"I don't suppose we're anywhere near London yet, are we? I'm not sure whether I can put up with much more of this," replied Faith, unperturbed by Davenant's embarrassment.

Underhill hadn't taken his eyes off Betterton, who sat opposite him, sporting several wild bruises, the largest of which had almost sealed his left eye. "Why did you do it, Thomas, I thought we were friends? But you're nothing more than piss in the wind!"

Betterton sank his head into his chest. "I will make it up to you all. I promise."

"Why lie to us?" spat Elizabeth.

Everyone was listening now as Betterton timidly took centre stage.

He appreciated that his answer to Elizabeth's

question had to be a bloody good one, and he took a deep breath in an effort to compose himself. "I have not lied to you. Yes, I have made a terrible mistake that I shall always regret, but I have not lied. What I saw was beyond the pale. I swear as God is my witness that I saw a young girl of no more than twelve years of age, stagger towards me with her head barely attached to her body. As she died in my arms, a group of men attacked me. I could see in their eyes that they weren't alive..."

"Weren't alive?" Elizabeth interrupted, abrasively.

"If you had seen them, you wouldn't think to question my integrity. Their eyes were as vacant as the expression on their faces. And as I turned to run, the young girl, who not a moment earlier was dead in my arms, was standing next to me, completely reanimated with blood still seeping from her wound."

There was a deathly silence. Even the creaking wheels of the carriage seemed to respect the situation and offer no interruption.

"You've taken several blows to your head, Thomas. You're concussed and what you're saying is a result of that," said Davenant, appealing for rationality.

"No! I saw her as clear as I see you now!" Betterton cried, as he looked desperately in Mary's direction, frantically trying to find a believer. She closed her eyes, much to his dismay.

"This is nothing more than a futile attempt to gain sympathy," said Charles, still smarting from Betterton's betrayal. "Let us hope that Cromwell has the good grace to chop off your head first."

Betterton shook his head glumly and turned to face the window. He was left in no doubt that any chance of him collecting the reward had vaporised into thin air. It was raining harder now, fierce droplets pounding rhythmically against the smoky glass and gushing through the crack in the roof. Betterton could no longer make out the mounted soldiers though they had been perfectly visible not five minutes prior to his chastisement. He could have sworn he had heard several gasps or squeals, but soon came to the conclusion that it must have been the carriage wheels again. He closed his eyes and prayed for sleep, even if it was for just ten minutes.

As they left the sodden village of Bishop's Cleeve behind them, Davenant could feel the carriage begin to slow and the thud of hooves on the wet terrain begin to ease in their ferocity. Eventually they came to a halt by a dense copse. The soldiers duly pulled up alongside the carriage, dismounting hurriedly, and the sound of a muted conversation between the General and the driver began to filter into the carriage. As Davenant appealed for silence from his comrades, he was alarmed to find the conversation build into a heated and animated exchange. As he put his ear to the window, he could pick out several words. "Crowd" and "trouble" seemed to be the most common plus the occasional obscenity thrown in for good measure. And then, for the briefest, most fleeting of moments, he could have sworn he heard one of the men utter the word "bloodshed."

He rubbed the sleeve of his jerkin on the window to remove some of the filth. To his bewilderment, there were only three mounted soldiers in their party, where previously there had been six. The three soldiers that remained looked as though they had come face to face with the Devil himself.

Davenant could see the driver hastily retake his seat and heard a viciously urgent crack of the whip rain down upon the horses' backs. As the carriage wheels jolted into action, he couldn't help but wonder whether there might be an element of truth in Betterton's implausible account after all. Perhaps their arrival in London would shed some light on this bizarre chain of events, he thought.

CHAPTER TWENTY-ONE

The Tower of London

It was exactly as he remembered it. The same repellent smell, the same sense of trepidation and apprehension – although Davenant was grateful that this time his entrance into the Tower was over its drawbridge and not through the murky waters of Traitors' Gate. As the weary carriage driver and the even wearier horses plodded through the portcullis of the Lion Tower, Davenant cast his eye at the ominous clouds gathering over the Thames. It had been another wretched day full of biting winds and rainstorms, but these black clouds brought with them an altogether more threatening atmosphere. The distant rumble of thunder and flashes of lightning had woken Elizabeth, who had been asleep since they passed through Abbots Langley more than three hours earlier.

"Where are we?" she muttered.

"The Tower of London," replied Davenant, keen not to make its name sound any more menacing than it already was. It was of no use, the look of fear that was already fixed upon the faces of his companions was clear for all to see. Even Charles and Middleton, men accustomed to the threat of death on a daily basis, looked pale.

The depleted convoy of soldiers followed the carriage and as they came to a halt outside the White Tower, they dismounted and unbolted the carriage doors. As Davenant was hoisted from the transport by one of the soldiers, he peered up at the gigantic building that loomed over them. He took a moment to remember the torpid months that he had been incarcerated here. But then he fondly remembered the friendship he had struck up with dear old Bray, and their ridiculous escape through the same gates that they had just passed through. Every cloud has a silver lining, he thought. Although the clouds hanging above him now were far darker than he ever remembered them being on that day. He pondered what might have become of Bray, the peculiar old seadog, and hoped that wherever he was and whatever he was doing he was enjoying every minute of it.

As he watched the others being hauled from the carriage, he tried to ascertain what was different about the Tower this time – was it the new armouries, or a change to the Queen's House? No, it was something else. He couldn't quite put his finger on it. And then it hit him, how could he have possibly forgotten? There was no sound of the squawking of ravens; the incessant din that they used to make would keep him awake for hours on end. And then he remembered the legend – that if the ravens ever left the Tower then the entire Kingdom would fall. He wasn't a great believer in folklore, but perhaps there was an ounce of truth to this one.

Cromwell and the gaunt artist sat within his luxurious chamber in the White Tower. The artist, in his drab workaday gown, had a dark, sporadic beard and drawn out features which looked as though his skin had been pulled tightly over his face. Despite the dingy weather outside, the cold marble floor was still able to gleam beneath the many burning lanterns and the glow of the fire burning in the grate.

The artist was putting the finishing touches to Cromwell's portrait. He was fortunate that the enigmatic lighting favoured Cromwell's new-found vanity, although what he thought of his portrait remained to be seen. There was no denying that Cromwell did look strikingly regal in his long golden gown trimmed with ermine, a surcoat of silver cloth, and a shirt of exquisite linen. Attendants hovered by to offer him wine, hold his gloves, move his chair or, at nod or lift of a finger, take some muttered message from him.

Footsteps resonated along the corridor outside the chamber. Cromwell's tubby General soon appeared, sheepishly, in the doorway.

"Excuse me, Sir. I'm sorry to disturb but..."

"Can't you see I'm busy!" snapped Cromwell.

"Yes, Sir, but I thought you would like to know that they've arrived."

"You will leave us." Cromwell said, curtly, to the artist.

The artist doffed his hat, holding it to his chest as etiquette required. He knelt to Cromwell with a few soft words of parting and slithered from the room.

"Would you be so kind as to send them up to me?" asked Cromwell, his eyes flickering with devilish glee.

"Yes Sir, right away."

Cromwell motioned for his attendants to leave the room. Within a minute he was alone in the vast chamber. He composed himself. Cromwell could feel his heart beating in his chest like a pair of castanets. It angered him to think that Davenant and Charles were having such an adverse effect on his nerves. The sounds of footsteps were becoming more insistent as they approached and Cromwell could distinguish the sound of several heavy boots amongst them. As he looked up, his General re-appeared in the doorway.

"William Davenant and Charles Stuart, Sir, plus several other... parasites we picked up en route."

"Send them in."

The two defiant figures strode purposefully into the chamber, unperturbed by its luxuriant peril, followed by the rest of the group.

Davenant was immediately struck by how hideous Cromwell had become, the warts that infested his face were like nothing he'd ever seen, even on the most stricken of pox-sufferers. Cromwell, already irritated by his bold entrance, could see the appalled reaction in Davenant's eyes and this angered him further.

"Good evening, Sir William, it's been a while, hasn't it? I trust you had a pleasant journey down?" he said.

"It was delightful. May I convey my thanks for sending your finest carriage and your most reputable of soldiers," replied Davenant.

Cromwell fixed his glare upon Charles. "Charles Stuart as well! My, my, this is quite a gathering. I've no doubt your father would have been very proud of your little rebellion, in particular escaping the Battle of Worcester unscathed. The good it's done you..."

"Go fuck yourself, you pox-ridden twat!" spat Charles.

Davenant let out a loud guffaw.

Cromwell was dumbfounded. "I see you display the legendary Stuart temper," he eventually managed.

And then it happened again – to begin with only

one or two droplets, but within a few seconds blood was pouring from Cromwell's nose. He motioned frantically for one of his attendants to re-enter the chamber. A tall, elegant woman rushed over to him and handed him a scented handkerchief which he duly snatched from her. He placed it carefully over his nose as Davenant and Charles looked on in unreserved astonishment.

"This happens from time to time," muttered Cromwell from behind the handkerchief, evidently embarrassed, and conscious that it had seemed an age since someone last spoke.

"I daresay it does," said Charles. "And I must say that it gives me great pleasure to watch you bleed."

Cromwell dabbed at the blood, thinking long and hard about his retort. "And it will give me great pleasure to finally end this war of ours. And to watch your head roll! I wonder if you will bleed as much as your father did. I was told they were mopping up his blood hours after his execution."

Charles lunged forward but was held back by Davenant before Cromwell's soldiers could apprehend him. Davenant winced under the pressure of Charles' anger. Eventually he backed down and stood pensively by Davenant.

"I suppose you have your people call that your throne? And your everyday robes your regal gown? Lord Protector is but another name for a King, and the country shan't tolerate your stealing the crown forever." Charles growled.

Cromwell brushed it off. "Before I have you all executed, I must ask a favour of you, Davenant. Consider this a temporary reprieve for you all. It is my wife's birthday tomorrow and to celebrate this she wants a cursed play put on for her. As luck would have it, I have your troupe to take care of this for me. I don't give a damn what play you decide to perform, and don't think for one moment that this is a chance for you to escape. Any funny business will see you executed on the spot. Think of this as your one final hurrah."

"Where are we to perform?" asked Davenant.

"The theatre, you damned fool!"

"With respect, you've destroyed all the theatres."

"There might be one or two left on Drury Lane," said Elizabeth, piping up.

Cromwell peered around Charles to get a better view of Davenant's daughter. He was instantly taken by the young, naive beauty that she displayed.

"And who are you, my pretty one?" he asked, as he made his way towards her.

"My name is Elizabeth Davenant," she said hesitantly.

Cromwell let out a wicked cackle. "Well how fortunate for you that you look nothing like him. Your mother must have been a very beautiful woman."

Elizabeth could smell his foul breath and noted his yellow, decaying teeth and bleeding gums. "I believe she was," she replied, already regretting her interruption.

Cromwell took her hand and planted a kiss upon it. "Do not worry, my dear. You shan't suffer at the hands of the executioner the way your father shall. I'll make sure he is swift with you." Elizabeth began to weep, as if the enormity of the situation hadn't hit her until Cromwell's sadistic statement.

Davenant put a comforting arm around her and glared at Cromwell with a blazing look of utter hatred. "The Phoenix Theatre," he said, in between gritted teeth. "I used to manage it and I made sure it was left... untouched."

"Excellent. The Phoenix Theatre it is!" cried Cromwell, as he turned his attention back to Davenant. "I shall leave it in your capable hands to arrange the entertainment. Oh, and William, I've doubled the sentry at your cell so there's no chance of you escaping this time."

"That's very kind of you."

"In which case, I shall bid you all a good evening." Cromwell sauntered from the chamber, his long gown trailing behind him.

Davenant turned to look out of the window. The sky was black, not even the moon was visible through the murkiness. With the fog came the cold and Davenant dreaded the night ahead, knowing full well how bitter the cells became when the Thames mist rolled in. They'd be lucky if they all saw the morning in, he thought.

As the group were frogmarched from the chamber and towards the cells, Davenant could see the General and Cromwell in the middle of an animated conversation at the furthest end of the corridor. He wondered whether they were discussing the strange circumstances surrounding the disappearance of the three mounted soldiers.

At least they were still together. This way they were able to stay as warm as possible, making use of one another's body heat as they huddled together. Cromwell had confined them to the Salt Tower and a smaller, more uncomfortable chamber than they would have received elsewhere. The cells were exactly as Davenant remembered them. The same stink of damp and mould, the same carvings adorning the walls, some drawn in beautiful calligraphy, others coarse profanities. Indeed, many of the inscriptions were left by Catholic and Jesuit priests during the reign of Elizabeth. And there was the same prevailing sense of sorrow that couldn't possibly be explained unless you'd spent a night within the same unforgiving walls of this torture palace.

Davenant could hear the rain lashing down outside. The cell would occasionally be illuminated by a flash of lightning accompanied by a grumble of thunder so severe, it sounded as if it had originated within the bowels of Hell itself. Davenant noticed that the majority of his group had somehow fallen asleep. He was grateful for that although he couldn't fathom how they could sleep in such conditions.

Davenant knew only too well that he would spend the entire night wide awake with worry, only his thoughts and Turnbull's ceaseless snoring to accompany him. He jumped when he felt a hand brush against his shoulder. He turned to face Faith, who had crept up next to him.

"Sorry if I startled you," she said.

"I thought I was the only one awake," replied Davenant, shifting along the wall to make more room for her.

"No, there's not much chance of me getting any sleep in here." She turned her face to his.

"I'm sorry for getting you involved in all this," whispered Davenant.

"You have nothing to be sorry for. You saved our

lives, Sir William. You mustn't forget that."

"I daresay you won't feel that way when we're up on Tower Hill staring the executioner in the eye."

Faith smiled tenderly. "Of course I will. I've enjoyed meeting you and your family, and spending these few days with you has been an experience to say the least."

"Yes, it has been an experience," he said, glancing over at Mary who was asleep in the furthest corner of the cell.

"You mustn't blame Mary," replied Faith. "She can't help the way she is."

"How did you get put on trial alongside her?" asked Davenant.

"It was a case of being in the wrong place at the wrong time. Anne and I went for a walk in the woods when we came across Mary performing some strange ritual. We hid behind a tree to watch her. When then the soldiers came to take her away they found us loitering nearby. They assumed that we were part of her witchcraft. Still, you have to admit that she is good."

"Yes, a little too good. She lifted the lid on me." said Davenant.

"Why are you so ashamed of your past?" Davenant didn't answer immediately. "I'm sorry, I should not have asked, it's none of my business."

"Because of the stigma and the dishonour surrounding my birth. I'm a bastard child and people don't like bastard children."

"Yet you follow in his footsteps."

"Yes. I already loved the theatre before I discovered that Shakespeare was my father. I cannot deny that having him as my father did help in my becoming recognised on the circuit, though."

"So why resent him?"

"Because I wanted to be known for my own plays and soon realised that mine weren't a patch on his."

"Let us perform one of your plays for Cromwell's wife tomorrow then!" said Faith encouragingly, trying to lift his spirits.

"No."

"Then what shall we do?"

Davenant cast his eye over his troupe and took a deep breath. "What about a play by my father? Now is as good a time as any."

"Are you sure?" asked Faith, taken aback.

"As sure as I'll ever be, it's just a question of which one."

"What about *Richard III*? That would send Cromwell into spasms of anger! After all, it might as well be about him."

Davenant's mind was racing at the possibilities. And then he spoke, a whispered murmur at first that went unheard.

"I beg your pardon?"

"*Macbeth*... the Scottish Play."

Faith looked puzzled. "Isn't that a little... depressing for a birthday celebration?" Davenant got to his feet unsteadily. "No, no, think about it. It's perfect. We've got three witches, a Scottish soldier and a King already amongst us. It is meant to be," he gasped.

"And you're sure you can do this?"

"My good lady, I was born to do this!"

CHAPTER TWENTY-TWO

Greenwich

Something was leading them towards the capital. The horde of men, women, children, soldiers, drunkards, housewives and whores staggered and lurched their way along the banks of the Thames. The stench of the London River was overwhelmed by the reek of rotting flesh, the smell penetrating the hovels nearby and rousing people from their sleep. If they listened carefully they could just make out the soft groans of the dead, many dismissing it as the sound of the wind and returning to their slumber, unaware of the horrors that lurched mere feet from their doors.

The banks of the river were crowded with the dead, some falling into the water as their brethren shuffled relentlessly on. Those lost to the river merely floated on the surface, occasionally twitching, staring dispassionately from empty eye sockets.

Eventually the dead came to a square, across which light spilled from the doors of a slaughterhouse, the scent of animal and human flesh drawing them quickly onwards. Soft groans now turned to feral growls of hunger as they spilled into the building. A man looked up as he slaughtered a pig, the knife dropping from his hand as a thing with half a face clawed into his stomach and pulled out his guts. Just before the darkness closed in, he saw the thing feasting on his steaming intestines.

The dead tore open animal pens, feasting on the squealing livestock within, pulling apart cows, sheep and chickens in their frenzy. Soon the sluices were overwhelmed with gore and the blood began to spill from the slaughterhouse into the square. The cobbles shone pitch black in the moonlight.

Within a matter of minutes all living flesh in the building had been consumed and the horde wandered back to the banks of the river and continued in their shuffling march into the capital.

In the distance the curtained walls of the Tower of London crouched over the Thames like a castle nestled over its moat. It was illuminated briefly by a flash of lightning, revealing the White Tower in all its ostentatious glory. In spite of their seemingly directionless ambling, there was no confusion amongst the dead – they knew exactly where they were heading and who they wanted to slay.

CHAPTER TWENTY-THREE

The Tower of London

It was morning. At least Davenant could have sworn it was – his body seemed to confirm it, but were his eyes deceiving him? As he stirred, the murky clouds that were so prevalent the night before were still hanging low in the dense sky, turning dawn to night. Davenant had never seen such a gloomy morning and he yearned for the bright countryside daybreaks that he had often enjoyed in Oxfordshire. He truly felt miserable. He even began to welcome the thought of his execution, for at least then he would be put out of his misery.

As he turned his head from the window, he became aware that Elizabeth and Betterton were also awake and in the middle of a muted quarrel. He closed his eyes and pretended to fall back asleep, eager to establish the cause of their disagreement.

"How many more times do I have to tell you?" asked Betterton.

Elizabeth sighed. "Don't take that tone with me. You forget your actions."

"Perhaps, but I have had enough of telling you the same thing, over and over again!"

"But it's so far fetched, Thomas. Put yourself in my position, would you believe what you're saying?"

"I daresay I wouldn't," replied Betterton sullenly. "But I want you to believe me more than anyone else."

Elizabeth allowed herself a reluctant smile. "I want to, really I do."

An uneasy silence fell upon the cell.

"All I thought about when I left was you."

"Yet I wager you wouldn't have returned to us unless you were forced to."

"Listen, Elizabeth, I am destitute. Your father hasn't paid our wages in weeks and I've had to steal to make ends meet. If there had been any other way..."

"My father keeps you in food, drink and shelter, isn't that enough?"

"Look, we shouldn't argue, we've only got one last day together. Let us make the most of it."

"Very well," Elizabeth replied.

A fleet of heavy footsteps broke her train of thought. Elizabeth got to her feet and peeked through the bars of the cell door. She could see several of Cromwell's soldiers and Cromwell himself marching down the corridor towards them. She quickly sat back down, seeking refuge in between her father and Turnbull, trembling at the thought of any further contact with the repulsive Cromwell.

The heavy lock on the door clunked open.

"Good morning, one and all. I trust you had a pleasant night's sleep?" asked Cromwell mockingly as he entered the cell.

"As well as could be expected," replied Davenant.

"My soldiers shall accompany you to the Queen's House. You can have the afternoon to rehearse. We meet at the Phoenix Theatre this evening."

"Come on! Get up!" bellowed the tubby General, as he banged his cudgel against the bars on the cell door.

The group got to their feet gingerly and walked in single file out of the chamber. Cromwell leered as he admired Elizabeth. He couldn't help but cup his hand around her pert buttock as she eased past him. She let out a faint yelp of disgust as her pace quickened. As Cromwell followed the actors, he allowed himself a fleeting glance into a cell to his left, a small chamber, little more than a privy. To his surprise, its single occupant seemed startlingly familiar. He saw his ashen, ghostlike face first, his sunken and sallow features drawn over his skeletal cheekbones. And then he saw the brown hooded cloak that shrouded the prisoner's pallid face. Cromwell turned and strode briskly up the corridor, feeling an icy breeze on the back of his neck, and his heart pounding in his chest.

CHAPTER TWENTY-FOUR

The Phoenix Theatre, Drury Lane

Given the circumstances, it had been a splendid afternoon. Davenant was able to forget his troubles as the group set about their rehearsal, and as the crowd began to convene in the pit of the old theatre for the evening's entertainment, Davenant felt a sense of palpable excitement – the kind that only performing in front of hundreds of people can give. They had done a good job in tidying up the place, bringing in new seats from Whitehall Palace and repairing the old timber of the stage. Several seamstresses had patched up the velvet of the crimson curtain and Cromwell had even allowed for several props and costumes to be taken over from the Red Bull Theatre in Clerkenwell.

It had been almost a decade since Davenant had last set foot in the Phoenix, and despite its neglect, it had managed to retain its unique atmosphere. He looked up at the ornate Inigo Jones designed ceiling that hung high above the first gallery. This wasn't some shabby little tavern full of drunken low-life. This was the real thing, and Davenant took a moment to breathe it in.

He was surprised by how adept his new-found members were at acting. Middleton's Macbeth was one of the finest he'd ever seen and Charles' Duncan was almost as polished, although their performances were no doubt aided by their real life similarity to the characters. The same could be said of Faith, Anne and Mary, who were unnervingly convincing as the three witches whilst Elizabeth was radiant as Lady Macbeth. Davenant still couldn't quite comprehend that he was allowing women on the stage for the first time, but the more he thought about it, the more it seemed to work, and to see Elizabeth so cheerful made it worthwhile. And it would give Cromwell a nasty shock too.

To complete the casting, Davenant decided to take the part of Banquo and Betterton the part of Malcolm. He had even drafted in Underhill and Turnbull to portray Donalbain and Macduff respectively, although from what he'd seen in rehearsal his optimism for those two was not quite as well founded.

Oliver, Elizabeth and Richard Cromwell greeted their guests with arrogant delight as they swept into the auditorium. They weren't the usual vermin that used to frequent the playhouses of London. These people were the dignitaries of the Parliamentarian campaign. As Davenant witnessed their entrance, he wished he were able to load the cellars with dynamite and blow them all to Hell, for as far as he could tell, his entire enemy were all encamped under one roof. And the most absurd part about it was that he was about to perform a play for them.

Everyone was in costume and the excitement amongst the troupe was tangible. Davenant's apprehension about performing the most legendary of his father's plays soon disappeared when he saw Middleton and Charles run through their lines in costume.

"The rest is labour, which is not used for you. I'll be myself the harbinger and make joyful the hearing of my wife with your approach; so humbly take my leave."

"My worthy Cawdor!"

Davenant stood and watched in admiration. He could scarcely believe just how accomplished the two of them were. "I am loath to interrupt gentlemen, but we are to start shortly," he said, before turning to the three witches. "Ladies, if you would kindly take your places on stage. We're ready to begin."

There was a glimmer of satisfaction in Davenant's eyes that had long been missing, and both Turnbull and Elizabeth noted it. They exchanged a brief smile. Elizabeth had fond memories of growing up in Turnbull's care when her father was imprisoned. They would for ever be getting into trouble in one way or another. As a child, Elizabeth always enjoyed the thrill of the chase, but as she faced the daunting prospect of the gallows, she longed for the days of riding on the back of Turnbull's steed, feeling the country air blow through her hair, fleeing the clutches of some scoundrel to whom Turnbull owed money. He had quickly become something of a second father to her.

She looked back at Davenant, who was surveying her costume. "Do I look suitable?" she asked.

"You look every bit the Lady Macbeth," replied Davenant proudly. "I look forward to seeing the look on Cromwell's face when he sees you ladies on stage. He won't know what hit him."

Betterton ambled sheepishly up to Davenant. "Sir William, I'd just like to thank you for giving me one last chance to perform a play by William Shakespeare. I know this must be difficult for you."

"Thank you, Thomas. It's quite all right. Now let's give them a show they'll never forget!"

Faith, Anne and Mary took centre stage as the loud muttering from the audience quickly descended into several gasps of whispered conversations. They couldn't quite believe what they were seeing, women on the London stage?

Faith stepped forward defiantly, carrying a suitably witchlike hunch. "When will we three meet again, in thunder, lightning or in rain?"

The whispering amongst the audience very quickly died down and they began to watch in enraptured silence.

"When the hurlyburly's done, when the battle's lost and won." It was Anne who took the role of the second witch and delivered her line just as confidently as Faith.

It was now Mary's turn to deliver and she didn't disappoint, her voice rasping and echoing around the vast auditorium. "That will be ere the set of sun."

"Where the place?"

"Upon the heath."

"There to meet with Macbeth."

"I come, Graymalkin."

"Paddock calls."

"Anon."

"Fair is foul, and foul is fair, hover through the fog and filthy air."

Davenant was just as entranced as the audience. The three women owned the stage. As he peeked around the side of the curtain to survey the reaction of the crowd, he could see a soldier walking briskly down the aisle towards Cromwell. He whispered something in his ear and Cromwell got to his feet, made his excuses and followed the soldier out of the theatre. Something was wrong.

Duncan, Malcolm and Donalbain had taken to stage beside him, unaware of what had just taken place in the auditorium.

"What bloody man is that? He can report, as seemeth by his plight, of the revolt the newest state."

"This is the sergeant who like a good and hardy soldier fought 'gainst my captivity. Hail, brave friend! Say to the king the knowledge of the broil as thou didst leave it."

Davenant's attention was once again drawn away from the stage. The soldier and Cromwell came storming back up the aisle, the sound of their heavy boots resonating around the auditorium. Davenant let out a faint gasp as Cromwell climbed the steps up to the stage itself.

Sensing something was dreadfully amiss, Betterton's eyes flickered towards Davenant and Charles began to muff his lines.

Cromwell quickly put him out of his misery. "I am sorry to interrupt the proceedings, but we have a problem. I have just been informed that there is an army attacking the city and we must seek refuge in the Tower immediately." He turned and looked accusingly at Charles, who responded with a confused shrug of the shoulders.

Elizabeth ran up to Davenant. "What's going on?"

"Something about an attack, apparently," replied Davenant, clearly heartbroken that his swansong had been so tragically cut short. Whoever was attacking the city had better be worth their attention, he thought.

"Come on, all of you! We must get back to the Tower immediately," bellowed the soldier who had come on stage with Cromwell.

"What's going on?" Davenant asked.

"Something about an army attacking the city. And I don't suppose you have anything to do with that?"

"Absolutely not."

After the initial shock of their theatrical sabotage had passed, his mind began to process the bizarre sequence of events. He remembered what Betterton and Mary had proclaimed, coupled with what had followed on their way down to London and the disappearance of the mounted soldiers. And who were those mysterious men lurching their way through the field in Evesham? In a moment of beautiful lucidity, what had been but a dim suspicion, a vague conjecture suddenly became as clear as countryside air. Despite its absurdity, its grim and brutal irrationality, Betterton must have been telling the truth.

The theatre was in chaos. The guests who had arrived so regally were now barging and clawing their way to get to the doors. Within a minute, Davenant had been herded outside. A nearby carriage had been prepared for the prisoners and the actors were shoved unceremoniously inside. Turnbull was the last in. The carriage doors were slammed shut, the driver's whip cracked into life and the wheels creaked into motion.

Davenant peered out of the window and could see that up ahead, Cromwell was bellowing orders. Just before he clambered into his own carriage, Davenant could hear him cry out:

"Unleash the Kryfangan!"

CHAPTER TWENTY-FIVE

Fleet Street

The carriage rattled through the cobbled streets of the Strand and Aldwych. Usually two of the busier areas of London, now they were all but deserted. It couldn't have been any later than eight o'clock, the time when the taverns should have been at their busiest. Yet as they passed the Boar's Head, one of Fleet Street's more notorious hostelries, not a soul was inside, no music or drunken singing radiating from within.

"This is what it was like in Kempsey!" cried Betterton. "A ghost town!"

"Except we're in London," replied Davenant. "And London should be a damned sight busier than Kempsey."

There was something terribly wrong in the capital and it frightened Davenant to his core. He was surprised to find the Thames similarly deserted, with only a smattering of watermen gracing the river in their boats. Cries of "Westward Ho!", "Eastward Ho!" would usually resound from the water but there were no calls tonight, just the sound of the wind beating against the side of their carriage.

Davenant could hear the sound of the wheels grinding to a halt. He caught a quick glimpse of his surroundings and saw that they'd stopped right in the heart of Cheapside.

"Why have we stopped?" asked Charles.

"I don't know," replied Davenant. "But no one stops in Cheapside unless they're spoiling for a fight."

"I'm scared, father," said Elizabeth, as she huddled up next to him.

Davenant was scared too, but he was damned if he'd let her know it. As he looked out of the window, he suddenly became aware of two or three muffled shrieks from up ahead. Davenant pressed his face to the glass and spied several of Cromwell's Generals and soldiers engaged in a skirmish with the locals of Cheapside.

"They're here," whispered Mary.

Suddenly, the carriage driver appeared at the window, his face ashen with fear and his eyes wide with terror. Davenant jolted backwards in fright, falling off his seat and onto the carriage floor.

"Ye Gods!" he cried, shuffling as far away from the window as possible.

"Everyone get out! We need to leave immediately!" The driver bellowed, throwing open the carriage doors.

"What the devil is going on?" asked Davenant.

"We're under attack!"

"Surely they're just a group of local ruffians," said Charles. "Aren't Cromwell's men more than sufficient to take care of them?"

"Them things ain't ruffians!"

Davenant shot a glance at Mary, who was shaking her head despairingly. Another cry echoed from further up the street and Davenant peered around the side of the carriage to get a better view of the commotion. What he saw would forever be etched onto his memory.

A group of soldiers were tearing Cromwell's men apart.

Davenant watched a General cry out in agony as a

ragged man plunged his thumbs into his eye sockets and tore out his throat with rotting teeth. Cromwell's man dropped, blood jetting against the tavern wall behind him and Davenant saw the feral soldier in all its horror. As it knelt down to tear strips of flesh from the General, Davenant could see that there was a hole where the soldier's chest should have been. Its ribs glistened in the lamplight.

How was it possible to suffer such a wound and live?

The soldier looked up, flesh and offal dripping from its mouth, and its terrible dead eyes turned on Davenant. Behind him more of the ragged soldiers were surging up the street. Already the second carriage was besieged by the reeking ghouls.

Where is Cromwell? Davenant thought. Has he already fallen in battle?

"We need to leave, now!" cried Davenant, aware that their driver was already hurrying away from the carnage. As they followed him, a thunder of horses' hooves filled the narrow street and their way was suddenly blocked by dark riders straddling horses as black as night, their eyes glowing diabolically. The carriage driver tried to turn and run as the dreadful cavalry pounded towards them, but his efforts were futile and he was obliterated beneath their hooves, his skull shattering as they rode over him.

There was nowhere to hide. From one side came the hideous groans of the dead feasting on human flesh; from the other came the riders bearing down on them like a ferocious black tide.

As the riders drew closer, Davenant could see the strange crab-like armour they wore, the black chitinous shells completely covering whatever lay beneath. In great clawed hands they wielded enormous swords, far bigger than any weapons Davenant had ever seen. He held tightly to Elizabeth's hand and closed his eyes, praying that their deaths would be swift and painless.

Turnbull and Middleton quickly bundled the group into a side alley, seconds before the riders swept past them.

Davenant didn't open his eyes immediately.

"You're alive! We're alive!" Elizabeth cried.

"Thought that just standing there wasn't one of your better ideas, Sir," Turnbull said. "Saw the alleyway and got us moving sharpish."

"Look!" Elizabeth pointed to the battle that was raging further up the street. Davenant watched part in awe, part in horror, as the horsemen clashed with the undead. Swords carved through flesh like knives through butter, spraying Cheapside with blood and guts. Davenant had given up trying to hide Elizabeth from the horror as she, along with everyone else, watched with their mouths agape, hypnotised by the massacre.

"What the hell!" gasped Betterton, pointing at one of Cromwell's fallen soldiers. The corpse had begun to twitch. Slowly, it levered itself up, one arm hanging by a mere scrap of tendon. Crawling along the cobblestones it began to feed on the lumps of flesh and offal that were strewn there.

Charles watched the ghoul feeding for a moment and then gasped. "We need to leave now!"

"Let's take the carriage," Middleton said, surprised to find that it had escaped unscathed, horses still intact.

Davenant ushered everyone inside as Middleton

clambered into the driver's seat.

Charles was the last to enter and slammed the door tightly shut behind him. "It's almost as if they're not interested in fighting us, only each other," he said, gazing out of the smeared windows at the two armies engaged in battle. It appeared to be very much a one-way conflict, as the horsemen decapitated wave after wave with their vast blades.

Davenant turned to Betterton. "I'm sorry, truly sorry that I didn't believe you."

"And I'm sorry for my actions, but there is no time for apologies now, we have to leave!" cried Betterton, as Middleton gave a vigorous crack of the whip, sending the horses into a frenzy. They ploughed straight through the battleground, mowing down anyone or anything that stood in their way, almost slipping several times on the blood-drenched cobblestone. Windows were smashed open and rotting arms groped into their carriage. A hand grabbed hold of Anne's hair, stubbornly refusing to let go. Underhill jumped to her aid, pulling her in the opposite direction. A clump was torn from her scalp and she let out an agonised scream. The hand, still holding the tuft of hair, remained in the carriage, bouncing its way over the carriage floor.

"For God's sake, somebody throw it out!" cried Faith.

Eventually Turnbull was able to grab hold of the writhing hand and threw it from the broken window. There was a collective sigh of relief followed by a marked silence.

It was Betterton who spoke first. "Have we left them behind?" he asked, his eyes darting around the carriage.

Davenant reluctantly peered out of the smashed window. "Yes, I think so." He looked back in the other direction and suddenly saw a lone figure standing in the entrance to an alleyway. "Wait! There's someone up ahead!"

He felt the carriage slowing as they approached, and it wasn't long before it became strikingly apparent who the figure was.

"Well, well, well," said Charles through gritted teeth. "If it isn't our friend Oliver Cromwell, I do hope we're not slowing down to carry him to safety?"

"I say we let him rot in Hell," spat Elizabeth.

"No, I want answers! Middleton, stop the carriage!" cried Davenant.

"No, Middleton, carry on! Sir William, you cannot make this decision on your own. We all have a say in whether we stop or not."

Davenant could see the look on Cromwell's face as they passed – the look of defeat. "I want answers from him. I want to know who those horsemen were."

"And what makes you so sure that Cromwell has got those answers?" asked Charles, unwilling to back down.

"Because I heard him summon them, and because there is a look in his eye that tells me that he is frightened to his marrow."

The two men shared a long, lingering stare. It was Charles who broke rank first.

"Very well, but promise me that I can kill him as soon as you've finished your interrogation."

Davenant nodded. "As long as I can help you," he said, smiling for the first time in a while.

"Middleton, stop the carriage! Let us see how he feels with the boot on the other foot."

"Are ye sure this is a wise idea, my Lord?" he shouted.

"No, but do as you're told!"

Middleton shook his head ruefully and reluctantly pulled the carriage up two hundred yards from Cromwell, who turned and ran towards them. There was a marked sense of unease as he clambered inside. Faith and Anne quickly slid over on the seats as far as they possibly could to make room for him, the thought of sharing a carriage with Cromwell as abhorrent to them as it was to Elizabeth. As he sat down next to her, she caught a waft of his odour, like a festering wound.

Cromwell's eyes drifted around the carriage, surveying the disgusted expressions on the faces of his companions, until they fell on Charles in the furthest corner, carrying a look of pure, unmitigated hatred.

"And to which one of my thespian friends do I owe my gratitude?" asked Cromwell.

Charles felt for the knife that was concealed in his belt and wrapped his hand tightly around its ivory handle. "I don't think any of us particularly want you in our carriage..."

"It's my carriage."

"Be that as it may, no one is here to look after you, so if I were you I'd think long and hard about how to start addressing people," said Davenant.

"Or else...?"

"Or else we'll throw you out of the window and happily watch as your 'horsemen' come back and rip you to pieces."

"Ah yes, my horsemen, my New Model Army, I wondered how long it would take you to mention them. They are quite remarkable, are they not?"

As much as it pained him, Davenant was impressed with his resilience. "Yes, they are. Yet I couldn't help but notice that their enemy were... well, already dead."

Cromwell's eyes swung back to face Charles. "No doubt you would have recognised the soldiers; after all, they've already been killed once before at Worcester."

That was it, the final straw. Charles couldn't take any further snide remarks, so he leapt across the carriage, withdrew the hunting knife from his belt and held it to Cromwell's throat, his hand shaking with rage.

"We want answers, Cromwell!" he yelled. "Or I might just have a little accident with this here knife."

"Go ahead and slit my throat. I'll thank you for it. I'm dead already."

"I say you slit his throat," said Elizabeth venomously.

"My, my, you are a little poisonous one, are you not? I daresay another character trait she has picked up from her mother..."

It was Davenant's turn to lose his composure. He leant in to Cromwell and planted a fierce blow across his jaw, sending him sprawling at Betterton's feet.

"Who are they, Cromwell, and where did you get them? I'd wager they didn't come with conscription!"

Cromwell shakily climbed back onto his seat. "You've no doubt heard several rumours about me. I know they've been circulating around the taverns and inns of Whitehall, I daresay started by my enemies in Parliament."

"There have been whispers," said Davenant, conspicuously rubbing his bruised fingers. "Something about a pact with the Devil is the one that I've heard."

Cromwell took a deep breath. "Yes, I've heard that one too. It is true, the rumours are true."

"How can that be possible?" asked Charles, shaking his head in disbelief.

"Please, let me finish. It was at the Battle of Marston Moor. My army were a shambles, a rambling mess of drunkards and low-life vermin. They'd barely the knowledge of which way up to hold a sword, let alone how to wield one. The night before the battle I decided to drown my sorrows in a local tavern. I fully expected it to be my last drink as a free man as I had no hope of winning the battle the following day. It was in the tavern that I was approached by a strange crooked man in a dark brown robe. I can vividly remember his wasted face and in his eyes seemed to shine a glimmer of dark red. This peculiar stranger offered me a deal. In return for my soul, he would give me his 'Legion', the Kryfangan, an ancient army of unbeatable evil..."

Charles scoffed at his words.

"Mock me all you like, but I tell you no lie. I stupidly agreed to his... pact, shaking the man's hand, praying that he would leave me alone. As he hobbled from the tavern, I fully expected to never see him again and nothing to ever come of our strange conversation. Like you, I derided his comments and dismissed them out of hand. That was until the following day. My army were being slaughtered; it was a bloodbath, a massacre. I had all but surrendered when the horsemen appeared from nowhere, counter-attacked under the cover of darkness and won the battle with ease. I soon realised that I wielded a weapon such as no man has ever used in all the grim history of warfare and that victory and control of the country was finally within my grasp. But victory wasn't achieved without a price and without suffering on my part. I see this strange, crooked man in my dreams, and I see him sometimes in the street, amidst the crowds. And I am dying inside; I cannot step onto consecrated ground without being sick and my body is rotten to the core."

"At last, some honesty!" spat Charles, struggling to keep his emotions in check.

"Please, my Lord! Let him finish," replied Davenant.

"You don't believe this nonsense, do you?"

Davenant didn't answer immediately. His eyes worked their way back over to Cromwell, who was sat despondently with his head in his hands. "I'm not sure. But let us show the good grace to allow him to finish his story."

"Very well," said Charles.

Cromwell took a deep breath. "Although at first I was happy to let the identity of my bloodthirsty soldiers remain a secret, after a while I couldn't help but conduct some research into their shrouded mystery. I found an old manuscript in the Westminster library that shed light on the subject. What I discovered was almost the death of me. I have unleashed onto the country the darkest, purest evil." There was genuine sadness in his forlorn eyes. "And they've taken my family from me. You have heard of the Four Horsemen of the Apocalypse? The Bible makes reference to them in the Book of Revelation. You must ignore their traditional interpretation. In fact, the four horsemen are the four beasts mentioned in the Book of Daniel. They represent four kings, the last of which will devour the world. The Kryfangan are lead by four soldiers, the most powerful and the most terrifying of them all. They do not ride the time-honoured white, red, black and pale horses. No, they ride black, jet-black steeds, and they represent the Antichrist, Plague, Famine and Death. One interpretation is that Satan has control over when the horsemen end the world – when the victims at the hands of horsemen rise from the dead to fight in a battle that will end all mankind. Well, that time is now. And that is why I bare my soul..."

"You have no soul," whispered Elizabeth.

"Why you, Cromwell? Why did he choose you?" asked Davenant.

"It wasn't just me."

"There are others too?"

"Yes, there have been others. During my research I discovered reports of a dark army on horseback fighting in Ancient Greece and then again in Mongolia in the thirteenth century."

"What happened on those occasions?" asked Davenant earnestly.

"I don't know about Greece, but in Mongolia, eyewitnesses claimed to have seen Genghis Khan unite the country with the help of a mysterious dark army on horseback. It was only after he had created his Empire that things started to take a turn for the worse. The statements went on to say how those who were killed by the horsemen rose from the dead and sought their vengeance upon them. They called them a plague army."

"How did it end?" asked Charles.

"They said a great fire ended the plague and the Kryfangan disappeared as quickly as they came."

"So this would explain why these... soldiers came to London, to seek the Kryfangan, to seek their revenge. And before the horsemen turned up, I saw them feast on the flesh of the living. Those slain by this unholy army in turn rose from the dead. Their hunger was terrible to observe."

Cromwell nodded. He was only too aware of the truth behind Davenant's observation. After all, he had been conspicuously rubbing the wound on his arm, a bite mark, for the past twenty minutes. He had even felt the disease course through his veins and prick at his skin. His vision had become blurred; no doubt a symptom of the same affliction.

"I can see the Tower up ahead!" yelled Middleton.

At last, Cromwell thought, he could seek sanctuary, for the time being at least...

CHAPTER TWENTY-SIX

The Tower of London

"Do I take it you're not going to imprison us this time?" asked Davenant.

Cromwell didn't satisfy him with an answer and instead began the arduous task of fortifying the defences of the Tower. He'd already lowered the portcullis of the Lion Tower and had strengthened its ramparts by moving the cannons from the nearby armouries of the Middle Tower. The group had set up camp in the adjacent Byward Tower from where they had a perfect vantage point of any intruders or would-be attackers.

"We must get some rest," said Davenant, peering out of an arrow loop. "I propose we take it in shifts."

"I agree," replied Charles. "I'll gladly take the first one."

"Very well, I shall take the second, Turnbull the third and Middleton the fourth."

"What about me?" Cromwell asked. "Surely I can take one of the shifts?"

Charles let out a chuckle. "You will forgive my impertinence, but I can't say I'm comfortable with sleeping whilst you watch over me."

"And I with you," spat Cromwell.

"Yes, but I have a say in the matter. And you don't."

"Enough! We must formulate a plan should our defences be breached. Have we any riverboats?"

"Yes, they are moored at Traitors' Gate," replied Cromwell.

Davenant felt a shudder run down his spine at the mere mention of its name. He turned back to the arrow loop and gazed over the Thames. The unspeakable savagery he had witnessed today seemed to pale in comparison with a journey through Traitors' Gate and its dark waters. And the very real prospect of Elizabeth having to endure its horrors occupied his thoughts more than any impending attack.

"I wonder whether word has reached any other town yet?" pondered Davenant, as he cast his eye over the dark sky looming high above him. For the briefest of moments he could have sworn he saw a shooting star fall into the stinking Thames. He concluded that his lethargic eyes must have deceived him.

He let out a vast yawn and rested his tired hand against the cold stone wall. It had been the longest day of his life.

"Sir William, will you please oblige me by taking some sleep," said Charles.

Davenant smiled. "Gladly, my good man, gladly." He ambled over to the fire, careful not to wake his sleeping companions. "Have we any firewood, Cromwell? This chamber is freezing cold."

"Yes, I think so. There should be some in the Queen's House," he replied, clambering to his feet and scurrying from the chamber, clutching his arm as he did so.

"Should we be letting him go?" asked Charles. "As far as I can see, he's our prisoner and should be treated as such. I know we're under extraordinary circumstances, but we shouldn't extend him the courtesy of wandering unaccompanied around the Tower as and when he pleases."

Davenant nodded in agreement. "I won't let it

happen again."

He rubbed his hands together in a fruitless attempt to warm them. As he leant against the wall and closed his eyes, he suddenly became aware of a faint rustling noise at his feet.

"Sir William, you should not trust him," whispered Mary, sidling towards him.

"Should not trust who?" he asked.

Mary's eyes flittered around the room before returning to meet Davenant's. "I'm sorry, Sir William."

"Sorry for what, Mary?"

"For treating you with disrespect. You're a good man, I can see that now."

"Thank you Mary, but whom shouldn't I trust."

Mary took a deep breath. "Cromwell. He's one of them."

Davenant's eyes widened with anxiety. "One of the plagued?"

"I saw him clutching his arm in the carriage. There was blood seeping through his sleeve."

"He could have acquired his wound from a weapon. What makes you so sure that the disease has been passed on?"

"It's in his eyes, Sir William, I can tell."

Davenant leant back against the wall, knowing better than to question her judgement, and hurriedly assessed his options. With Cromwell's return with the firewood imminent, Davenant took his chance to liaise with Charles. "My Lord, we've got a problem."

"I'll put the wood in the grate."

Davenant turned to find Cromwell standing in the doorway, his arms full of well-seasoned timber. "Very well," he replied.

Cromwell shuffled across the chamber and placed the wood in the grate.

"What problem?" Charles asked.

"Oh, it's nothing. It can wait. I say, Cromwell. Can you fetch us some bread and wine?"

"Can it not wait until I've got the fire started?"

"No, it can't. I'm famished," replied Davenant, noticing for the first time how Cromwell was favouring his left arm.

"Very well then, I shan't be long."

"Sir William! Someone must accompany him!" hissed Charles.

Davenant turned and shook his head, motioning Charles to stay quiet. Oblivious to what was going on around him, Cromwell brushed past the two men, sauntered back outside and down the narrow staircase of the turret, his heavy footsteps echoing back up into the chamber.

Davenant waited patiently until he was sure Cromwell was out of earshot. "For God's sake, do not let him back in here! He's one of the infected!"

Charles grinned. "You don't have to ask for my permission to lock him out."

"I'm deadly serious, he's been bitten by one of them! Mary saw it!"

The expression on Charles' face changed dramatically. "Middleton, Turnbull, get up!" he barked.

"What's wrong, my Lord?" asked Middleton, his voice faint and fatigued.

"What does a man have to do to get some bloody sleep around here?" Turnbull grumbled.

"Help us barricade the door, you big oaf!" cried Davenant, his eyes darting around the chamber, desperately trying to locate something to utilise. To his horror, there was nothing available to him apart from a couple of battered old stools.

Charles inspected the lock on the door. "Is there a key?"

"I haven't seen one," replied Davenant, testing the durability of one of the stools against his hand, a leg snapping off.

Mary was waking those who were still asleep. She gently tugged Elizabeth by her shoulder. "Wake up, you must wake up," she said.

Faith, Anne, Underhill and Betterton had begun to stir too amidst the commotion.

"What's going on?" asked Underhill, rubbing his eyes.

His question went unanswered.

"Where's Cromwell?" asked Middleton more forthrightly.

"Outside, and we mustn't let him back in! We need to get this door secured. Can we not just stand against it?"

"Stand against it? I say we leave immediately and board the riverboats," replied Davenant, hurling the broken stool back across the chamber in frustration.

"Not that I have a problem with the decision, but why exactly mustn't we let him in?" demanded Middleton. "Someone had better tell me what's going on!"

"Cromwell's been bitten, he's one of them," said Davenant.

"Where is he now?" asked Elizabeth, backing away from the door.

"I asked him to fetch us some bread and wine as a ruse to get him out of here. But he will be back any moment."

The sound of approaching footsteps echoed up the turret stairs. They weren't the same as the steps that had been heard making their way down earlier. No, these were far different – a rough, dragging of the feet that shuffled awkwardly against the hard granite. After what seemed an eternity, the steps reached the top of the turret and shambled up to the door. Middleton and Turnbull pressed their backs against the ageing timber, frantically beckoning the others into the furthest corner.

Suddenly, the door handle started to shake violently. Anne let out a scream, which seemed to encourage the handle to shake more fiercely than before.

Betterton thrust a hand over her mouth to quieten her. "Be quiet, it'll only make it worse," he whispered breathlessly.

She nodded apologetically and Betterton eased his hand away. Silence – no footsteps, no murmurs or groans, just the sound of the ever-present wind.

"Do you think he's still outside?" muttered Faith.

Davenant shrugged his shoulders, half-tempted to open the door and see for himself. "What shall we do?" he asked, turning in Charles' direction.

The door impacted inwards with a sharp crack, sending Middleton sprawling to the floor, his large frame bouncing off the hard stone. Davenant and Charles surged forward to give Turnbull much needed support. They could now hear a low growl from the other side of the door, as, with another thunderous crack, one of the timber panels splintered. "The door won't hold for much longer!" cried Davenant, as Cromwell slammed against it again. A panel shattered and Cromwell forced his arm through, his doublet

The Devil's Plague

tearing on the sharp splinters and piercing his flesh. Davenant could see him now. The boils that had had so markedly covered his skin had burst, spilling blood and pus all over his face. Blood poured from his nose, and his eyes had rolled up into his skull.

Cromwell grabbed hold of Davenant's jerkin, pulling him against the door. Elizabeth let out a gasp of horror as she saw her father come face to face with Cromwell, who had forced his head through the broken panel and leant into the chamber.

"For God's sake somebody help me," cried Davenant, as he arched backwards to avoid Cromwell's bite.

Elizabeth picked up the broken stool and smashed it over Cromwell's head, sending him stumbling backwards. He looked up and caught a glimpse of her, his eyes, although vacant and wasted, seeming to spark with a hint of recognition. He forced his hand through the hole in the door, and then his shoulder and Cromwell growled in triumph as he smashed through the last of the wood and stumbled into the chamber. The weapons they had raided from the armoury were drawn – Turnbull's axe, Charles' knife and Middleton's sword.

As Cromwell shambled forwards there was a loud bang and the sound of splintering wood from the courtyard. The whinnying of horses and the sound of hooves on cobbles stopped Cromwell in his tracks.

"It's the gates," gasped Davenant.

Cromwell, mouth agape, turned sluggishly on his heel and barged back through the splintered door, lurching his way down the turret steps.

Betterton's eyes lit up. "The Kryfangan, he's after the Kryfangan! Remember what he told us?"

"We must get to the boats. We're in a real danger

of being caught up in the middle of this devilish conflict, especially once Cromwell opens the gates to them all," Davenant said.

"How far is Traitors' Gate?" asked Charles.

"Not far, some two hundred yards or so."

As a group, they tentatively made their way from the chamber and down the turret steps. Before long they were outside in the cold, rain was beginning to fall.

"We've got to go that way!" shouted Davenant over the wind.

He pointed towards the narrow passageway that led to St Thomas's Tower; a small, one-storey half-timbered building that squatted over Traitors' Gate. Davenant took a quick glance over his shoulder as they raced up the passageway – the dead had breeched the portcullis of the Lion Tower and were forcing their way over the moat of the Middle Tower. The wind was blowing icy rain into their eyes now, impeding their vision and making it harder for them to see where they were going. Davenant ran his hand along the wall, feeling instinctively for the gap that opened up into Traitors' Gate. Eventually the wall turned into a stone archway that encompassed a small jetty. Beneath the archway sat a large imposing wooden gate, the same gate that had long plagued Davenant's nightmares. As he looked down at the water, his heart sank. There was only one boat.

"There won't be enough room for us all!" he cried, looking helplessly at Charles.

There was a loud thump that reverberated all the way down the passageway.

Charles peered through the heavy rain, covering his forehead with his hand. His eyes widened as he spied the shadows of a hundred men staggering towards them, fending off the swords of the Kryfangan. "They're past the Byward Tower and coming this way! We must go, now!"

There was a mad dash as the troupe descended and boarded the vessel. As Betterton finally managed to squeeze himself aboard, Turnbull slashed the weathered rope binding them to the jetty. It snapped with ease, the boat catching a gust of wind which took them away from the landing platform. Middleton passed him an oar and the two men desperately heaved the craft towards the gate.

As Davenant looked back, he saw two or three soldiers stumble onto the jetty before jumping in after them. "Quickly, open the gates!"

Summoning up all the strength they could possibly muster, Underhill, Betterton and Charles forced the gates open, which groaned against the pull of the water. The half-open doors grated against the hull of the boat as it squeezed its way through. Davenant looked back once again and, to his relief, the undead soldiers had sunk to the bottom.

The boat bounced its way off the tunnel wall before taking a straight course through the dark water. The lanterns that usually greeted those travelling through the river entrance to the Tower had been extinguished by the wind, plunging the whole tunnel into darkness.

"What's that smell?" asked Underhill, gagging at the stench.

"If I told you, you'd panic," replied Davenant, conscious that the weight in the boat was allowing the vile water to slowly trickle onboard.

A flash of lightning lit up the tunnel, briefly

exposing the horrors that bobbed in the oily water.

"I wish I hadn't seen that," Elizabeth breathed.

"We'll be out of here before you know it," stammered Davenant.

Charles felt the water begin to lap at his boots. "Sir William, we're too heavy! We're not going to cross the Thames, let alone get out of this hellhole without sinking!"

Another flash of lightning, this time accompanied by a roll of thunder that was so severe, it seemed to shake the water. Once again, the tunnel lit up, revealing more horrors from within the belly of the Tower. Rats were tearing at the scraps of meat clinging to bleached skulls, some fighting each other for the leftovers.

"Oh please, God, I can't take much more of this," whimpered Anne, as a rat clambered into the boat.

Middleton used an oar to shove the vermin back into the water.

"Everyone calm down!" cried Davenant. "We can't afford to take on any more water."

To his relief, the boat had finally passed through the mouth of the tunnel and onto the open Thames. However, the horror, the turmoil of the rats and decapitated heads were merely the beginning, as the storm had whisked the river up into frenzy, sending their boat crashing from side to side as it hit wave after wave. The rain came down hard, adding to the water in the already deluged vessel.

"We need to moor the boat and empty the water!" yelled Middleton, amidst the storm. "We will drown in minutes if we don't!"

Davenant nodded in agreement, and Turnbull and Middleton rowed towards the riverbank. Davenant reached out to grab hold of a wooden strut. He dragged the boat next to the dock and clambered out, examining the damage to the hull as he did so. It had taken a lashing, but would probably be strong enough to get them out of London. The rest of the group were frantically scooping water out of the boat with anything they could make use of – hands, hats and boots.

"Behind you, father!" Elizabeth suddenly cried out.

Davenant turned, fear already tightening its grip as he let out a shuddering breath.

They shambled towards the dock, their pale eyes full of a terrible, ardent hunger.

"We're leaving now!" he bellowed. Davenant jumped back into the boat, followed by the rest of his troupe. Hauling on the oars with Turnbull, they managed to put just enough distance between them and their pursuers. "Look, over there!" said Charles, pointing to the southern side of the river.

Davenant could make out several hundred walking corpses gathered at the riverbank, desperately seeking a way over the water to engage in battle with the Kryfangan. Some had worked their way across London Bridge, and through the warren of timbered buildings that were built on top. Others weren't quite as intuitive, and attempted to cross through the river itself, before being swept away by the vicious tide.

The Kryfangan had made their way to Tower Hill and their battle had moved eastwards towards the northern shore of the Thames. Both riverbanks were now teeming with the dead, like bees around a honeycomb.

It was at that moment, when there was no escape on

either shore, no possible way of swimming to safety through the strength of the deadly current, when it finally dawned on Davenant and his company.

They were sinking.

"Abandon ship!" Davenant yelled.

Elizabeth began to sob uncontrollably. "No, no, please God, no," she whimpered through her tears.

"No, Sir!" cried Turnbull. "I'm the heaviest onboard; if I leave the boat then you can go on!"

"For God's sake Turnbull, do as you're told for once!"

"It's been an honour, Sir William, an absolute bloody honour." Turnbull brushed aside Davenant's desperate outstretched arm. He smiled tenderly at Elizabeth before plunging into the dank water, the boat rising almost immediately.

Davenant's eyes filled up with tears. "Turnbull, get back over here now!" He leant over the side, his head almost touching the water, desperately scouring the river for any sign of his manservant. He could hear Elizabeth, Betterton and Underhill weeping behind him. "It should have been me," he whispered. "It should have been me."

"I hate to interrupt your moment of grief, but we're still going under," spluttered Charles.

Betterton clambered clumsily to his feet. "I'm going over too. It is my fault that we're in this mess, so it is only fair I sacrifice myself as well."

"No, please Thomas, no, not you as well. I couldn't bear it," cried Elizabeth.

Davenant could see the desperation in her eyes. He cursed Cromwell for what he'd done. "Betterton, stay where you are, I am responsible for this, it is my duty. You make sure you look after Elizabeth for me, do you hear? Look after her!"

Betterton stood with his mouth agape, scared to back down, but equally scared to brave the icy water of the river. Before he could make his decision, Davenant was on his feet too, stripping his doublet from his body and grabbing hold of a knife.

He leant in to Elizabeth and kissed her tenderly on the cheek. "I love you, Elizabeth, always remember that."

There was a splash and Davenant looked up in bewilderment. "What in the name of the Lord was that?"

"I do believe Mary has just thrown herself overboard," replied Charles. "I expect she was bored of your theatrical exit!"

Davenant shook his head. "My God," he said finally. "No one else is jumping off this boat! Do you all understand? That is an order!"

The boat had risen another couple of inches and with some frantic bailing they were able to stabilise the craft.

"Thank you, Mary," muttered Davenant under his breath. "You bloody lunatic."

"There's Turnbull! On the north shore!" shrieked Underhill. They peered into the darkness and could just distinguish his vast frame and pot belly amidst his scrawny attackers. He swung a sword, no doubt pilfered from one of the soldiers, decapitating anything that closed in upon him, spraying the riverbank with body parts and saturating it with diseased blood. Eventually the sheer number of the dead swamped him, and Turnbull disappeared beneath a pile of bodies.

Charles grabbed hold of an oar, and together with

Middleton, gained control of the boat once more. They glided past Custom House, the tall, proud buildings of Billingsgate on the north side of the river, under one of the archways of London Bridge and alongside the borough of Southwark on the south side of the Thames. Davenant could see what was left of the theatrical district of Bankside, and although the Globe had long been destroyed, he had fond memories of the place. In the shadow and amidst the rubble of its more famous sibling, he was glad to see that the Hope Theatre had survived Cromwell's tyrannical regime, and cast his mind back to his days in which he and his father had trod the boards together. He prayed that he would see the theatres of Bankside again one day, under happier circumstances.

As he settled back against the side of the boat, Davenant spared a fleeting glance back to the north side of the river. Funny, he thought, despite seeing Turnbull desperately and courageously fight for his life, Mary had seemed to vanish into thin air.

CHAPTER TWENTY-SEVEN

Oxford

It was the sun that woke him, piercing through a break in the clouds. He had almost forgotten what it felt like to have its warmth on his face. As Davenant stirred, he became aware that the boat had become entangled in the reeds of the riverbank. With one eye open, he glanced over at his sleeping companions. He took a moment to remember the events of the previous evening and his heart sank. Amidst the chaos of their escape from London, he hadn't been able to grieve for his friend. Even as he saw Turnbull being overcome by the hordes of soldiers, his mind was preoccupied with the thought of getting everyone else to safety.

Davenant broke down in tears. He had tried to remain strong, but losing Turnbull, his trusted friend and manservant was just too much for him to bear.

His sobs woke Elizabeth, who wrestled herself free from beneath Underhill's legs, and crawled her way across the boat to grieve with her father, placing an arm around his shoulders.

"He loved you very much, father," she said, wiping away her own tears.

"I never thanked him enough. I was always whinging at him, always..."

"Ssssh! I won't hear another word about it," replied Elizabeth.

Davenant eventually managed a smile and leant in to embrace his daughter. He held her tightly, unwilling to let go. He looked up at the rolling green pastures and the surrounding fields, brimming with crops and fresh produce. He filled his lungs with the countryside air and let out a sigh of relief.

Thank God they were out of London!

Davenant looked around, trying to establish their whereabouts. He couldn't believe how far they'd come – the Thames had become narrower, so narrow in fact that there was barely enough room for two riverboats to pass one another. He smiled at the sight and sounds of the wildlife: the quacking of ducks, the warbling of a nearby woodlark, and even the splashing of an otter. He couldn't recall when he'd fallen asleep, but remembered passing the last of the London bridges and dockyards. As he looked around he could see a church and a cluster of buildings to the east. There was no doubt in his mind that they were in desperate need of food, water and rest. He was fairly certain that the danger seemed to be restricted to London for now, yet at the same time was aware that Cromwell's men outside of the city would still be on the look-out for Charles Stuart and his mercenary friends.

As much as it pained him to wake his companions from their well-earned sleep, Davenant felt it best they were on the move once more.

He gently shook Charles' shoulder. "My Lord, you must wake up."

"What... what's going on, Sir William?"

"We must have fallen asleep and drifted here. I don't know where we are, but there's a town over there," replied Davenant. "We need food and rest, my Lord. And it would be wise if we were to vacate the boat as soon as possible."

Charles nodded in agreement. "Yes, yes, quite

right," he said, pulling himself upright to get a better view of his surroundings.

"Just one other thing, my Lord, we must be wary of Cromwell's men. I doubt word of what has happened in London would have reached them yet, neither would they have heard of our arrest in Evesham. Their orders to capture us are still very much their priority, so we must tread carefully."

The others began to stir.

"Can we not stay here for a while?" Underhill said. "It's so warm."

"No, we can't," replied Charles sternly, grabbing hold of one of the oars and pulling the boat round. Davenant leapt onto the bank, holding the boat in place whilst his companions were able to step carefully to safety.

As the group approached the settlement, Davenant was surprised to find that the cluster of dwellings that had seemed to form part of a small village from his view on the riverbank had opened up into a larger town. It wasn't until they had ambled halfway across the field that it suddenly struck him – it wasn't a town, but a city, and the church he had seen from the boat wasn't a church at all.

It was a cathedral – Christ Church Cathedral.

And the all too familiar city they were advancing on was Oxford – his birthplace, the home of a million memories both happy and sad.

CHAPTER TWENTY-EIGHT

Tower Hill, London

Black clouds boiled above the raging battle below. The Thames shimmered with the crimson of the streams of blood that were washed from the streets by the driving rain. Lightning lit up the unholy war that had laid siege to the capital, the undead and the Kryfangan locked in combat. Any remaining human was quickly despatched either by the dark riders or by the hordes of zombies that washed up into the city with the stench of rotting flesh.

Two of the undead fought over the flesh of one of the Kryfangan, tearing away its cloak and armour to reveal the creature beneath. The two soldiers took great delight in sinking their decaying teeth into the coarse flesh, wrestling with it as if they were dogs fighting over a bone. There was no blood, just dry, raw tissue.

Amidst the howling winds and the sweeping rain, fires raged and buildings crumbled. In just over a day, London, the once proud and thriving city full of heritage and hope, had been reduced to little more than a battlefield.

On the banks of the Thames something twitched. Oliver Cromwell sat up and, clutching a sword in his right hand, rose sluggishly to his feet. Despite his repellent nature, his vulgar face that teemed with scars and his lifeless, vacant eyes, there seemed to linger a glimmer of intelligence that wasn't prevalent in his ungainly brethren.

The pounding of hooves made Cromwell's head

turn. As the horseman bore down on him, Cromwell swung his sword, connecting with the forelegs of the mount, sending horse and rider screeching into the dark water of the river. The horse squealed as it died, thrashing as the current took it out of view.

Suddenly, the Kryfangan burst from the water. It threw its dark robe to one side and withdrew a sword from an elaborate scabbard. Even its armour was ornately crafted, with religious symbols and inscriptions embossed in its dark iron chest plate. Its icy breath filtered through the gap in the mask covering its face, another intricate design of twisted metal inlaid with gold. Despite his stricken intellect, Cromwell realised that this must be one of the Kryfangan leaders he had read about. If this was the case, its skills with the sword were likely to be more masterful than any of its platoon.

The Kryfangan lifted its weapon and charged. Gripping his sword tightly, Cromwell parried the first blow with ease, knocking the Kryfangan off balance in the process. He had gained the initiative; taking three strides he swung his sword down on the skull of his opponent. The Kryfangan twisted its body, just before Cromwell's sword crashed down. Somehow, from the jaws of defeat, it had regained the initiative as the force of Cromwell's wild swing sent him tumbling into the shallows of the river, his sword dropping to the bank. Before Cromwell could get back to his feet, the Kryfangan had waded in after him, eager to end their brief skirmish. Cromwell looked up at the demon standing menacingly above him with his emotionless, lifeless eyes – the Devil's eyes. There was no pleading or begging for mercy, just unreserved, unapologetic ruthlessness.

Once more the Kryfangan raised its great sword. At that precise moment, Cromwell rose from the water, his eyes coming alive and burning a vivid red. He took one enormous leap to the shore, there gathering his fallen sword.

The two warriors circled one another, swords outstretched, both waiting patiently for their opponent to make the first move.

And then it came. Cromwell lunged with vicious ferocity, the tip of his blade piercing the chest plate of the Kryfangan.

It drew no blood.

The Kryfangan responded with a similarly vicious swipe of its blade, narrowly missing Cromwell's abdomen. This was followed by several rattling blows in quick succession as blade met blade; each strike lighting up the riverbank with sparks. The battle had become so fierce that it had caught the attention of the nearby undead, who were busy combing the riverbank for any sign of food.

Cromwell planted a ferocious blow on the Kryfangan's faceplate, sending it sprawling in the mud. With another sweep of his sword, he knocked the Kryfangan's weapon from its hand.

A cluster of the undead had convened around the battleground, and seemed to watch intently as Cromwell mercilessly plunged his sword through the neck of his adversary. The zombies' eyes seemed to gleam with respect. Could this man lead them? If he could defeat a Kryfangan General single-handed, could he win the war for their kind?

As they lurched forward to share in the demon flesh, their somnolent bodies seemed to suggest a mixture of gratitude and fear towards the provider of their feast. Whatever their sentiment, there was no denying that they had found their new King.

CHAPTER TWENTY-NINE

Oxford

As they entered the city, Davenant was pleased to see that it hadn't changed one bit. It was market day and the calls of traders selling their goods echoed through the streets. Women in headscarves tussled over bargains while men lounged outside taverns at a safe distance, watching the proceedings with wry amusement through a pall of pipe smoke. Davenant cast his eye over the wares on sale and saw that one enterprising stall-owner was selling Royalist memorabilia. Highly illegal of course, but it would appear that Cromwell's men were willing to turn a blind eye for a small cut of the profit.

Charles picked up a silk scarf with images depicting the famous Royalist victory at Kilsyth. "I don't understand," he said. "How can these people get away with selling such items without ending up in the stocks?"

Davenant smiled. "Ah, my Lord, but this is Oxford, the Royalist capital of England! By the way, keep your identity hidden. They may love you here but if Cromwell's men notice you you're as good as dead."

Charles nodded and paid the tubby market trader. The group sauntered through the hustle and bustle of Market Street, avoiding any contact with the mounted soldiers that paraded the busy cobblestone lanes. Before long they had worked their way to St Giles', bedraggled and in desperate need of respite.

"We must rest soon, Sir William. A night spent in a boat has left me rather weary," said Charles.

"Let's see if we can find rooms in the tavern you were brought up in," said Elizabeth excitedly. "I would love to see where you were born."

Davenant shook his head. "The Crown Tavern? No, I don't think I could face that. Revisiting Oxford is strange enough without having to endure the memories of that wretched place. But I have a better idea. There's a modest inn just around the corner that will provide us with comfortable enough rooms."

"Is it reputable?" asked Charles.

"I daresay you've heard of it, the Eagle and Child. It acted as a headquarters for your father during the early part of the war."

"Well that sounds remarkably suitable!" exclaimed Charles.

"That's settled then." Davenant led the group along a dark, tapered passageway, which opened up onto another cobbled street. Standing opposite them was a tall, proud and narrow building, the Eagle and Child.

Davenant couldn't quite believe how little Oxford had changed as he cast his eye over St Giles' Church in the distance. He spared a thought for his parents who had been buried next to one another in the churchyard there. They had died only two weeks apart from each other. He felt a warm hand slide into his own and looked up to see Faith smiling tenderly at him. She gently guided him into the tavern where the others were waiting.

"You lot stay here," he said to them. "I'll try and secure us some rooms."

Davenant approached the innkeeper, an elderly man with greying sideburns, who was sleeping behind the bar, an empty tankard and plate in front of him. Davenant rapped sharply on the counter.

"Ah, good evening," Davenant said as the publican stirred. "I was wondering whether you may be able to accommodate myself and my friends for the evening? There are eight of us in total."

The innkeeper's eyes narrowed. "My, my, that's some crowd you've got. You lot from the circus?"

"We're just a weary group of merchants who are in desperate need of food and rest. You'll find our money is just as good as anyone else's."

"Very well," replied the innkeeper, clambering off his stool. "I have three rooms that you can take. There's fresh linen and I'll prepare some supper for you. It won't be much; just some bread and cheese."

"That's very kind of you, Sir. Elizabeth, could you fetch the others please, my dear?"

The innkeeper opened an old leather bound book, blowing the dust from its pages. They were filled with signatures from past guests, with a date alongside each faded scribble. As Davenant signed his name, he couldn't help but notice that the signature above his, a MR. D. SYMS, was dated the 24th February, 1647.

"Is business slow?" asked Davenant.

The innkeeper smiled. "No, no, not at all, we just haven't used this book for a while, that's all."

Davenant nodded and finished writing the name, MR. WILL DAVENPORT, on the register.

"Here are your keys, Mr Davenport. Enjoy your stay."

"Thank you, Sir." Davenant received the large iron keys gratefully and ushered his tired troupe up the narrow staircase and towards their rooms.

Once they were out of sight, the innkeeper pulled out a crinkled leaf of parchment from underneath the bar. He read the wanted poster again, grinning at the sight of the princely reward on offer, his toothless smile widening as he saw the names that were printed there.

The rooms were poorly furnished and maintained, but they had been cheap. Woodworm had begun to eat its way into the shabby furniture and creaking floorboards. Davenant shared a room with Charles and Elizabeth, separating her from Betterton who grudgingly shared with Underhill and Middleton. Faith and Anne took the third room.

Davenant stirred when he felt the sun cascading through the moth-eaten curtain. He must have been asleep most of a day, he thought to himself. He craned his neck to peer out of the window, his rickety bed creaking as he rolled over. The sun was beginning to set in the cloudless sky, giving Davenant the impression that it was late afternoon or early evening. He turned to find that Charles was stirring in the bed alongside his.

"My Lord, are you awake?" he asked, his voice a hushed whisper.

"Yes, Will, I am now," replied Charles.

"Ah, I am sorry if I woke you."

"No, no, it was the damned creaking of your bed! Now, what is the plan for today?"

"Well, firstly I plan to get out of this bed before it kills me. Then I propose we leave the city immediately. If my experiences with Cromwell's troops have taught me anything, it's that we must keep on the move. We ought to head south. After all, I insist on keeping my part of the deal we struck in Bewdley Woods."

"The deal?" asked Charles, running a tired hand through his unkempt beard.

"My Lord, you've forgotten!"

"It seems as though years have passed and empire's have crumbled since we first met in Bewdley Woods," said Charles ponderously, allowing the slightest smile to pass over his lips – no doubt replaying the scarcely believable events of the past two weeks over in his mind.

"Then you've forgotten that I promised to ensure that you and Middleton reached Portsmouth unscathed." Davenant said.

"I didn't forget. I just didn't expect you to see it through. What you promised was foolhardy Sir William, and I will not hold you to it. Middleton and I have already cost you the life of dear old Turnbull and I'll be damned if we will cost you another. And neither of us could have possibly imagined what was going to happen, could we?"

"Turnbull's death was no one's fault, and I am a man of my word, my Lord. I will see that you reach Portsmouth, whether you like it or not. Besides, I can hardly return to London now, can I?"

There was a ferocious clatter and shouting outside.

Middleton rushed into the room, almost smashing the door from its hinges in his haste. "We must leave at once! Cromwell's men are outside!"

Charles leapt to his feet as Davenant shook Elizabeth awake.

"Elizabeth, we need to go right away!"

Her eyes flitted wildly around the room, over its ramshackle walls and archaic decor. She was finally able to compose herself and clambered clumsily out of bed. As Anne, Faith, Underhill and Betterton all poured into the small bedroom, a flurry of heavy footsteps began to ascend the staircase. Davenant threw a quick glance at the window and could see that the soldiers had left their horse-drawn carriage unattended by the tavern entrance. In a moment of reckless abandonment, he threw a chair through the window, smashing the glass and sending its shards scattering over the steep tiled roof.

"Out of the window!" he cried, picking Anne up and forcing her through the gap.

"Are you out of your mind?" gasped Underhill, as he reached out to stop his sister from falling.

"For God's sake, Cave! It's the only way!" He lifted Underhill and shoved him out of the window after his sister, receiving a blow in the face from Underhill's boot for his troubles.

Just as the soldiers' footsteps had reached the top of the stairs, Davenant hoisted Elizabeth through, her hand catching on a shard of glass still lodged in the frame. She cried out in agony as blood dripped from her wound. Davenant had no time to tend to it now – besides it was just a scratch – and urged Elizabeth onto the roof to join the others, who were now perched perilously close to the edge. Several tiles gave way underneath her, skipping over the others, smashing onto the cobbled street below.

As she clutched hold of her wounded hand, Elizabeth could see that Betterton had emerged onto the roof close behind her. Another tide of tiles gave way beneath him, dragging him down towards the ledge as if he were riding on the crest of a wave. Just before he fell, Elizabeth reached and grabbed hold of his arm. She screamed out in agony, alerting a cluster of nearby locals to the troubles above. Betterton was hanging on to Elizabeth, his grip lessening with every passing second. He shot a glance over his shoulder to see that one or two of the more sturdy onlookers had positioned themselves beneath him, their arms outstretched, waiting to break his fall.

"Jump you silly beggar, or you'll take her with you!" shouted one of the onlookers.

Betterton let go and landed in the arms of a man. Getting unsteadily to his feet, he noted Underhill, Faith and Anne being helped down by various other strangers. Elizabeth remained on the roof, looking down nervously. "Elizabeth, for God's sake jump! I'll catch you."

Behind Elizabeth, Charles and Middleton had made it onto the roof, the shouts of Cromwell's men issuing from the room behind them. Another line of tiles broke away underneath Charles, this time dragging him all the way over the ledge, dislodging Elizabeth as he came plummeting downwards. Betterton caught her as she fell, and as he looked up, he could see Charles hanging by his tunic from an outcropping of guttering.

"Don't move, my Lord!" yelled Betterton as he clambered to his feet, placing Elizabeth gently on hers. He could see that the burly man who had caught him was positioning himself for a second rescue attempt. Charles winced as his tunic tore fibre by fibre, until he fell into the arms of the man; the two sprawling across the street as he landed.

"Thank you, my good chap," said Charles through gritted teeth, clutching his shoulder in pain. He pointed up at Middleton who was perched awkwardly

The Devil's Plague

on the roof. "Now, if you wouldn't mind helping me catch that big brute, we'll be on our way."

The man nodded apprehensively just as Middleton threw himself off the roof. Somehow Charles and the burly man together were able to take Middleton's weight, although Charles grimaced in pain once more as his weakened shoulder was wrenched around. He dropped Middleton to his feet and let out a loud gasp of agonised pain.

"There's no time for that, my Lord," cried Middleton, seeing the soldiers hurriedly making their way back through the tavern. "Quickly everyone, get in that bloody carriage!"

The Parliamentarians' carriage had stood abandoned while the men did a sweep of the inn. As the one means of transport available it was their only option. Middleton clambered onto the driver's seat, clasped hold of the whip and cracked it down as hard as he possibly could. The horses whinnied and reared into action. Middleton allowed himself a fleeting glimpse over his shoulder as the soldiers came rushing from the tavern, a grin painted on his face.

"That'll teach the bastards a lesson!" he cried out, laughing, little realising that they had left Davenant on the roof in their rush to get away.

CHAPTER THIRTY

Oxford Castle Gaol

It wasn't quite as bad as the Tower, but it ran a close second. Although much of the Castle had been destroyed by Parliamentary troops, keen to remove this symbol of Royalist loyalties, Cromwell had recognised its advantages as a gaol and much of it had been repaired and extended. Thus Davenant had woken to find his hands bound by rusting iron cuffs and his ankles fastened together by metal clasps, which were secured to a sturdy shackle in the cold, clammy cell wall. He realised that he must have been knocked unconscious as his cheek was swollen and there was a pronounced bump on the back of his head.

By now, Davenant was utterly sick of incarceration. As he slumped in despair, he could hear footsteps making their way along the passageway outside. Davenant had no doubt that he was soon to be tortured until he gave up his secrets.

It occurred to him that if he were to tell them the whole truth, in all its gruesome, devilish detail, then he would most likely be sent to the Bedlam, and his imprisonment in the Oxford gaol would come to seem as paradise in comparison. He had heard some horrific tales about the Bedlam – such as the guards being as demented as the inmates and the physicians carrying out hideous and unnatural experiments on the poor souls incarcerated there. Davenant decided that he would tell Cromwell's men what they wanted to hear, with one or two little white lies thrown in

168

for good measure. After all, he could hardly give up the whereabouts of Charles, as he had no idea where his troupe had gone, although a small part of him prayed that they would launch some foolhardy rescue mission, not least because of his urge to see through his pledge that Charles and Middleton reach Portsmouth. His thoughts then turned to Elizabeth. He was accustomed to leaving her in Turnbull's care, but without him around, he was naturally concerned for her well being, especially with Betterton so unashamedly lusting after her. In the end he decided to give him the benefit of the doubt.

A key was turned and the heavy door was pushed viciously open. Charles Fleetwood stepped into the cell, followed by two soldiers, little more than boys.

"I see that Cromwell has spared his most senior officers," mocked Davenant.

Fleetwood planted his fist into Davenant's midriff. "You will regret your choice of words when you're on the rack!"

Davenant let out a faint wheeze. "Perhaps you would indulge me with a goblet of your finest wine first?"

Fleetwood launched a wad of spit at Davenant. "There you go," he replied, venomously. He knelt down and looked him square in the eye, holding up his chin between thumb and forefinger. "Where are Charles Stuart and the rest of your ragbag collective?"

Davenant shrugged his shoulders.

"I'll ask you one more time and take heed that if you fail to answer my question this time, I will flay the skin from your body," said Fleetwood icily.

"I told them that if we were to be split up, the Crown Tavern was where we were to reconvene."

It was the first building that came to mind – his birthplace.

"Very well," said Fleetwood. "But if I find that there is no sign of them there, then I will personally see to your torture and execution. And no doubt my Lord Cromwell will take great pleasure in your demise."

As Fleetwood and his two boy soldiers strode from the cell, Davenant appreciated that he'd only delayed his death sentence, but he felt optimistic that his temporary reprieve might somehow give him enough time to find a way out of his predicament. Either way, he knew that Fleetwood's men were racing their way across Oxford to the Crown Tavern and it wouldn't be long until they discovered his deception.

CHAPTER THIRTY-ONE

St. Martin's Church, Oxford

As soon as they had realised that Davenant had been left behind, Charles had taken over the role of leader. In doing so he had made his first decision – instead of seeking refuge outside of Oxford, he suggested that they hide in the Carfax Tower of St. Martin's Church in the middle of the city. In his opinion it was the last place Cromwell's troops would have expected to find them, thus being the last place they would look. Underhill wasn't as convinced, and had personally taken the role of sentry.

The church tower itself was a tall, proud and elegant building that offered picturesque views of the city. It rose over Oxford like a blessing. The troupe had climbed the ninety-nine steps and enjoyed the panoramic view of Oxford's dreaming spires as the sun was setting, its skyline shaped by the golden stone buildings of the University with their towers, spires and domes.

Now they were encamped behind the pulpit on the ground floor, the moonlight shafting in from the thin windows, forming a kaleidoscope of colours that settled upon the nave.

Charles looked up at the magnificent ceiling. Of the few buildings he had seen in his short time in England, this was by far the most impressive, and it gave him a feeling of pride that one day he would lead a country with such magnificent heritage.

"There's someone coming," Underhill gasped. "I told you we should have left Oxford!"

Middleton shot to his feet. "Wait here, I'll go and see who it is."

As the thick door of the chapel creaked open, Middleton allowed the intruder to take five or six paces inside before pouncing on him. The intruder let out a groan as Middleton landed on him, before turning him over onto his back to reveal his identity. Much to Middleton's horror, the man he was gripping viciously by the throat was an elderly priest.

"Who are you and what are you doing in my church?" asked the priest. "Is it money you're after?"

"No, no, it's not like that," replied Middleton, somewhat ashamed that he had assaulted a member of the clergy. "We are in need of shelter you see."

"Would you please get off me? I might be of some help if you allowed me to breathe!"

"I'm sorry. I didn't mean to hurt you."

"That's quite all right. If you wouldn't mind helping an old man to his feet, we can discuss this situation as gentlemen."

"My apologies once again," Middleton said, helping the priest up.

"It would appear that you have some questions to answer. I have no wish to involve those dreadful soldiers in our business and, should you offer me a sincere and honest reply, I won't have to. Please, take a seat. My legs are weary and I've no desire to stand unless I very much have to."

Middleton sat. "It's been a long time since I offered a confession."

"Is that what this is? A confession?"

"Of sorts, although I am at peace with what I have done recently," replied Middleton.

"Then I ask again, what is your business in my church tonight, and why the need to assault me upon me entering my place of work?"

Charles stood up, revealing himself. "I am sorry for our breaking into your place of worship. Please forgive my solider, he means you no harm. He's got a fiery temperament, no doubt a symptom of his Scottish ancestry. And we're all a little tired to say the least." Charles beckoned his companions to reveal themselves. "Father, it really is not how it appears."

"Well then, how do you think it appears?"

"That is a good question. It might be wise if I started from the very beginning," replied Charles, taking a seat beside Middleton.

"You look very familiar. Are you a wanted man?" asked the priest.

"In truth, yes, yes I am. I have had to go under the cover of a disguise much of the time. My name is Charles Stuart, the rightful heir to the throne of England. I am hunted by Oliver Cromwell's soldiers..."

"What are you doing in Oxford then? You should be hiding in the countryside!" exclaimed the priest.

"I am beginning to wonder the same thing."

"I knew your father very well," the priest said, getting to his feet. "You do look startlingly similar. And your accent, no doubt you picked it up from your time abroad?"

Charles nodded and the priest dropped to his knees.

"You've stumbled upon an old man who has a Royalist heart, my Lord! We heard that you had been killed in battle! I can't tell you what a relief, and what an honour it is to make your acquaintance."

Charles helped the priest to his feet. There were tears glistening in the old man's eyes. "My name is Runcible and I am your humble servant."

"You're not my servant, Father. All I need of you is your secrecy and your sanctuary. We are missing a member of our faction. He was taken by Cromwell's soldiers earlier today, but we are not leaving Oxford without him."

"How can you be sure that he is still alive?"

Elizabeth winced at Runcible's words.

"I do not know for certain. But I won't be satisfied until we've at least explored the possibility that he is."

"Well, there's only one place around here where they would keep him and that's in the old castle gaol. But you can't just expect to walk in unannounced and spring your friend to safety."

"Yes, yes, quite right, so we must go dressed as Cromwell's soldiers."

"And how exactly do you plan on doing that?" asked Middleton incredulously.

Charles grinned. "It's quite straightforward, really. Father, you look like a drinking man. Where is the nearest tavern around these parts?"

CHAPTER THIRTY-TWO

The Bear Inn, Oxford

Charles and Middleton loitered outside the Bear Inn until they had settled on their plan. They had left the rest of the group with Runcible who had proven himself something of an invaluable ally, not least because of his extensive knowledge of the Oxford streets.

"So, let's run through this one more time," whispered Middleton. "You want us to go in there, attract the attention of two soldiers, hope they follow us, attack them, steal their clothes and then go and rescue Sir William, disguised as Cromwell's men?"

"Yes." Charles could see the trepidation in Middleton's eyes. "Come on, Middleton! Where's your sense of adventure?" Middleton double-checked that his weaponry was secured as they stepped warily into the saloon, Charles removing his disguise as they did so. They were immediately struck by how small the inn was – several of the more intoxicated locals were perched precariously on the tables to make room for more of their comrades. The wattle and daub structure was exposed in the plaster on the walls, occasionally taking a beating from one of the stumbling drunkards, the wattles creaking inwards with a groan. Carvings of heraldic beasts had been etched deeply into the tobacco-stained plaster above the fireplace, perhaps the legacy of a previous era. Garish replicas of Flemish tapestries were hung nearby, similarly coated in grime, which almost made them appear genuine.

Charles spied a gathering of lantern-jawed soldiers in the furthest corner of the inn, far more sober than the other groups of reprobates. He nudged Middleton and they made their way through the throng towards the bar. They were now only feet away from the soldiers and Charles swaggered up to the bar and rested his arm upon it.

A plump old crone approached him. "What can I get you two gentlemen?"

"Two mugs of your finest ale, please," replied Charles, his voice loud and concise, as if he wanted the nearby soldiers to take note of his tangled accent. He could see in the corner of his eye that it had piqued their interest and they began to draw themselves upright. The serving wench soon reappeared with two pewter tankards of frothy brown ale. Charles and Middleton received them gratefully and each took a hearty swig. Middleton took the opportunity to observe some of the other tavern dwellers – two ostlers engaged in a heated exchange by the entrance over the whereabouts of one of their master's horses, a one-eyed cutpurse guzzling a flagon of wine whilst sifting through his booty and a foreign sailor ignoring the offensive comments being hurled his way by a group of cartwrights.

"Middleton, are they still looking at me?" asked Charles under his breath.

Middleton turned to face the soldiers, placing his ale on the bar. He could see that their gazes were still ardently fixed upon them.

He turned back to Charles. "Aye."

"Finish your drink, we're going," said Charles, allowing himself a sidelong glance at the soldiers. He could see that they were monitoring his every move.

Charles finished the last sip of his ale and eased his way back through the crowd with Middleton close behind. They barged past the arguing ostlers obstructing the door and into the night. Middleton's hand was tightly gripped around his knife handle.

And then the patter of footsteps came in chase. Charles distinguished three separate footfalls, less than twenty yards behind them. He realised they could utilise the alleyway to their advantage, engaging the soldiers in a skirmish before they made it onto the busier High Street. Charles turned to face his pursuers. He withdrew a cudgel from his belt, prompting Middleton to unsheathe his blade. The three soldiers were caught off guard, clumsily reaching for their own weapons as Charles and Middleton came rushing back up the alley.

The largest of the three soldiers was able to remove his sword from its scabbard just before Middleton bore down upon him, parrying Middleton's wild swing with his blade. Charles smashed his cudgel down upon the head of the first solider, his head cracking and blood gushing from his nose. He was immediately dead.

The second solider, evidently distraught at the death of his friend, thrust his sword at Charles, its tip piercing the silk of his doublet.

No harm done, just a scratch, Charles told himself, as he swung his cudgel back round until it came into contact with the soldier's knee. There was a crack and the soldier fell in a crumpled heap onto the filthy cobblestone, writhing in agony. Charles could see that the broken bone had pierced through his skin and the cotton of his trousers. He then mercilessly smashed the cudgel down upon the soldier's head, putting him out of his misery.

Seeing his two companions sprawled out across the alleyway, Middleton's adversary turned to run. He got as far as the mouth of the alley before Middleton's knife pierced his throat, a throw of pinpoint precision. The soldier swivelled sluggishly on his legs, a look of disbelief crossing his ruddy face, before sinking to the floor with a gurgle.

"I wondered when you were going to help me!" Charles said to Middleton as he hauled two of the bodies into an adjacent alley. Middleton dragged the last soldier from the cobblestone before anyone could find him lying there.

Charles was already in the process of stripping the clothes off the larger of his two victims. "Come on Middleton, we haven't got all day!" he said, cajoling his lumbering comrade into action. Middleton reluctantly removed the soldier's uniform and boots before taking off his own sweat stained jerkin and tunic. He squeezed, somewhat uncomfortably, into the red overcoat, which was about three sizes too small for him, and discarded his own clothes over a wall. Charles hurriedly swapped his own apparel, having little trouble fitting into his new garb. Once he had hurled his own clothes out of view, he ushered Middleton back up the alleyway and onto the High Street.

They headed for the gaol.

CHAPTER THIRTY-THREE

Oxford Castle Gaol

Davenant hadn't heard a sound for over an hour; not a footstep, a mumble or a foul-mouthed tirade from one of his fellow prisoners. The silence frightened him, not least because he was alone with his thoughts, and it was his thoughts that scared him the most. His eyes had worked their way around the cell time and time again, searching for something he could use to break his shackles. But there was nothing.

Davenant thought that it wouldn't be long until he heard the wrought iron gates creaking open and heavy footsteps thundering along the corridor outside his cell. Cromwell's men would soon discover that he had lied to them.

He started to pray, appealing for Elizabeth's safety and his own salvation, and that was when he heard the footsteps approaching. Davenant knew he was for it this time: no escapes, no trickery, no bribes, just the rack, manacles and the grip of the torturer. He buried his head into his chest as the pounding rhythm of the footsteps drew closer. He suddenly found himself sobbing. Despite the horrors in London, the terrifying escape through the Thames and incarceration in the Tower, this was the first time he had been truly afraid. It was not the fear of death, but the fear that he would never see Elizabeth again.

The footsteps came to a halt outside his cell. There was the scrabble of a key being clumsily fitted into the lock and the door opened.

Davenant didn't look up immediately. It wasn't until he heard a familiar voice that he lifted his head from his chest.

"Sir William, we're here to rescue you!"

His eyes were blurry from tears, but he could just about make out two figures stood in the doorway.

"Well, you could look a little more grateful than that!"

"Middleton, is that you?" Davenant's tears dried almost immediately. "What in the name of the Lord do you two look like?"

"Do you not like our new attire?" asked Charles, kneeling down to unlock Davenant's shackles.

"They're very fetching! But how did you get them? And how did you get in here?"

"We took the keys off the old guard at the entrance. The stupid fool thinks we're real soldiers. The rest I'll explain later, but we need to smuggle you past the guard and—"

"—and before the other guards return. I sent them on a wild goose chase around Oxford looking for you," replied Davenant, removing the clasps around his ankles. He rose sluggishly to his feet with the aid of Middleton's arm, a spasm of pain shooting through his legs as he stood. There was a riot of dark bruises on his wrists and ankles. Charles and Middleton supported Davenant from the cell and along the narrow corridor outside. They worked their way slowly past the other cells, the inhabitants a rough-looking group of drunkards and thieves. They soon came across the elderly guard perched somewhat uncomfortably on a stool at the end of the corridor. He looked up as they approached.

"We're to take this prisoner to London immediately,"

said Charles.

The old man nodded. "Very well, perhaps whilst you're there you could enquire as to what has happened to the other guards? They should have returned by now, and I shouldn't have to work such long hours at my age."

Charles nodded and proceeded to drag Davenant past the guard and into the torch-lit courtyard.

They were greeted by an all too familiar darkened sky and a driving rain as they made their escape.

CHAPTER THIRTY-FOUR

Hampshire

Much to Davenant's relief, the rain stopped shortly after they left Oxford. In its place came a dry, bitterly cold wind and a sudden frost, which froze the muddy ruts in the lanes down which they rode. The wheels of their stolen carriage and the horses' hooves struggled to acclimatise to the conditions, occasionally slipping and sending the carriage careening dangerously to the side.

The further south they travelled, the narrower the roads became, set deep beneath lofty banks with little paths leading off to remote villages and hamlets. The group kept a lookout for thieves, wary that the isolated highways of southern England had a reputation for such nefarious activity.

Leaving Oxford had been surprisingly easy. Davenant, Charles and Middleton had made their way back to the Carfax Tower, having managed to avoid Fleetwood's troops. Runcible had been true to his word, and had kept the others hidden until their return. Davenant was touched by the relief on the faces of his troupe as he stepped jadedly into the church. Even Betterton was overjoyed to see him. Davenant embraced Elizabeth with more than the usual tenderness. The priest had offered a tearful farewell as the group left the tower, and Charles made several promises to him that he would be rewarded for his loyalty on Charles' return to the throne.

The carriage trundled its way onto the South Downs, the rolling hills dotted with ancient ruins.

Davenant ordered Middleton to stop the carriage in the small hamlet of Selborne to purchase some more suitable clothing for the suddenly inclement weather. Charles and Middleton were markedly happier once they had got rid of their soldier's uniforms.

As night began to fall, the weary travellers found themselves in the small market town of Petersfield, half a day's journey from the south coast and Portsmouth. It was a pleasant enough town, dominated by a vast market square and the surrounding taverns, with more than adequate amenities on offer. Being short of money for accommodation for the entire party, the group decided to set up camp in a nearby field.

Middleton, Charles and Betterton decided to explore more of the town as Davenant and the rest of the group prepared for the night. As Davenant spread the woollen rugs out on the grass, he became aware that they were sharing the pasture with a variety of wildlife and cattle. A herd of sheep grazed contentedly nearby and there were cows in the adjacent field.

Davenant rummaged through his pockets for a flint with which he could start a fire. To his annoyance, he realised that it must have fallen out somewhere along the trail. Elizabeth, Anne and Underhill were sitting nearby, huddled together for warmth.

"Will you sit with me?" called Faith, as he looked over

Davenant nodded and managed a smile. "I'd be delighted to," he said, settling beside her and wrapping a blanket tightly around his shoulders. "Are you warm enough?"

"Not particularly. It may be an idea to build a fire."

"I'm afraid that I have misplaced my flint and we

have scarce any wood."

"In which case we'll have to make do," she said, resting her head on his shoulder.

Davenant felt a thrill at her touch.

"If you don't mind me asking, Sir William, how did your wife die?"

It took Davenant a few moments to compose himself before he could answer. "My wife died during childbirth. As you can probably tell, it is not something I am terribly comfortable talking about."

"Sir William, a thousand apologies. I should not have pried," she said.

Davenant looked into her crestfallen eyes, their striking blue seeming to shine bright despite the darkness. "No, no. Perhaps it is something I should try to talk about. Not even Elizabeth knows the circumstances of her mother's death."

"Does she look like her?"

"They could be twins," replied Davenant, gradually feeling more at ease with the conversation and Faith's presence next to him. "It is quite remarkable."

"I have no doubt your wife would have been very proud of the way you have brought her up. She is a credit to you."

Davenant stared out over the pastures. "Yes, I hope so. It is strange, is it not?"

"What is strange?"

"That these last two weeks have brought us ever closer, even under the most trying of circumstances. Do you not feel it?"

"I would like to think that we share a bond, not only forged by what has happened but by—"

Davenant leant in to kiss her soft lips. The time for waiting was over – he had been dying to do this

ever since their first conversation at Evesham Abbey.
He felt certain that his darling Anna would not have
disapproved of his finding love elsewhere. No matter,
for the time being he wanted to enjoy this intimacy.

He heard the approach of footsteps from behind,
accompanied by drunken muttering. He broke away
from Faith and turned to see the silhouettes of three
staggering men closing in upon them.

"Who goes there?" demanded Davenant, mindful
that he'd already had enough trouble with undead
soldiers, cloaked horsemen and Cromwell's troops, let
alone having to contend with drunkards.

There was no reply.

Davenant got to his feet. "Who goes there?"

"Is that Sir William Davenant?" asked a voice.

"Yes, yes, it is. Who is speaking?"

"King Phillip IV of Spain. I have come to claim
your horses and your women..." The sentence trailed
away into a spasm of drunken laughter. Only then
did Davenant realise that the prowler was none other
than Charles Stuart.

"God's son, you had me in fits!" he said. "We have
barely enough money for accommodation but you
manage to find enough to get utterly ruined!"

Middleton, grinning drunkenly, aided Davenant
in hauling Charles towards the camp. He had fallen
asleep, and the sound of his snoring reverberated
against Davenant's shoulder. The two men dropped
him on a rug, landing in a crumpled heap by Faith's
feet.

"I told His Majesty that my father worked as
his father's cook! Can you believe it, Sir William?
We're practically brothers." Betterton said, swaying
drunkenly.

"You have the future King of England in your care and you let him get as drunk as a choirboy on rum!" Davenant was incandescent. "What if you got into a tavern brawl? I don't know whether you have noticed but this future King is supposed to be travelling incognito."

Middleton and Betterton shuffled awkwardly as if they were being chastised by a parent.

Davenant threw a blanket at each of the men "You drunkards get some sleep; hopefully the cold frost will sober you."

Davenant could almost smell the salt-tang of the ocean as he woke and stirred Faith, who slept beside him. They had managed to get the carriage to themselves, the rest of the group managing to start a fire and provide much needed warmth for those sleeping under the stars. Faith rolled onto her side revealing the scars on her back from the witchcraft trial that had so viciously ruined her otherwise perfect complexion. They would heal in time, Davenant thought, although he appreciated just how painful it must have been for her.

"Good morning," he said, bending over to kiss her. "We should leave soon. The sooner we reach Portsmouth, the sooner we can complete our mission and make our own plans."

Faith smiled and Davenant left the carriage to chivvy the rest of the group awake.

"Will you desist!" she heard Charles shout. "I have quite possibly the worst hangover I have ever had."

"I want to reach Portsmouth by nightfall, and if

you're not up in five minutes, you can make your own way to the south coast," Davenant replied.

"You're an utter bastard, Sir William." The future monarch groaned.

With every judder of the carriage wheels, Charles seemed to turn a deeper shade of green. Davenant had decided to drive, as Middleton and Betterton were in no better a state than their royal comrade. As they ploughed straight through another rut, Charles rose shakily to his feet, knocked viciously on the roof of the carriage signalling Davenant to stop. He barely made it out of the door before he let go of his breakfast and last night's libations. Wiping his mouth he looked up and saw a large bird hovering above them. It called out and Charles realised that it was a seagull. He hurriedly wiped the spittle from his mouth and climbed back inside the carriage.

"It's a seagull!" he exclaimed, collapsing back into his seat next to Anne. "We must be close!"

For the next two hours, all thoughts of bad heads and hangovers were forgotten. As the carriage wound its way along the coastal road to Portsmouth, animated conversations issued from the carriage as those inside realised that they had almost achieved their hard-fought for objective. Davenant heard the laughter radiating from inside and wished he could be a part of it. Not least to protect himself from the biting gales and the dark skies that had begun to set in. No matter, he thought, he would soon be able to revel in his freedom with the others.

As they clattered onto another road, a smoother

version of the previous one, Davenant could spy a collection of dwellings up ahead, a series of lantern lights guiding him towards them.

They had finally made it to Portsmouth.

CHAPTER THIRTY-FIVE

Portsmouth

Now that they had reached the coast they were going to have to find a ship willing to take Charles and Middleton on the final leg of their journey. They would more than likely be forced to spend another evening camped out, as no vessel would risk setting sail for France in darkness. But at least this gave Davenant, Charles and Middleton a chance to run their eyes over the various ships that were moored in the harbour. They hadn't much money left, but Charles felt that his and Middleton's experience as sailors would more than compensate in securing them a bark. Charles also felt confident that no one would recognise him, secure in the knowledge that the copies of his portrait had only been handed out to Parliamentarian soldiers in and around London.

"How can we be sure that any of these boats are travelling to France?" asked Middleton, holding aloft an oil lantern.

"Take a closer look at their names, you dumb oaf!" said Charles, pointing at the painted hulls.

Juliet, Dives-sur-Mer.

Augusta, Insigny-le-Buat.

Blanche, Cayeux-sur-Mer.

Middleton shrugged his shoulders and raised his eyebrows, suggesting that the names meant nothing to him.

"Where do you think those ships came from?" Charles asked in exasperation.

"Spain?"

Charles ignored Middleton's obtuseness and proceeded along the dock. At the far end he could see several sailors and shipwrights heaving huge wooden crates onboard a large vessel. As he looked closely, he could make out the name Sa Majesté painted in bold white letters upon its stern.

"That looks like a far more suitable craft."

Charles approached the crew, little reflecting on why they were making ready for departure under the cover of night. Davenant watched as Charles spoke to a thuggish looking sailor who was rolling a barrel crammed with bales of cloth along the dock. As Davenant drew closer Charles laughed, said something to the sailor in French and shook his hand before turning to face Davenant and Middleton. "Louis, please meet my good friends, John Middleton and William Davenant." The hulking Frenchman, who was only marginally shorter than Middleton, offered his hand.

"A pleasure to meet you," said Davenant, as he took the sailor's hand in his own.

"It is my pleasure to make your acquaintance."

"As luck would have it, they're setting sail for Le Havre within the hour and have agreed to take us with them," Charles said.

Davenant immediately felt a tinge of sadness. "Oh, I see, as soon as that."

Charles picked up on his melancholy and placed a hand on his shoulder. "Yes, as soon as that. Let us go back to the carriage and say our goodbyes."

Davenant nodded.

"That seemed surprisingly easy," said Middleton, as they made their way back up the dock. "Will they not suspect that we are spies?"

"Perhaps, but as luck would have it, they're short on crew. And neither of us have an English accent," replied Charles.

"Be that as it may, are you sure you shouldn't at least wait until the morning? Perhaps there might be an English crew amongst this lot." Davenant said.

"It is settled, Sir William. We leave tonight."

As they left the wooden gangway, Davenant realised that there was no way of talking Charles out of leaving on the Sa Majesté. "Very well," he said, seeing the carriage up ahead. "In which case, we will bid you farewell."

"Please, Sir William. Do not make this any harder than it has to be." There was marked sadness in Charles' tone now, his voice wavering with a hint of emotion. "I promise that I shall return with an army to reclaim my throne." As they stopped by the carriage, Charles could see the look of restlessness in the eyes of the troupe. "With much sadness, Middleton and I are to leave tonight on a boat traveling to Le Havre. I would very much like to extend my thanks and gratitude to all of you for helping us to reach Portsmouth unscathed."

Davenant could see tears in Charles' eyes as he stepped forward to embrace him. Middleton, who was similarly glum, shook the hands of each man and took the liberty of hugging and kissing each woman.

"I will come back and I will seek you out, Sir William." Charles said. "I promise." It was at that moment that Davenant realised with a shudder that some day they would have to return to London.

He tried to put it to the back of his mind as he shook Middleton firmly by the hand and patted him heartily on the back. Charles picked up his few belongings and, with his manservant in tow, headed for the docks.

Although utterly crestfallen, Davenant prayed that it wouldn't be too long before he saw his friends again. He turned and looked at Faith, her warm smile immediately lifting his spirits. It was there and then that he hoped she would be a part of his future.

Fifteen Years Later
1666

CHAPTER THIRTY-SIX

Shanklin, Isle of Wight
28th August, 1666

Little Charles Davenant looked up at the imposing cliff that loomed over the small fishing village, separating it from the old village above. To a seven year old it looked like a mountain. A waterfall thundered down a gorge in the rock, its slippery walls garlanded by a vast array of flora and fauna. It really was a magical place, especially to the children of the village who would watch its majestic grandeur in awe. Unbeknown to Charles, the gorge also had its uses for those who weren't quite as innocent. It was well-known amongst the locals as a haunt for smugglers, with a tunnel having been dug between the old village and the Chine Inn.

And that was why his mother refused to let him go there at night.

Faith caught a glimpse of her son through the mullioned windows of their thatched cottage; he sat transfixed by the sight of one of nature's finest splendours. She would often find him there, and no matter how much she warned him of its perils, he would continue to risk her wrath by sneaking out for one last glimpse before bedtime. His obstinacy reminded her of his father's stubbornness. Certainly one character trait that she wished he hadn't inherited.

Faith hastily removed a pan from the range and dashed outside, the warped cottage door left swinging on its rusty hinges.

"Charles! How many more times must I tell you? Do not leave the cottage without telling me!"

Charles turned to face his mother, his rosy red cheeks and bright blue eyes melting her heart. How could she possibly stay angry with him?

Faith turned to the beach as she heard a patter of weary footsteps dragging through the sand. It was her husband, dressed head to toe in his fisherman's garb and clutching a handful of mackerel. His mass of grey hair poked out from beneath his hat and his beard was soaking wet.

"I've caught a veritable banquet tonight, my dear!" He called out. Thomas Betterton stood next to him, clasping hold of two fishing rods which bowed in the strong wind.

"It was a joint effort!" called Betterton.

"What's Charles doing out here so late?" Davenant asked.

"He sneaked out whilst I was tending to the stove."

Davenant knelt down beside his son, running his hand through his thick mass of blonde windswept hair. "Come on; let's get you inside before it starts to rain. Are you hungry?"

Charles' eyes lit up and he nodded happily. Davenant ushered him back towards the cottage before turning back to Faith. "Remember Elizabeth and Alexander will be eating with us tonight."

"Am I not invited too?" asked Betterton, bending down to avoid clouting his head on the frame of the door. "As the father of your grandson, the husband of your daughter and the provider of the feast, I feel I have every right to sit at your table."

"What utter rot! You caught one fish!"

"Of course you're invited Thomas. Ignore this gruff old seaman, he's getting far too big for his boots," interjected Faith, shutting the cottage door against the brewing storm.

Betterton smiled, removed his boots and collapsed into an armchair by the roaring fire. Davenant followed suit and looked out of the window as the waves began to churn. The mizzling rain began to turn into a hard downpour and thunder joined the crashing of the sea.

The smell of steamed mackerel and vegetables drifted in from the kitchen. "That smells delicious!" Davenant said, looking at Betterton and finding that he had fallen asleep. He gently placed a blanket around his shoulders.

Over the years Davenant had managed to grow accustomed to Betterton and Elizabeth being together, and by the time they became man and wife, the two men had forged a new relationship based on mutual respect. They still enjoyed making fun of one another, but the tension that had been present from their time on the run had eventually dispersed. Davenant wouldn't admit it, but he was a little hurt when they named their son Alexander and not William, after his grandfather. Still, he hadn't been as foolish as Davenant himself and named his son after Charles Stuart. The traitor who had broken his word.

Davenant had waited patiently for his friend to return to England, but after fifteen years he had all but given up hope that he would ever see him again. As they had said their farewells to Charles and Middleton in Portsmouth, Davenant thought it best the group stay on the coast and as far away from London as possible. By the time word had begun to sift down about the horrors in the capital, more and more families had fled south, and before long Portsmouth had become overrun. It was the same in all of the coastal towns and cities, and Davenant would hear rumours of all sorts of goings on in places such as Southampton and Bournemouth. After a while, new laws were introduced to stop the looting, raping and pillaging, and new committees were elected to oversee that the judicial system remained intact. A small army was raised to maintain order, a platoon composed of the very best soldiers the southern cities could spare. They had enough resources to mount an attack on London with a view to reclaiming the capital should the call come. Having seen the horrors for himself though, Davenant was in no doubt that their efforts would be futile. Already several small-scale operations had been mounted, but not one man had returned.

Eventually Davenant had felt it best that they relocate to the Isle of Wight, fearing that conscription would see Betterton, Underhill and himself drafted up. It was never a place he was overly fond of, but in comparison to the heaving mass of unruly louts that overran Portsmouth, it seemed like paradise. Very few people had cottoned on to this idea, so Davenant insisted their exile be kept secret. By this time, Faith was already pregnant with Charles and Elizabeth and Betterton were married, so it seemed fitting that they came with them. He had even persuaded Underhill and Anne to come too. Although they put up some resistance, they could see for themselves just how infested Portsmouth had become.

Davenant had left word with one or two trusted innkeepers of his plan and told them that should two men named Charles and Middleton come looking for them; they could find him in Shanklin on the Isle of Wight. It was more an act of blind optimism than expectation, but he felt it best he covered all his bases. As the years slipped by, the chances of Charles and Middleton returning seemed to lessen with every passing Christmas. Davenant knew he was an old man now, without the agility he once had, and Charles couldn't have been much younger. If they were to return to England, it would have to be soon, or not at all.

A tapping on the door broke Davenant out of his reverie and woke Betterton with a start. Davenant groaned as he got out of his chair, hobbled across the room and unlocked the door. As it creaked open Elizabeth appeared in the doorway, her hair soaking wet and baby Alexander cradled tightly in her arms.

Davenant ushered her in from the cold and removed the sodden shawl from her shoulders. "My darling, take a seat by the fire. You must be freezing!"

"This storm seems to have come from nowhere," replied Elizabeth, taking a seat, her face illuminated by the flames. Despite the passage of time she had still maintained the same unmistakable beauty.

"Something smells good," said Elizabeth. "Where's Charles?"

"He's in his room. I found him by the gorge again," replied Faith, coming through from the kitchen. "It's good to see you Elizabeth."

Davenant looked on with pleasure as Faith embraced his daughter. He had feared that she would be wary of their relationship, but to his surprise Elizabeth treated her every bit like the mother she never knew.

He glanced back out over the bustling waves

crashing onto the sand and spied a small, solitary vessel being tossed around as it approached the shore. A group of several men climbed frantically over the sides and into the shallows; wading the rest of their way onto the beach, their vessel capsizing as a big wave struck it from the stern. Davenant pitied those fishermen who had stayed out late. In such conditions as these, death was never far away. He just hoped that the men who made their way up the beach hadn't lost any of their comrades.

It was almost as if the storm from the previous night had never happened, little debris littered the beach and the sun beat down relentlessly, making the sand almost too hot to walk on.

Davenant, Betterton and Underhill had risen early once they realised that the storm had passed. It was cooler and easier to work the sea at this hour – before the sun reached its zenith and made the already difficult work twice as hard. It had been a stiflingly hot summer, bringing with it shoals of weird and wonderful fish that were rarely seen in English waters. It did wonders for their trade and Davenant had managed to make a tidy sum from the unusually warm conditions. If Bray could only see me now, he thought, the old sea dog would be proud. Davenant had gone from seasick landlubber to hardened sailor in a remarkably short time.

"We should think about heading back soon. I don't want to miss the service," he said, reeling in his line.

Davenant had had plenty of time to mull over what

they had witnessed in London, not least Cromwell's declaration regarding the Devil and the events that seemed to corroborate his claims. Over the years, Davenant had formed the belief that if there was such an evil, an evil that could manifest itself in human form, then there must be a force that represented all that was good. Since their arrival in Shanklin, he hadn't missed a Sunday service, thus a devout believer was born. Slowly and surely, the others began to follow him, no doubt driven by their own conclusions as to what had happened all those years ago.

Underhill took off his hat and leant against the starboard rail, happy to bask in the glorious sunshine. "Did you hear the stories of a strange boat appearing overnight? Apparently it was full of foreign smugglers," he said.

Davenant stiffened. "No, no, I didn't hear a thing."

Betterton replied with a quizzical shrug of the shoulders. "Whoever they were, I'm sure they'll come to light soon."

The line of Underhill's fishing rod jerked taut, sending busy ripples across the water. "Another one for me!" he said, with a smug grin stamped across his face. "At this rate you two will be going hungry."

The jollity passed Davenant by as he stared out over the ocean, transfixed by its serenity. His mind raced at the thought of who those sailors were who had barely made it to shore in the night. It sounded as if they hadn't been normal fisher-folk at all.

That night Davenant tried to fight his way into

sleep. It wasn't the reappearance of the howling winds whistling round the cottage that bothered him, it was something else entirely. Davenant could hear Faith's sleep-heavy breathing beside him and he longed for the same release. He hated his constant insomnia. Spending the small hours alone with his thoughts, listening to the wind and rain beating down upon the cottage drove him wild with frustration.

He rolled out of bed, doing his best not to wake Faith in the process, and tiptoed across the cold stone floor and into the living room. Elizabeth, Betterton and Alexander, who had once more joined them for supper, had returned to their own dwelling further along the seafront, leaving the cottage in silence.

Davenant ambled up to the window and took in the view. The moon was obscured by thick clouds, but he could still make out the waves grinding up the beach. His thoughts soon turned to the capsized boat and the men he had seen the night before.

Who could they have been?

Davenant nestled into his chair by the fireplace, its fading coals providing little heat, and picked up his clay pipe, stuffing it with tobacco. He lit his briar and sat back in his armchair, contentedly puffing away. As his eyes drifted back towards the window, he suddenly became aware of a cluster of shadows skulking close to the cottage. He leapt out of his armchair with the agility of a man half his age and backed into a darkened corner, concealing himself by a chest of drawers. He listened closely; keen to discern any audible words amidst the wind and rain.

"This is the place," said a voice in a muted whisper.

Davenant saw the outlines of the men moving to

the front door. His hand fumbled for a poker and he clutched it tightly, wondering whether he would have enough time to get back to the bedroom and alert Faith and Charles before the door burst open. But instead, there was a polite knocking.

"Who is it?" he asked.

"Is this the home of Sir William Davenant?"

He hadn't been called Sir William in years. "Yes, yes it is. I ask again, who is it?"

"An old friend," said the voice in reply. "So could you do us the greatest of services and let us in?"

The voice sounded familiar, but Davenant hesitated as he shuffled towards the door, his hand fumbling as he turned the key in the lock. He eased the door open and came face to face with a shabbily dressed middle-aged man.

"Charles?"

Davenant heard Faith come into the room behind him and she let out a gasp when she saw the man standing in her doorway.

"Do not be alarmed, my dear," said Charles, taking a step inside the cottage. "It is I, your long lost friend, Charles Stuart."

Faith lifted her lantern, its light revealing the contours of Charles' wrinkled face. Davenant could scarcely believe his eyes. The man had the same voice, the same mannerisms and the same gruff countenance, but the years had been unkind to him. Charles edged forward and embraced Davenant who, dumbfounded, reciprocated.

"Fifteen years, it's been fifteen years," he said, beginning to sob. "What took you so long?"

Charles didn't answer straight away. Instead he shuffled sheepishly up to Faith and offered her the same warm embrace. Davenant could see a group of men ambling idly outside. One of them took a timid step into the cottage, revealing his vast bulk and imposing stature.

"Middleton, is that you?"

"Aye, Sir William, it is. And can I say what a pleasure it is to see you again!"

"It is wonderful to see you both again!" Davenant's voice began to break, emotion taking hold and eventually getting the better of him. He could see Middleton properly now – age hadn't shrunk him in the slightest, although a shock of white hair had replaced his once proud black mane.

"I am so very sorry to disturb you at this hour, and my sincere apologies for leaving it so long before I returned," said Charles, turning back to face Davenant. Young Charles had emerged in the doorway, the commotion having woken him. "You have a son, William?"

Davenant looked lovingly towards Charles. "Yes, my Lord, we have a son. And we named him after you."

"Well then, I am indeed delighted for you both, and appreciate your kind gesture. I have had several children of my own, all bastards of course. I have yet to be so foolish as to get married," replied Charles flippantly as he took a seat. "Yes, you are wondering why it has taken me so long to return, Sir William."

"We have grown old, my Lord. Any chance of us reclaiming London and your throne has surely passed."

"The truth of the matter is this. I was reluctant to commit myself and my men to a cause until I had received word from the spies I had sent over from

France. I must have sent at least fifty men these past few years to report back to me. And only one of them returned, last week in fact, hence my arrival at your cottage tonight. Henri, could you step forwards please and introduce yourself?"

A slight, impish looking man eased into the cottage, taking off his soaking, weathered hat before bowing to Faith and Davenant. "I am at your service, Sir William," he said in perfect English, with only a trace of a French accent.

"Would you be so kind as to tell them what you told me?" asked Charles.

Henri took a moment to compose himself. "Sir William, what I saw was beyond the pale. I arrived in London by carriage, having to pay the carriage driver a princely sum to take me to the outskirts. After narrating his own grisly stories of what he'd seen and heard, he naturally refused to take me any further than Dulwich Wood, and as he left me I had never felt more alone. It was at the Thames that I saw the first signs of destruction and chaos. As I hid in the ruins of a tavern, I saw groups of the undead roaming the streets in search of food. There were thousands of them I tell you!"

"Was there any sign of the horsemen, the Kryfangan?" Davenant asked.

"No, I didn't see them. Although I must confess that I didn't hang around long enough to seek them out."

Davenant turned back to Charles. "Where is your army based?"

"There is no army," replied Charles solemnly.

"No army? Then how in God's name do you expect us to mount an attack?"

"I tried, Will, really I did. But it is very hard to raise an army to fight the undead! Most of the time they laughed in my face. France is sadly lacking in lunatics who are willing to risk their lives for me, unlike Henri over there."

"So what do you propose we do?" asked Davenant.

"I have brought over a group of five of us. Are Betterton and Underhill still around?" Davenant nodded, seeing for the first time the other two men in Charles' group, little more than fresh-faced schoolboys. He noted that one of them was dressed as a clergyman. "Then we few could attempt to get into the city." Charles said.

Davenant admired his bravery and recklessness, but at the same time was entirely unconvinced that a group of middle-aged men and schoolboys would make the slightest difference.

Yet Davenant wasn't prepared to sit idly by whilst London crumbled. "How will we defeat them, my Lord?"

Charles could see the fire burning in Davenant's eyes; perhaps a symbol of what was to come. "Oh, worry not Sir William, for I have a plan."

CHAPTER THIRTY-SEVEN

The Chine Inn, Shanklin

The following afternoon they gathered at the Chine Inn. The storm of the previous night had disappeared and in its place returned the beautiful sunshine, highlighting the splendour of the island, its glorious cliffs and lush green forests contrasting one another majestically.

Davenant had requested that Betterton and Underhill join them in the inn as well as a group of local fishermen. Elizabeth, Faith and Anne had all been left behind, much to their annoyance. Davenant could easily imagine them, along with the other women of Shanklin, all gathered around bellyaching about their respective husbands, brothers and fathers, but Davenant didn't care. He wanted them as far away from London and danger as possible.

Betterton and Underhill were still in the dark as to what was going on, and it wasn't until Charles and Middleton had entered that the situation became clear to them. As happy as they were to see their compatriots again, they were only too aware of the reasons behind their visit. The men huddled around the largest table that the inn had to offer and the innkeeper locked and bolted the door behind them, keeping their conspiracy safe from regular customers.

"Thank you for agreeing to come at such short notice gentlemen. It is a most terrible matter that brings us all together," said Davenant.

"Come on Will, out with it!" cried one of the

fishermen, a robust gentleman with a bushy grey beard.

Davenant gestured towards Charles. "This gentleman beside me is none other than Charles Stuart, the rightful heir to the throne of England."

There was a collective gasp and then one of the fishermen got to his feet. "You call us here today and you interrupt our work to tell us ridiculous lies!" he cried.

"For pity's sake, they are not lies!" replied Davenant, banging his fist angrily on the table. "And that is not the half of it, for I will tell you a story that will make your skin crawl."

Davenant had won their attention. After calming himself, he proceeded to recount the events from London. The group listened intently, occasionally shaking their heads in disbelief. Like everyone else, they had heard the rumours of what was happening in the capital but had never been privy to a first-hand account. As Davenant came to the end, he nodded to Charles to take over.

"It's as simple as this," he said. "We make our way into London under the cover of darkness and set fire to the city." Charles turned to Davenant. "You remember what Cromwell told us about the plague in Mongolia? He told us that Genghis Khan had united the warring tribes of Mongolia with the help of a dark army on horseback. When their victims rose from the dead to seek their vengeance upon them, it started a civil war in which those who weren't afflicted by the blight were caught in the middle. It was a great fire that eventually ended the plague."

"And you want us to help you get to London?" asked one of the fishermen. "We are only simple folk, we are not warriors."

His comrades nodded in agreement and Charles slowly retook his seat, a glum expression on his face.

"What would it take for you to come?" asked Davenant.

"We've got families, Will. We can't just leave them and our livelihoods, especially when there is the very real chance of us not returning."

"I've got a family too! Don't you see that this is a chance for you all to reclaim what is rightfully ours, and become heroes in the process? This is the future of England we are talking about. The future of us all! The rot at the centre of our country cannot be allowed to spread and trust me, if we don't so something about it, it will!"

The fishermen sat in silence, all of them weighing up the enormity of the situation.

"When I become King, your actions now will not be forgotten and I will bring stability back to this country," said Charles. A sudden knock on the door broke their train of thought. The innkeeper grimaced as he shuffled across the stone floor to unlock the door. As he tugged it open, he came face to face with a group of local smugglers. They barged past the innkeeper and into the lounge bar.

"God's wounds, Jack, we're dry here! What are you doing locked up at this time of day? Hang about, what have we here?" asked a grimy man as he barged his way into the pub. He strode aggressively up to Davenant and looked him in the eyes with a stern, unbending gaze. "Is this your doing Davenant?"

Davenant nodded. "Yes it is, Tom. What we're discussing here doesn't concern you."

"Hold on Will, do you not think that Tom and his boys have every right to know?" asked one of the fishermen. "Perhaps they might be of some use, provide some more manpower. I know we'd be happier with them coming."

Davenant considered what the fisherman had to say, gesturing for Tom and his band of smugglers to sit.

"It's been the hottest summer in years and London's buildings will be tinder dry. If you want to start a fire, you've got the perfect catalyst right there," said Tom, much to everyone's surprise. "Don't look shocked, we were listening at the door. And we want in."

"It might not be an army, and I might not agree with their morals, but it's the best we've got," said Davenant to Charles, almost cracking a smile in the process. Deep down Charles knew it too. It was the best he had, a collection of ragtag fishermen and smugglers would just have to do.

"Fine," he said. "Say your farewells because we leave at dawn tomorrow."

CHAPTER THIRTY-EIGHT

Portsmouth

It had been at least a decade since Davenant had last set foot on the mainland. The group had set sail from Shanklin in a fleet of fishing boats, aided by a strong wind that got them across the choppy Solent in what seemed like no time at all. Davenant knew only too well that it would be a tearful farewell, and as he had said his goodbyes to Faith, Elizabeth, Charles and Alexander, he had a gut wrenching feeling that he would never see them again. Faith and Elizabeth had expressed a mixture of anger and sorrow, but did their best to put on a brave face for the sake of the children. They didn't want the last time they saw their husbands to be filled with resentment. It was just as hard for Betterton and Underhill to say goodbye to their friends and family, but they knew in their heart of hearts that they were doing the right thing, and the thought of returning as heroes seemed to bolster their courage.

Portsmouth's dock hadn't changed in the slightest, its weathered timber creaking and groaning as the group of men strode purposefully along it. Davenant heard several insults being thrown their way from the locals, belittling the intelligence and breeding of the 'islanders'. He was glad to see that his men were ignoring the jibes, although Tom the smuggler couldn't resist reciprocating with a few offensive hand gestures of his own. Davenant had noted that the fishermen and the smugglers kept well out of each other's way, causing a slight tension in the group.

Nevertheless, he was happy that the smugglers had decided to come along, and it was their muscle that had persuaded the fishermen to throw their lot in with the group.

"If you gentlemen wouldn't mind occupying yourselves for a while, we have some business to attend to," said Charles, as he and Middleton headed towards a blacksmith's shop. After a short rest spent loitering by the sun-drenched docks, Davenant saw the two men re-emerge. Middleton let out a piercing whistle which got everyone's attention, and beckoned them over. Davenant led the group to the blacksmith's shed. Inside, a vast array of weaponry shimmered in the meagre sunlight filtering in from outside. All types of swords, daggers, axes and maces were being prepared by the smithy, including three or four claymores, battle axes and machetes. Davenant could also see an array of peculiar body armour along with dark hats that were fixed upon complex masks. The masks were fitted with glass visors to protect the wearer's vision, and long beaks moulded from bronze, stuffed with fresh herbs to purify the air. A selection of waxed gowns and leather boots of all sizes completed the collection. Charles admired the arsenal and handed the hunchbacked blacksmith two bulging pigskin purses.

Middleton could see the bemused expression on Davenant's face. "We placed our order before we came over to the island," he said, grinning wickedly. "We are the plague doctors now, Sir William."

"Our carriages are through there," said Charles. "If we're quite ready gentlemen I propose that we start loading up. I'm certainly more than ready to get out of this shit-hole. We shall be in London in two days!"

The good weather aided their journey from Portsmouth and through the sunken lanes of the Hampshire countryside. Betterton, Underhill, Henri and Charles' men were travelling in one carriage with the smugglers, whilst Davenant, Charles and Middleton occupied the other carriage with the fishermen. Davenant admired the fine craftsmanship of their transport. There were no cracks or holes in this beauty. As he peered out of the carriage windows, the little thatched-roofed dwellings they passed reminded him of his own cottage by the sea, and he immediately felt a tinge of sorrow.

"Sir William!" cried one of the fishermen, a fat, bushy-bearded simpleton. "How comes you got that in front of your name then?"

"He was knighted by my father," replied Charles.

"Well, well, we'll make sure we treat you with the respect you deserve," replied the man, accompanied by snorts of laughter from his cohorts.

Davenant shook. "I don't need to be treated any differently."

"Don't be so modest, Sir William. You should be proud of your knighthood," said Charles. "And who knows, if any of you survive this conflict, perhaps you will get one too."

That shut them up. Davenant turned back to the rolling countryside. Strange, he thought. They hadn't heard one bird or seen any animals since they'd set out.

As night began to fall, Charles called for the party to set up camp. A chill breeze stirred the trees around them and a smattering of rain began to fall as they prepared for the night. Davenant glumly pondered whether it was a sign of things to come.

"I don't mind admitting that I am a little scared," said Tom the smuggler once they had got settled.

"It's the waiting that's the worst part, don't you think?" Davenant replied. "Wondering what might happen, what it's going to be like when we get there."

"I'm a hardened man, Will, and I have seen a great deal of bloodshed in my time. Yet your corroboration of the rumours from London sent shivers down my spine."

"Then why do you risk your life? If you don't mind me asking."

"I may be a smuggler, but I am also a patriot."

"I am indeed grateful for your bravery."

"We laughed at you when you first came over to the island," said Tom, a smile now crossing his lips. "You were totally unaccustomed to life on the sea, flouncing and floundering your way around the ocean on that ridiculous little rowboat of yours. But over the years, we all saw you change from a city man into a bona fide islander. I don't mind saying that you're one of us now, Will."

Davenant nodded his appreciation.

He was surprised by how well he slept and as the group set off the following morning, Davenant felt remarkably revitalised. It was more than could be said for Tom's smugglers, who looked suitably gnarled after a hard session in a nearby tavern.

Half an hour's journeying took them around the

twisting, winding lanes of the Devil's Punchbowl, a large hollow of dry sandy heath which commanded spectacular views. Davenant overheard two of the fishermen talking of its legend, how the Devil spent his time tormenting the god Thor by pelting him with enormous handfuls of earth, leaving the Punchbowl the way it was. With what he had already been through, Davenant could just about imagine that to be true.

As the carriages trundled onwards through Guildford and towards Epsom, Davenant could feel his eyelids getting heavier with every turn of the carriage wheels, although he did note another change in weather before he eventually fell asleep.

Dark clouds were gathering.

Somebody nudged him awake. He couldn't have been asleep for more than an hour, he thought to himself, but as he stirred he could see Charles looking at him, his face pallid and etched with anxiety and apprehension.

Davenant quickly turned to look out of the carriage window. The sky was now so dark that he had difficulty discerning their surroundings, although the shimmering of water that ran alongside the carriage must have been the Thames. As he looked up, he could just about make out the outline of several tall buildings that looked in desperate need of repair. In the distance lay a charnel house, a city in ruins.

London.

CHAPTER THIRTY-NINE

Wandsworth, London

The two carriages had become trapped; the road blocked by fallen masonry and churned earth. The horses whinnied in terror as lightning lit up the sky. They were in Wandsworth on the outskirts of the city. The original plan had been for the group to commandeer some boats near Putney and row their way into the capital, but now they would have to go on foot. The various buildings that made up Wandsworth lay mostly in ruins, including the old church. Gravestones had been hauled out of the graveyard itself and the crypt door had been shattered.

The group stepped cautiously out of their carriages, the sudden chill of the weather hitting them like a hammer blow. Middleton handed out the weapons and armour, keeping aside a particularly vicious looking sword for himself, and Charles ushered them along the street. Occasionally someone would trip on a stray brick or a piece of timber, but Charles was loath to light the lanterns, fearing their flames would draw the attention of any nearby undead.

Even though the sky was as black as night, and an icy wind howled through the streets, no rain fell. Charles reached out to feel a timber support on a nearby house and, to his relief, felt that it was dry and cracked. It wouldn't take much to get a fire going, especially with the vicious crosswind to aid it. As soon as they made their way to the centre of the city they would get a conflagration of historic proportions going.

Tom and his band of smugglers brought up the rear of the group, each of them clasping a mace, their eyes, accustomed to the darkness of caves and nightfall, darting around the surrounding buildings for any sign of movement. The fishermen, Underhill and Betterton were in the middle of the group, clutching an array of swords, daggers and axes, and Henri and the clergyman were nestled behind their King.

"This is what it was like from Dulwich to Southwark, empty and rotting," whispered Henri. Another gust of wind swept down the narrow street, bringing with it a foul stench.

"From the smell I would suggest that we want to go that way," said Betterton, covering his face with a nosegay. The group swiftly fastened their gowns and placed the masks over their faces, the scent of the fresh rosemary overpowering the putrid stink of rotting flesh. They were now indistinguishable from one another, only Middleton's formidable bulk recognisable beneath the strange attire.

Charles led the way into the dark abyss unaware that something was following them.

Before long the group found themselves at a crossroads, the road to the left leading to Bankside and the Thames, the road to the right to Lambeth Marsh and the road ahead to Greenwich.

"We want to head towards the city and the river. They should be in their thousands around there," said Charles, his voice muffled by the mask.

It was stifling in the plague suits and Davenant

could feel the sweat running down his arms and onto his wrists. As the group took the road to the left, Davenant's heart thumped manically in his chest and the exhilarating pulse of adrenaline coursed through his ageing veins. He felt the nervous excitement that only soldiers experienced, staring death in the face, not knowing whether God would spare him and allow him to make it back home and to the sanctuary of his family.

"Should I become one of... them, you must make sure you kill me," he said to Charles resolutely.

Charles nodded. "Likewise, Sir William, but it won't happen. We will prevail. God is on our side."

Davenant heard them before he saw them – a chorus of wheezing groans drifting to them on the wind. He was frozen to the spot in terror, the horrifying memories of what had happened fifteen years earlier flooding back in a wave of awful recollection. Davenant's heart skipped a beat as they appeared in front of him, a group of four shambling undead emerging slowly from the shadows and lurching their way towards them. He turned to see the fishermen and smugglers backing away. As well as they could have possibly prepared themselves for this moment, the sight of the marauding zombies scared them half to death and every part of them wanted to flee.

"No! We stand and fight. Let's send these bastards back to hell!" Charles cried, leading the charge.

Middleton and Underhill swung their clubs at the lead zombie and its withered corpse vanished in a cloud of powdered bone and flesh. One of the fishermen, seeing how easily his compatriots had taken down the creature, mistimed his attack and gasped for air as a cold, dead hand clamped itself around his neck. Even through the leather of the cape its grip was ferocious. In one final act of desperation, he planted his axe into the zombies' back. It didn't seem to notice the blow and snapped its jaws down on the fisherman's throat, tearing through leather and flesh, moaning in pleasure as blood jetted over its hideous face. The fisherman let out an inhuman, gurgling scream and dropped. He was dead before he hit the ground. Davenant turned and separated the zombie's head from its shoulders as it bent to feast – the power of the blade surprising him. He saw Betterton and Charles hack another of the undead to pieces, whilst some of the smugglers saw off the final zombie.

Davenant looked down at the body of the fallen fisherman, the blood pooling black around his head. "I'm sorry, Paul," he said. "I'm so sorry."

Charles removed his mask as he strode over. "If we don't do something, Will, that man is going to return."

Davenant nodded, but couldn't bring himself to desecrate his friend's body. This was a man he had drunk with at the Chine Inn, a man he had braved the seas with in foul weather. As he looked down sadly at Paul's body it twitched, blood trickling from the broken windpipe. Just a reflex action, Davenant told himself, just muscles relaxing. But then Paul let out an agonised scream and rose, unsteadily, to his feet. Time seemed to stand still for Davenant. He looked into Paul's clouded eyes and saw the hunger there. For a moment they stood watching each other, the living and the dead. Then with a growl Paul launched himself forwards, his lips pulled back in a terrifying snarl. Davenant swung his sword, closing his eyes as the blade connected, keeping them closed as the headless corpse staggered against him. He sobbed as his friend's body sank to the floor, covering him in blood and gore as it dropped.

"It had to be done," said Charles, placing a hand on his shoulder. "And I would expect all of you to do the same for any one of us." He said, turning to the group. Davenant could see the disgusted expressions on their faces.

"His Majesty is right, if you get bitten or killed by any one of these abominations then you shall become one yourself. You have seen what they can do. Even these gowns and our armour are no guarantee against them. Always, always be on your guard."

As Davenant watched his harsh words sink in, the awful realisation beginning to dawn, he could have sworn he saw something moving quickly through the ruins of a nearby house. It couldn't have been one of the undead, he thought. They weren't that fast. Davenant shrugged it off, concluding that it may just have been a trick of the light or a pall of fog. Even so, he checked his armour was secured before he moved off with caution.

As they made their way towards Bankside, Davenant remembered the promise he had made to Elizabeth that he would ensure that he and Betterton return to Shanklin alive. It was a foolish promise to make as the odds were stacked firmly against their survival, yet he never let Betterton out of his sight. Years before he would have happily seen the man hang for his betrayal, but now he was protecting him as one of his own.

They were now passing the ruins of St George's Church – its elaborate stonework engraved with gargoyles – and heading downhill. In the distance Davenant could see a shimmer of water and realised that they were nearing the Thames.

"Whatever you do, make sure you keep your masks on!" Charles said. "As we get closer to the centre of the city the stench will become overpowering. Be on your guard, soon we will be surrounded by the dead."

They soon found themselves by the water's edge and Davenant looked nervously out over the river. What he saw would haunt his dreams for years to come. It was far, far worse than he remembered it being. In the distance he could see London Bridge teeming with the dead, scavenging for food. Several skirmishes had broken out between rival factions on the opposite side of the Thames, the dead tearing at each other in their desperate hunger. In places, the crowds of zombies were so dense that occasionally one of them would tumble into the water and be swept away. Armageddon had come to the city, the darkest passages of Revelations being played out before their eyes.

Davenant noticed that the Kryfangan were nowhere to be seen. Was that why the dead were now turning on one another?

Whatever the reason, Davenant was left in no doubt that the situation was now more dangerous than it had ever been.

"It's just as I remember it," breathed Henri at his shoulder.

"We must cross the river," said Charles. "The

buildings on that side are grouped closer together and it will be easier for a fire to spread from there."

"And how do you expect us to get over there?" Betterton asked.

"We need to cross the bridge. It's our only way in."

Davenant clutched the silver cross hanging around his neck and muttered a few words in prayer.

"I never had you down as a religious man, Will," said Tom.

"Oh, I never used to be, but when we came to London fifteen years ago, it was hard not to see the evidence of evil incarnate before our very eyes. It was then that I stared to pray. What about you, Tom, do you have faith?"

"Some may have us down as godless men, but it's not true."

Charles drew the group together and outlined his plan.

"We move quickly and we do not stop. Speed is the one thing that they do not possess. If you stop, you will die. Should you get bitten, you stay on the bridge and kill as many of them as possible before they take you down. Now, if we are ready, gentlemen?" The young clergyman whispered a few soft words, blessing those who were about to go into battle.

As they made their way down the uneven stone steps and onto the riverbank, Davenant spared a glance to his left and over the Southwark skyline, trying to see what had become of the once thriving Bankside theatres. Not one was left standing. The monuments to Shakespeare, Burbage and Marlowe were nothing more than rubble and rotting timber. This act of theatrical heresy spurred Davenant onwards and he barged his way to the front of the group alongside Charles and Middleton, his blood-stained sword poised and ready. As they reached the steps to London Bridge, the zombies reacted to their presence, jerking their way towards them, their jaws snapping. Swords flashed and the steps were soon covered with withered, twitching limbs. They ran frantically up the timber stairs and proceeded quickly underneath the archway and its tall vaulted ceiling. The skulls of the traitors of yesteryear still topped the numerous metal spikes that adorned the southern gateway. As the group sprinted over the bridge, they came face to face with their next challenge, a group of zombies dressed in shabby soldiers' apparel, clutching rusting weapons. Davenant wondered whether they were the same soldiers sent by Charles to investigate London's downfall.

"Come," cried Charles. "They are nothing but dried bone and sinew. They will fall beneath our blades."

Davenant parried the dagger of an assailant before thrusting his sword through the chest of another undead soldier. The blow didn't impede the creature in the slightest and it lunged at him, jaws snapping. Before it could tear the flesh from him, Betterton charged in and decapitated the fiend. "Come on, old man!" he cried. "I've got my fair share to take care of without having to contend with yours as well!"

"Go for their heads!" Davenant shouted to his comrades. "It's the only true stopper."

There was a collective ring of steel on rotting flesh and bone – heads rolled along the bridge and fell into the river below. Davenant turned to see if there were any human casualties and noticed Tom and the smugglers leaning over one of their fallen men. "Was he bitten?" asked Davenant.

Tom shook his head. "No, he was stabbed through the heart by one of our own in the confusion. Poor Edward, his wife was expecting their third child."

Davenant saw the dead closing in on the scent of fresh meat. "We need to leave now. Say your prayers for Edward later."

They continued onwards through the old shops and archways of the bridge. They met little resistance until they reached the dark stone tunnel which ran through the half-timbered Nonesuch House. The mouth of the tunnel was crowded with zombies. Davenant estimated that there must have been at least three hundred of them.

"Oh God in heaven!" cried Charles. "We'll never hack our way through that."

Davenant turned and saw that their way back was similarly blocked. The press of rotting flesh was too dense to rush through. Only a miracle could save them now. He considered jumping into the Thames and chancing his luck at swimming to the bank.

And then a miracle occurred.

The pounding of hooves rang out along the north bank, drawing the attention of the undead away from them. Turning their backs on the group, they shuffled back along the cobbled path and towards the sound. There was just enough room for them to make a break for the tunnel and get off the bridge.

Davenant couldn't believe their luck. He could see the Kryfangan now and they were just as he remembered them. He watched as they shredded their enemy, saturating the riverbank with gore.

CHAPTER FORTY

They finally made it across the bridge, hacking at the undead as they went, their gowns and plague masks covered by the remnants of their enemies. Once they were in the city they ran for what seemed like an hour. Finally they pulled up, the dead left behind them for the time being.

"I am too old to be running around like this," gasped Davenant.

"Don't worry Sir William, our plan will soon come to fruition. I say that we start our fire right here." Charles said.

"And where is here?" asked Betterton.

"Pudding Lane, according to that sign. I propose we start with the bakery over there. It's in the middle of a cluster of buildings and these dried old timbers should take quite quickly."

As they entered the kitchen, Charles turned to Davenant. "Take the others upstairs and dispatch any undead you find. We must not be interrupted in our task."

Davenant nodded and motioned Betterton and Underhill to follow him. Charles found a pile of straw and started to stuff both ovens with it, adding firewood and discarded aprons to the blend. Next he scattered the floor with bags of old flour, making sure that it was evenly spread. Middleton returned from the cellar with some bottles of rum he had found and proceeded to liberally douse any exposed timbers. As he did so he could hear the three making their way up the stairs and onto the first floor. He heard their footsteps cross the ceiling before stopping, no doubt examining one of the upper chambers. Suddenly, another set of footsteps creaked their way across the timber, it now sounded as if there were four of them up there.

"Wait here, my Lord. I just want to check on something," he said, darting from the kitchen. As he reached the top of the staircase, his eyes struggled to acclimatise to the dark corridor. He could just about discern movement ahead.

"Sir William, is that you? Underhill, Betterton?"

There was no reply, just the howling of the wind outside. Middleton edged forwards, his sword at the ready. There was no one on the landing, but he could see three doors leading into rooms on either side of the corridor. His hand reached out for the first of the doors to his left. Middleton eased it open with infinite gentleness before creeping inside. To his relief, the chamber was empty, only a four-poster bed occupied the cramped space within. Middleton breathed a sigh of relief and tried the second door along.

He managed to whack Underhill in the face as he threw open the door, forcing Betterton and Davenant to cry out in surprise as he barged his way into the room.

"What are you doing, you great fool?" cried Davenant.

Middleton beckoned them to stay quiet and helped Underhill to his feet. "I think there's someone else up here with us," he whispered. And then they heard footsteps creaking from further up the corridor. Middleton put his finger to his lips and shuffled over to the open doorway. He peeked around the corner and could make out someone lurching towards him in the darkness. He turned back into the room.

"It's coming. Follow me and wait for my command."

Davenant nodded and gestured to Middleton to make his move, following him closely down the narrow corridor, with Betterton and Underhill covering their backs. The footsteps had stopped. All Davenant could hear was his heavy breathing and the pounding of his heart.

"Where's it gone?" he whispered.

"I don't know. But I think it's still—"

Charging footsteps suddenly bore down on them. Out of the darkness emerged a woman so vulgar, it would have taken away the lust from the most fervent of men. What was left of her breasts were visible through a shredded blouse, their soft tissue having been eaten away, the rest of the body riddled with deep bite marks. Her face was crooked, the nose long and pointed, the eyes dark and vacant.

Middleton was knocked to the floor, the snapping of sharp teeth and the pungent stench of dead breath bearing down on his face. "For God's sake, get it off me!" he cried, pulling the creature away by its long hair. But it was too strong for him and was able to force its head through his grip, losing several clumps of hair in the process, before clamping its teeth around Middleton's neck, piercing his dark cloak.

Davenant planted his sword through the creature's head. It spasmed once and then was gone. "Help me get him to his feet," he shouted.

"I've been bitten," said Middleton bluntly. "Give me a sword, one of you. Let me finish it my way."

"No, I can't do that," replied Davenant, draping Middleton's arm over his shoulder and dragging him back down the corridor.

"The dead are coming!" cried Henri from outside.

"God in heaven," muttered Davenant. "Help me carry him down."

Betterton and Underhill supported Middleton's other arm and carried him back down the staircase. Davenant then ran into the kitchen where Charles was frantically banging a flint against the stone wall.

"It's Middleton! He's been bitten!"

Charles stopped what he was doing and turned to face him, his pale face somehow luminous against the dark stone. "No, it's not true." He looked utterly crestfallen.

"My Lord, there's no time for that now. There are more of them coming and we need to get the fire started."

Charles nodded. "Yes, yes, quite right, where was I?" His hand trembled as he fumbled for the piece of flint.

"Please, my Lord. Allow me." Davenant took the flint from Charles' sweaty palm, wrapped several pieces of straw tightly around it and smashed it against the stone of the oven. A single spark immediately lit the straw. Davenant used some of the burning grass to ignite the rum-drenched timbers of the kitchen. "We're leaving now." He said as the inferno began to take hold.

Charles stared for a moment at the flames, then turned and ran, joining Betterton, Underhill and Middleton outside. Davenant came tearing out soon after and immediately saw the throng of undead shuffling their way up the narrow street towards them, no doubt with the Kryfangan in close pursuit.

Charles was more concerned with Middleton, who leant sluggishly against a wall. "They've said some

The Devil's Plague

terrible things, my old friend. They've said you have been bitten. They're liars, are they not?"

"You need to leave, your Majesty. But before you do, please can you do me the honour of killing me," replied Middleton.

"How dare you ask me such a thing? You will come with us!" decreed Charles, hauling Middleton to his feet and prompting him into a run.

"We can make our way back to the river this way," cried Davenant, leading them up the street.

As they ran, Middleton could feel a burning sensation tingling down his body and into his toes. He began to feel stronger with every step he took.

CHAPTER FORTY-ONE

Their journey back to the river didn't take half as long as Davenant had feared it would. Middleton was bravely marching on, although it was all too evident that he was severely hampered by his wound and the loss of blood. Charles hadn't left his side, closely scrutinising his every move. His hand was rested on the handle of his axe, although the thought of killing his closest friend made him feel sick to his stomach.

The roaring flames had taken hold of the dry timber of Pudding Lane, the yard of Fish Street Hill and St Margaret's Church with ease, and as they spread east along Thames Street aided by the brisk wind, they had begun to provide a slender light for the group running blindly through the dark wilderness. A red hue already hung above the north side of the city, the fire now engulfing anything in its wake.

"Have we any idea of how we're going to get out of here?" asked Davenant, panting in between his words.

"We make it back to the bridge, cross it and return from whence we came," replied Charles. "It is as simple as that."

Davenant could see the looming shadow of the bridge up ahead. The crashing sounds that drifted along on the wind suggested that there were still vast numbers of zombies battling with the Kryfangan nearby. Davenant hoped that at least their war had shifted as far along as Billingsgate, leaving the mouth of the bridge open for them to access.

There was a clattering of hooves nearby and an unholy demonic screeching. "Quickly, into the alley!"

Davenant cried, leading the group into the shadows of an inn. The vicious gallop descended into a steady trot – they were close now, less than twenty yards away. Within seconds, the dark stallions and their riders cantered slowly along the cobblestone lane, mere feet from where they were hidden. He spied four of them as they passed; bigger, heavier, more imposing than the rest of their platoon. Davenant calculated that they must be at least eight foot tall when standing. It was then that he remembered what Cromwell had told them that night in the carriage as they had fled the Cheapside streets.

Were these the Four Horsemen of the Apocalypse trotting past them? The true disciples of Satan?

As he heard the deep, grunting breaths of the horses as they went past, he had never felt more alive. It was strange, Davenant thought, this was the closest he had been to death and fear was no longer an obstacle. The only fear remaining for him now was how Elizabeth, Faith and Charles would cope without him should he fall.

He pulled himself together and waited until the Kryfangan were safely in the distance. "Come on, let's get going," he barked, looking over at Charles and Middleton as he tried to spur them onwards. Middleton hadn't uttered a word since they had left the Pudding Lane bakery.

They were now only a few hundred yards from the bridge and Davenant could see that the fighting had indeed shifted across to Billingsgate. There were no orders or commands from him this time – every man knew what they had to do, and ran as fast as their weary legs would carry them. As they crossed over the wooden drawbridge, Davenant dared to look over his shoulder. The fire had spread all the way down Thames Street now and was swallowing up everything that stood in its path. London was burning.

As the group clattered across the bridge, their exit was suddenly blocked by a heavy-set man, stood with a great sword clutched in his right hand. In the time it took for Davenant to blink, another group of men had emerged behind their leader, stretching the width of the bridge. Davenant halted, the others following suit, their hands reaching for their weapons.

The inferno blazing behind them illuminated the sallow countenance of the man. Amidst the rag-like attire of his cohorts, this soldier seemed smart and orderly in comparison, his hose and neat overcoat only showing three or four holes. And unlike his gaunt and lean followers, his stature had somehow retained its form and bulk.

With a sudden spark of irrational terror, Davenant could have sworn that it was Satan himself looking him in the eye. But then he was struck with the chilling realisation that it wasn't the Devil at all. It was someone else entirely. "Cromwell!"

Oliver Cromwell's withered upper lip peeled back from his rotting teeth in a sneer, recognition burning deep in his eyes. Much of his face had wasted away; even the many boils and pock marks that once blighted his features were now little more than open scars. But somehow his eyes retained knowledge, wisdom and a glimmer of understanding. They hadn't changed in the slightest.

"God's death, it can't be?" cried Davenant, turning to Charles, who pointed at the ragged army behind Cromwell.

"Look at them! They're following him, Sir

William!"

"These bastards are standing between us and our escape. Let's stick it to them!" Betterton cried, wielding his sword

The thought of returning home as heroes spurred the rest of the group on. Led by Tom, the smugglers made a mad dash towards the undead. Not wanting to be outdone, the fishermen followed hot on their heels.

Cromwell and his army tore them from limb to limb.

As Davenant saw another of the fishermen being sliced in half, he charged; Charles, Underhill and Henri piling in after him. Davenant tried desperately to fight his way to Cromwell, fending off blow after blow from the undead soldiers. Charles came to his aid, ramming the handle of his axe into the head of a zombie before hurling it over the side of the bridge. He had lost sight of Middleton, wary that he was turning and could be drawn into fighting for Cromwell at any moment.

The bridge was now covered in gore and Charles lost his balance, his boots slipping on a slick coil of intestines. Looking up, he found to his horror that he had landed at Cromwell's feet. Cromwell seemed to grin as he lifted his sword, the vast blade seeming to stretch into infinity. It shone with a terrible wrath as it reflected the fire that was consuming London.

Davenant looked over and saw what was about to happen. He tried to call out to Betterton and Underhill but they couldn't hear his cries amidst the tumult.

The sword came crashing down and there was a terrific clang.

Somehow Middleton had clambered around

Cromwell and parried his blow. He collapsed in a heap beside Charles, his weapon falling from his limp hand. As the mask slipped from Middleton's face, Charles could see that he had breathed his last.

Charles grabbed Middleton's weapon and rose to his feet, his face twisted with rage and the purest hate.

"You may remember me, Lord Protector. And I believe you knew my father."

He swung the sword with all his might and landed it between Cromwell's collarbone and neck, hacking his head from his shoulders in one perfect stroke. The sight of Cromwell falling to his knees seemed to stun his horde into submission, the rest of the group taking advantage of the lull and hacking the heads from the undead army.

Charles paused to survey the carnage, attempting to catch his breath at the same time. He had never seen so much blood, even on the battlefield.

Betterton, Underhill, Henri, Charles and Davenant looked at one another, none of them able to muster up the strength to speak. Charles picked up Cromwell's blooded head and rammed it down upon an empty spike secured to the timber of the bridge.

"Behold the head of a traitor! That is for my father," he shouted.

Davenant smiled. "Now shall we get out of here?"

Suddenly, Middleton jerked to his feet and Charles could see in his eyes that he had turned. He took four ungainly steps forward, driven by the desire for human flesh. Charles knew now that he owed his friend death. After all he had done for him and the numerous times he had saved his life, Middleton didn't deserve this terrible unlife. Middleton reached down and picked up a severed arm, tearing the stringy meat away from the bone. He looked up at Charles as he stood over him, axe raised, and there seemed to be a glimmer of recognition in his eyes.

"You must put him out of his misery, my Lord," cried Davenant. Charles lowered his weapon and removed his mask. He gagged as he took in the acrid scent of the city. Middleton backed away, lumbering to the side of the bridge and the balustrade. He looked back once again, and Charles could have sworn he saw a hint of a smile cross his lips before he threw himself into the river below.

"You stupid, clumsy, daft, foolish boar," said Charles under his breath.

Davenant stepped forward and placed a consoling hand on his arm. "He was a good man, my Lord, one of finest." Charles broke down into a frenzy of choking sobs. "But we need to leave; the fire is ravaging the city." Davenant could see that the blaze had stretched as far east as St Botolph's Lane. The heat was now so intense that it seemed to roast their backs.

Charles nodded in agreement, placed his mask back on and turned to run, prompting those stood beside him to move. As they left the bridge Davenant looked back one last time. He firmly believed that they had followed the right course of action and did what was necessary for the good of the country and its people. Yet as he saw the fire take hold of St Paul's Cathedral, he prayed that they would be able to return soon and restore London to its former glory.

The last thing Davenant remembered before losing consciousness was Charles and Betterton supporting his ageing legs as they shuffled through Southwark and out of the city, taking the path back to Wandsworth that had led them to the river. It was far more exhausting this time as they were walking uphill and had no food or water to provide them with sustenance. The ruins of a nearby fountain only added to their frustration, its stone basin was bone dry. They were all desperately thirsty and even the Thames muck had begun to seem desirable to them. Finally, though, they made it back to Wandsworth and its derelict buildings. Davenant had drifted in and out of their few conversations, and woke to find Charles in the middle of some sort of heartfelt monologue.

"This will be consigned to history as the great fire of London that ended this Black Death, this Devil's Plague of ours, and we will now prosper in a new and brighter future. I am eternally grateful to you all, particularly this old war horse, for all you have given up for the cause. I am seldom accustomed to such honour, bravery and dignity."

As they ambled along the causeway with its dilapidated buildings, Charles could spot what was left of their carriages in the near distance.

"Well, looks like we're on foot, gentlemen." He said.

"What's going on?" Davenant asked, waking fully now.

"We made it, Will, but we still have a good way to go."

"Then, my Lord, we will walk this road together."

Davenant's last memory was reaching Portsmouth by carriage. He then experienced flashing images, almost dream-like in nature. He could have sworn he saw darkened, leaden skies and remembered experiencing a rush of relief as they eventually faded into the morning sunshine, the sound of birdsong and lush green landscapes. He could feel the gentle breeze on his face.

Perhaps this was the afterlife?

As he woke for the third time, he was greeted by the monotonous rolling sounds of the sea and the beautiful scent of saltwater. He felt remarkably at peace and breathed a huge sigh of relief. He could tell that it was dark again, his eyes slowly becoming familiar with the stars and the moon in the cloudless sky. He could have sworn he heard Charles' voice beside him, its comforting, soothing tone sending him back to sleep again.

And as he woke for the last time, he found his wife by his bedside, lovingly tending to his wounds.

He had never been so happy.

CHAPTER FORTY-TWO

Theatre Royal, London
1st November, 1667

After so many years of Puritan Interregnum, Davenant could scarcely believe that he was witnessing such a beautiful sunny November's day in the heart of London. The crowds were flocking to the theatre in their hundreds. The poor were arriving on foot and the rich were arriving by carriage, coach or palanquin.

Davenant saw Samuel Pepys ambling towards him from the corner of his eye. He pretended to watch the flock of birds that were soaring high above the flag of the new theatre, its three tiers of the best timber providing the finest playhouse he had ever seen, even grander than the Globe.

"I am glad the King chose one of your baroque spectacles to put on as an opening performance, rather than one of Killigrew's talk dramas. Those who have attended your shows at Lincoln Inn Field's have informed me that you have moveable scenery and wings! My, my, Sir William, you have the monopoly on them all!"

"Thank you, Samuel," replied Davenant as politely as he could. In his eyes, Pepys was little more than a sycophant, a fawning monstrosity who would weasel his way into any event or occasion.

"Don't worry, Sir William. I'll be sure to give you a good review," cried Pepys, waving his little pocket diary in the air as he spotted someone else in the crowd.

As the last of the audience filtered into the theatre, Davenant was struck by a feeling he hadn't experienced in years: first night nerves. He decided to take a short walk down to the river to calm his anxiety.

Davenant was immediately taken by just how much London had changed in little over a year, with many of the dilapidated buildings now bearing the first symptoms of reconstruction. Since his coronation, Charles had been true to his word and had begun to rebuild much of what was destroyed by the great fire. He had even commissioned Christopher Wren to design and oversee the building of a new St Paul's Cathedral, its predecessor having been reduced to smouldering rubble. Charles had shown Davenant the designs, and he was left in awe by their magnificence, although a little sceptical that it could be accomplished. Nevertheless, Charles and Wren had seen through the construction of the majestic Theatre Royal, which could hold almost seven hundred theatregoers. So perhaps the Cathedral wasn't such a daring project after all.

Davenant took several deep breaths to calm his nerves. The air was refreshingly clean in comparison to what it had been like on that fateful night by the Thames. Once the group had left London and returned to the Isle of Wight, Charles and Henri had headed back to France to assemble a group to take back to London with them on a clean up mission. Davenant had decided to remain at home with Faith, Elizabeth and Charles, although Betterton and Underhill had agreed to revisit London. When they returned home Betterton informed Davenant of what had happened.

Much of the city had been decimated by the fire,

all traces of the plague had been consumed by the flames and there was no sign whatsoever of the Kryfangan, who had presumably perished alongside the undead. Charles had organised groups of his men to bury what was left of the corpses in designated plague pits, although rumour had it that he had found Cromwell's head and body and performed a posthumous execution on the thirtieth of January at Tyburn by hanging his body in chains. It was on the very same date that his father had been executed by Cromwell at Whitehall, years earlier.

Above all else, Davenant was glad to see that London was becoming repopulated. He could see a lone Thames waterman fighting against the current as he carried his fare from Bankside to Billingsgate, and even noticed a group of painted ladies flaunting their wares to a group of Merchant Tailors by the Pickleherring Stairs. As his eyes worked their way round to London Bridge, his thoughts immediately turned to the clash with Cromwell and his legion at the southern entrance. It gave him a peculiar feeling, and a sudden chill crept down his spine.

He turned around hastily, thinking it best he returned to the theatre, fearing people would start to question his absence. Tonight they were performing Macbeth, giving Davenant a chance to finish what he had started all those years ago in the Phoenix Theatre before he had been so rudely interrupted. Charles had lifted the ban on women performing in public theatre and had insisted that his mistress, Nell Gwynne, take the part of one of the witches. She was a rancorous little trollop, but Davenant didn't have any say in the matter, especially when Charles had just granted him an exclusive license to perform at the Theatre Royal and to establish a company of players. Davenant had formed his own troupe of players in Shanklin, which he still regarded as his home, but could hardly miss out on such an opportunity to act on the London stage again and in such a magnificent venue.

They had had several rehearsals at the playhouse in Lincoln Inn Field's, which seemed to go down a storm, giving Davenant hope that this would be the performance to end all performances. Faith and Elizabeth reprised their roles of the first witch and Lady Macbeth respectively and Nell took the part of the third witch, although her acting ability was limited at best. Betterton, on the other hand, had grown into one of the country's finest actors and now took the title role after Middleton's sad demise, with Underhill portraying Malcolm in his place. Davenant took the part of King Duncan, with Charles happy to be consigned to the Royal Box in the auditorium. Davenant completed the casting by filling the other parts with up and coming actors from the Duke's Players, such as the Noakes brothers, Robert and James, Thomas Sheppey, John Mosely and Edward Kynaston, and actresses such as Anne Bracegirdle and Mary Lee.

He cast his mind back to what his father had once told him.

"A part never belongs to an actor, but an actor belongs to a part."

Those words had always rung true, and tonight Davenant hoped and prayed that he did his father justice.

After slipping into his costume and applying some stage make-up, Davenant sidled into the wings from where he could observe the buzzing atmosphere of the crowded auditorium. All walks of London life were represented – shipwrights and fishmongers from St Dunstan's; drapers and haberdashers from Spitalfields; the skinners and silk weavers from St Giles Cripplegate, and the King himself in his green baize-covered box, ornamented with gold-tooled leather. Davenant noticed that many were without seats and were huddled together by the sides and in the narrow passages, increasing the capacity to at least eight or nine hundred. His eyes wandered upwards towards the glazed dome that allowed shards of sunlight to shaft into the theatre, lighting the stage and protecting the patrons from the wind and rain. They needed no protection today though, Davenant thought. It was a glorious afternoon.

His eyes worked their way back down over the semi-circular galleries crammed with doctors, lawyers and the incessant deluge of Protestant Frenchmen in exile from Catholic France, and onto the pit where there was a palpable hum of excitement. The poorer folk had packed themselves onto the backless green benches with the vendors, who were selling nuts and bottled ale, struggling to weave their way through the commotion. Davenant could hear the heaving, sweating anticipation, the excited noises of conversation and secretive whispers, and could smell the fetid stench of raw garlic; stale ale and Thames tobacco mingled together with the sharp tang of cheap perfume and oils. The rustling of silk and tunics, the clinking of bottle on bottle and the high-pitched giggling of the ladies in the third gallery only served to add to the atmosphere.

Davenant heard a clatter of footsteps approach from behind him and turned to face Nell Gwynne, dressed head to toe in a dark witch's cloak and wearing a thick layer of make-up. "Why can't I be the first witch, Sir William?" she asked, in a thick cockney accent.

"Because I want you to have the least lines, my dear," replied Davenant bluntly. He didn't enjoy a particularly fruitful relationship with Nell and didn't feel the need to placate her, simply because he knew that Charles with his notorious nocturnal habits would cast her aside in favour of a younger, prettier girl soon enough. He grinned as she turned her back on him, stomped her foot and disappeared in a sulk. He could see Faith and Elizabeth rehearsing by the tiring house. They were consummate professionals now, veterans of the stage. Davenant let out a broad smile. Never in a million years could he have ever dreamt that this would become reality – sharing the very finest London stage with his wife and daughter. He could remember a time when the thought of women on the stage was an abhorrent notion. But now he couldn't think of two more deserving actresses.

"Break a leg, Sir William," said Charles, having slipped into the wings.

"Thank you, my Lord, and I hope your head falls off," replied Davenant, grinning wickedly. Davenant noted a young stagehand, having walked past at that exact moment, carrying a look of pure astonishment, scarcely believing that someone would have the gall to address the King in such a way. Davenant chuckled heartily.

"Mind your tongue, Sir William. I have had more

important men than you hanged at Tyburn for saying less. And where is my pretty Nell? I was hoping to have my wicked way with her before the first act."

"I fear you may—"

Davenant was interrupted by the sound of a trumpet signalling the start of the play and a deathly hush descended upon the audience.

"Looks as though I will have to wait until the interval," whispered Charles. "Let us have the show of your life, Sir William," he said, patting Davenant on the back and disappearing back into the packed auditorium.

Davenant rolled his eyes. "No pressure then."

As Davenant took to the Drury Lane stage for the first time, he experienced a rush of pure adrenalin. He turned to face the audience and, to his relief, they appeared enraptured by what was happening before them. The beams of sunlight that were flooding the auditorium only served to augment the already flagrant sense of wonderment.

Davenant turned and watched as Elizabeth entered gracefully as Lady Macbeth. He was just as enraptured as the vagrants in the pit as she flitted elegantly across the stage with remarkable poise and breathtaking beauty.

"See, see, our honored hostess! The love that follows us sometime is our trouble, which still we thank as love. Herein I teach you how you shall bid God 'ild us for your pains, and thank us for your trouble."

"All our service in every point twice done and then done double were poor and single business to contend against those honours deep and broad wherewith your majesty loads our house. For those of old, and the late dignities heaped up to them, we rest your hermits."

Davenant left the stage and was able to watch the rest of the play from the sanctuary of the wings. What he saw was without doubt the finest display of acting he had ever witnessed from any company of players. Even Nell had somehow managed to avoid being upstaged in almost all of her scenes. That was an accomplishment in itself, Davenant thought. He could hear the gasps from the audience in all the right places, the occasional sob and the fleeting shrieks that accompanied the more gruesome scenes.

As Underhill took centre stage to deliver the final speech, there wasn't a sound from amongst the nine hundred people jammed together. Davenant prayed that Underhill would deliver his monologue the way he did in rehearsals. To his relief, his voice was strong and confident, and as he approached the final line, Davenant closed his eyes and held his breath.

"So, thanks to all at once and to each one, whom we invite to see us crowned at Scone."

Silence – not even a breath or a muted whimper.

Davenant dared to open his eyes and could see that Underhill stood with a bemused expression on his face. Just as Davenant was about to walk onto the stage and interject, a sudden shrill whistle of approval rained down from the top gallery. It was followed by a cluster of muted handclaps, which slowly and surely built up into a resounding ovation and deafening roar. Davenant frantically ushered the rest of his company onto the stage to join Underhill and meet their applause and approval.

Despite all his years spent away from the theatre as a hardened fisherman on the Solent and fighting all manner of ghouls in London, Davenant hadn't lost his lust for the spotlight. Calmly and ever so assuredly, he waited for the right moment, just as the applause had started to dip. Then he made his way onstage and the theatre erupted once more, its glass domed roof would have surely flown off had it not been fastened down.

Davenant took a deep breath and stood between Faith and Elizabeth, his eyes devouring these last few fabulous memories of the London stage.

"Bravo, Sir William, Bravo!"

Davenant could see that it was his King leading the standing ovation.

EPILOGUE

The Cabinet War Rooms, London
30th January, 1944

Winston Churchill had already stated that he was to direct the rest of the Second World War from the confines of the Cabinet War Rooms, a warren of interlocking chambers and tunnels set in a secret underground bunker opposite St James's Park near Westminster. It was from here that Churchill and his cabinet would enjoy the benefits of the dormitories, the refectory and even a shooting gallery whilst they negotiated the war from the hub of the Map Room.

Churchill lay down on a small bed in his own designated suite, the frame struggling to cope with his bulk. He settled himself and lit up one his trademark cigars. Contentedly, he drew its thick smoke into his lungs and made a small 'o' as he gently exhaled. The heavy burden that weighed down upon his raddled mind seemed to lift every time he lit a cigar. General Eisenhower had just laid out his plans for Operations Overlord and Neptune to Churchill. Overlord was to be the codename for the Allied invasion of northwest Europe and Churchill was only too aware of what was at stake. The thought of raising a huge army with over one million men scared Churchill half to death and he wasn't surprised to find that his cigar wasn't having its usual calming influence.

Floundering out of bed, he decided that he needed a stroll. "Clemmie, have you seen my walking cane?" he asked, calling out to his long-suffering wife, who was in the adjoining Map Room.

"No, why do you want your walking cane?"

"Because I want to go to a pub and have a stiff drink," replied Churchill, forthrightly. As he lifted the maps and papers somewhat carelessly off his table in search of his cane, Clemmie appeared in his doorway.

"Why can't you have a stiff drink here? You know it's not safe to go out there at the moment."

"My apologies, I failed to mention that I also want some fresh air. This claustrophobic atmosphere is giving me one of my heads. And besides, the blackouts won't start for another few hours."

"Then at least take someone with you," said Clemmie, reasonably.

Churchill's eyes lit up as he found his cane hiding beneath his bed. "Absolutely not, I want to be alone. It's a gentleman's prerogative, my dear." Churchill kissed Clemmie on the cheek before robustly marching down the main corridor, turning the heads of several of his staff and cabinet members in the process. He strode past the Mess Room and Cabinet Room and up the steps to the guarded entrance, his heavy footsteps echoing all the way back to the Transatlantic Telephone Room.

"Good evening, Sir," said the young man at the entrance, his immaculate dress and appearance displaying an evident pride in his work.

"Good evening, Stapleton," replied Churchill.

"Are you going for a walk, Sir?"

"Yes, so if you wouldn't mind opening the door?"

"Are you sure you don't want someone to accompany you, Sir?"

Churchill guffawed. "My, Stapleton, you are as bad as my wife! Now come on, son, do as you're told!"

Stapleton reluctantly unlocked the door for the Prime Minister and held it open for him as he strode defiantly onto King Charles Street.

"Thank you Stapleton, I shan't be long."

It was early in the evening and bitterly cold. Churchill was greeted by a mizzling rain as he turned left onto Parliament Street. He remembered a decent pub by the name of St Stephen's Tavern on Bridge Street, opposite Big Ben. It was a popular watering hole for Parliamentarians and lobbyists and Churchill had fond memories of drinking with Chamberlain within those very walls. As he ambled past Westminster Hall and the Houses of Parliament, the rain began to pour down and a blanket of darkened clouds seemed to appear from nowhere. A cold, keening wind cut through him like a knife. He quickened his pace upon seeing the tavern less than a hundred yards ahead. He had no trouble crossing the quiet Bridge Street and eased his way inside the pub, noting the splendour of its carved wood, etched glass, original fixtures and fittings. Although it wasn't busy by any means, Churchill decided to climb the stairs and settle down in a beautifully upholstered mezzanine alcove by the window, overlooking Westminster Hall and Bridge Street below. He removed his drenched overcoat and top hat, placing them carefully on the armchair beside him.

Within a minute, a tall, beanpole of a barman approached Churchill's table. "Good evening, Sir, and what can I get for you?" It was only as he finished asking his question that he realised he was talking to none other than the Prime Minister. He immediately lost the colour from his rosy cheeks, overcome, awestruck and speechless.

"I'll have a large whiskey, please. It's been a tough day."

The barman managed a reluctant smile and shuffled nervously back to the bar.

"Is anyone sat with you?"

Churchill was taken aback. He looked up to see a strange and crooked gentleman looming over his right shoulder, having seemingly emerged from nowhere. He had a pale, emaciated face that was sunk deep into his hefty, rain-soaked overcoat. The top of his head was obscured by a large hat, which bore a peculiar inscription embossed in its cloth trim.

"No, no, by all means, take a seat," replied Churchill. He was surprised to find himself stuttering and couldn't fathom for the life of him why he had allowed this strange man to share the table when there were plenty of vacant ones. He longed for a moment alone, yet at the same time felt strangely powerless to request it, even with his notorious bravado and forthrightness.

"Thank you, Prime Minister. And may I say it is a pleasure to make your acquaintance," replied the man, holding out his skeletal hand, revealing two elaborately designed rings on his forefinger and thumb.

"Your name is?" asked Churchill, accepting the man's hand.

"Cipher, Mr Cipher." Churchill could see that he was reluctant to remove either of his sodden garments, probably in fear of exposing his contorted features any further. He presumed he must have had some terrible childhood affliction, but daren't look too closely in fear of insulting the man. The barman scampered across the floorboards, placed Churchill's whiskey down in front of him, his hand shaking nervously as he did so, and flitted back to the bar.

"Thank you, my good man," said Churchill before turning back to Cipher. "I say, the silly fool didn't offer you a drink. I daresay he ignored you completely, almost as if you weren't even here. I wouldn't stand for that if I were you."

"It's not a problem, Prime Minister. I get it all the time."

Churchill was quite taken with the man's deep voice and saw for the first time a set of dark eyes that almost lurked too deep in their sockets. "As long as you're happy," he said, smiling and turning to look out of the window and back over Westminster Hall.

"A remarkable building, is it not? Are you aware of its history?" Churchill nodded resolutely. He could see the statue of Oliver Cromwell that was situated outside the Palace of Westminster.

"Ah, yes. Oliver Cromwell, a weak-minded fool. Look closely at the statue and you will see that his head is bowed in thought. According to one view, this is to avoid the accusing gaze of King Charles I, whose bust is on the wall of St Margaret's Church directly opposite."

"Is that so?" asked Churchill, genuinely interested.

"Indeed. And you are aware that your Cabinet War Rooms are situated on the site of Whitehall Palace, where King Charles was beheaded?"

"How do you know about the War Rooms?" barked Churchill.

"I know a great many things, Prime Minister. Please, calm down and enjoy your whiskey. You look in a great deal of stress." Churchill nodded and took a hefty swig. "Did you know that this very pub used to be called the Hell Tavern in the seventeenth century?"

Churchill shook his head. "Well, Prime Minister. That is where you are now, the deepest, darkest depths of Hell. You are worrying, are you not, about what the great British public will think of you when you send hundreds of thousands of their men into a battle that they can ill-afford to lose?" Churchill was paralysed.

"What if I were to give you an army, an unbeatable force for you to take into battle? Would that be of interest to you?"

Churchill managed to relax his rigid jaw. He could feel a thin sheen of sweat coating his head. "Yes, yes it would." He couldn't quite believe what he was saying – deep down in his heart he knew that this was ridiculous, but never had he been so terrified of one man. Never had he felt so unmanned, even after all of the perils he had witnessed. This is ludicrous, he kept on telling himself.

"Over the years my army has fought in numerous battles. They have massacred the Persians for King Leonidas of Sparta, united Mongolia for Genghis Khan, defeated the Royalists and the Monarchy for Oliver Cromwell and will now decimate the Nazis for you. In the first two cases, they had never witnessed warriors on horseback before."

"Horseback?" muttered Churchill.

"Oh yes, Prime Minister. Far more powerful than any tank, fighter plane or machine gun of yours. So now you'll be asking yourself who I am and what exactly do I want in return for such a favour?" Churchill forced his head into a slight nod, the sweat now dripping onto the table in front of him, the man's eyes now shining a brighter shade of red and the sound of the air raid sirens beginning to blare out in the near distance. "It is quite straightforward, Prime Minister. All I want in return is your soul."

THE END

HISTORICAL NOTES

When Charles II ascended the throne of England, he granted William Davenant and Thomas Killigrew a warrant to 'erect two companies of players [...] and to purchase, build, and erect [...] two houses or theatres with all convenient rooms and other necessaries thereunto appertaining, for the representation of tragedies, comedies, plays, operas, and all other entertainments of that nature.'

Whereas Killigrew's company were labelled the Original King's Players, Davenant's company were granted the title, the Original Duke's Players. They consisted of ten actors – Davenant himself, Thomas Betterton, Cave Underhill, Thomas Sheppey, Robert Noakes, James Noakes, Thomas Lovell, John Mosely, Robert Turner and Thomas Lilleston, and four actresses, Elizabeth Barry, Anne Bracegirdle, Elizabeth Currer and Mary Lee. Throughout the Restoration, both companies enjoyed a healthy rivalry, although Killigrew's incompetence as a manger coupled with Davenant's brilliance soon led to the downfall of the King's Players. Upon Davenant's death in April 1668, Thomas Betterton took over as manager of the Duke's Players and proved to be just as capable as his mentor and predecessor. He prospered in his duty until Charles Davenant, William's son, was old enough to take over. In the early 1670s, Charles Davenant invested vast sums of money in new theatres and the remodelling of existing ones.

On the 12th December 1660, Davenant and the Duke's Company were given the exclusive rights to nine of Shakespeare's plays; *The Tempest, Macbeth,*

Measure for Measure, Much ado About Nothing, Hamlet, Romeo and Juliet, Twelfth Night, King Lear and the very popular *Henry VIII*. He also regained the rights to all of his own plays and poems.

The Great Fire of London engulfed the City of London from Sunday 2nd of September to Wednesday 5th September, 1666. The fire rampaged through the medieval part of the city inside the old Roman City Wall. It was finally extinguished just short of the aristocratic district of Westminster (the modern West End), the Palace of Whitehall, and the majority of the suburban slums. In total, it consumed 13,200 houses, 87 parish churches, St Paul's Cathedral, and most of the buildings of the City authorities. It is estimated that the fire destroyed the homes of 70,000 of London's 80,000 inhabitants. It was believed to have been started in Thomas Farriner's bakery in Pudding Lane just after midnight on Sunday, 2nd September, and spread quickly thereafter. Experts now believe that Farriner failed to extinguish the fire in the bakery's oven which set light to nearby flour and fuel. Without decent firefighting techniques available at the time, the indecisiveness of the then Lord Mayor of London, Sir Thomas Bloodworth, crucially delayed the use of the creation of firebreaks by means of demolition. By the time he had ordered the large scale demolitions, a wind had already blown the fire across the city. However, for all the destruction it caused, the fire had ended the Great Plague that had ravaged the city throughout the previous year, killing up to 100,000 people, a fifth of London's population. The disease was believed to be a recurrence of the Bubonic Plague, or "Black Death", a virulent affliction that spread throughout Europe in the fourteenth century – the plague itself was carried by fleas, which lived as parasites on rats. Designated Plague doctors would scour the city, diagnosing victims, although the vast majority of them were unqualified doctors. They would look for the obvious symptoms on a patient, for example the victim's skin would turn black in patches and inflamed glands or 'buboes' would appear in the neck and groin. Vomiting, diarrhoea, swollen tongue and agonising headaches made it an altogether unpleasant demise. When the plague appeared in a household, the house was immediately sealed up with the inhabitants within, condemning them to suffer an appalling death together. These houses were always made notable by a painted red cross on the front door and the words, 'Lord have mercy on us'. Once dead, the corpses were brought out at night to the cries of, 'Bring out your dead'. They were then placed in wooden carts and carried away to the plague pits to suffer a dishonourable burial. One of these pits, the Great Pit, was at Aldgate in London and another was at Finsbury Fields.

MARK BEYNON has had screenplays in development with the UK Film Council and Screen South. He began his writing career with a succession of acclaimed theatrical productions before moving into the short film arena where he enjoyed making the official selection of some of the UK's top film festivals. *The Devil's Plague* is Mark's debut novel.

TOMES OF THE DEAD

I, ZOMBIE

Al Ewing

COMING JUNE 2008

ISBN: 978-1-905437-72-6

£6.99

WWW.ABADDONBOOKS.COM

CHAPTER ONE

Time slows to a crawl.

The broken glass around me hangs in the air like mountains of ice, floating in space in the Science-Fiction movie of my life. Like healing crystals in a New Age junk shop, hanging on threads, spinning slowly. Beautiful little diamond fragments.

For five minutes – or less than a second, depending on your viewpoint – I drift slowly downwards, watching the glass shimmer and spin. It's moments like this that make this strange life-not-life of mine seem almost worthwhile.

Moments of beauty in a sea of horror and blood.

I'd like to just hang here forever, drifting downwards, watching the shards of glass spin and turn in the air around me, but eventually I have to relax my grip or get bored. And I'd rather not get bored of a moment like this one.

I let go.

Time snaps back like a rubber band.

The moment passes.

Time perception is a trick of the human mind. The average human perceives events at a rate of one second per second, so to speak, but that doesn't make it the standard. Hummingbirds and mayflies perceive time differently. It's much slower for them, to match their metabolism – I'm pretty sure that's the case. I read it somewhere. In a magazine.

New Scientist, I think. Or *Laboratory News*. Maybe

Discover.

I read a lot of scientific magazines.

It might have been *Scientific American.* Or *Popular Science.* Or just plain *Science.* I go through them all.

I look for articles about decomposition, about autolysis and cell fractionation, about the retardation of putrefaction. About the factors that affect skin temperature or blood clotting.

Things that might explain my situation.

I know it wasn't the *Fortean Times.* Unless it was talking about an alien hummingbird kept under a pyramid. Or possibly building the pyramids. I read that one for the cartoons.

Anyway. Time perception is a trick of the human mind. It's possible to slow down the perception of time in humans, to perceive things in slow motion, experience more in a shorter time. Shorten reaction time to zero. Anybody can do it with the right drugs, or the right kind of hypnosis.

I can do it at will.

I concentrate.

Time slows.

The glass hangs in the air.

I look for articles about the basal ganglia and the superchiasmatic nucleus, about neurotransmitters and the subconscious. I've done research when I can. Heightened time perception burns a lot of adrenaline, apparently. A lot of energy stores. You can't keep it up for long periods without needing plenty of sleep.

But I don't need to sleep.

I don't need to eat either.

Or breathe.

Time rushes back in, like air into an empty lung that's never used.

The moment passes...

...and then the soles of the converse trainers I wear to look cool slap loudly onto the concrete floor of a disused warehouse in Hackney and four big men in badly-fitted suits are pointing guns at me. But that's okay. I've got a gun too. And if they shoot me, I won't bleed.

My heart doesn't beat, so the blood doesn't pump around my body. My skin is cold and clammy and so pale as to be almost blue, or green, depending on the light. My hair is white, like an old man's. My eyes are red and bloodshot and I keep them hidden when I can.

Let's see, what else do you need to know before we get started?

Oh yes.

I've been dead for the last ten years.

I don't have any memory of not being dead. The earliest thing I can remember is waking up in a cheap bed-and-breakfast in Stamford Hill. The room was registered in the name John Doe – the name generally used for an unidentified corpse. I'm sure somebody somewhere thought that was hilarious.

Still, it was the only name I had, so I stuck with it. To all intents and purposes, it was mine.

To all intents and purposes, the gun sitting by the sink was mine as well.

It's strange. I don't have any memory of feeling different, of anything being out of the ordinary. I got up, brushed my teeth even though they never need it, took a shower even though I never smell of anything. People hate that more than B.O., I've noticed. That smell of nothing at all, that olfactory absence. Cologne can't cover it, because there's just the cologne on its own, with that huge blank void beneath that rings all the subconscious alarm bells. Even your best friend won't tell you.

I don't remember being surprised that I was dead. I'm actually more surprised now than I was then, surprised at not being surprised. What sort of person was I, that I woke up dead and took it in my stride?

I remember that the first thing I did that day was shoot a man in the back room of a dingy pub in the Stoke Newington area.

Why did I do that? What sort of person was I then?

Obviously, I had a reason. I mean, I must have. I just can't remember quite what it was.

I had a reason. I had a gun. I had a mobile phone that was a bit clunky and crap and didn't even have games on it, never mind anything useful, and occasionally it rang and then I had a job to do that fit someone who was dead but still moving around. I had a bank account, and I had plenty of money sitting in it for a rainy day. I had a low profile.

No matter what, I always had a low profile. I always knew how to fit in, even though I was dead. Even though I killed people.

Even though I have occasionally...

Just occasionally... I may have...

I may have eaten...

You know what? I have better things to do right now than think about that.

For a start, the bad men are pulling their guns.

They're pulling their guns. My legs uncoil and I sail up, arcing forward, the first bullet passing through the space I've left behind me. I hold time in my mind, keeping it running at a reasonable speed, not too slow, not too fast. Behind me, the last shards of glass from the window hit the floor. At this speed, it sounds like wind chimes clanging softly in the breeze. The gunshots sound like the bellows of prehistoric monsters. The shells clang against the stone like church bells.

Did you ever see *The Matrix*?

Bit of a busman's holiday, I thought.

My own gun roars and I'm almost surprised. The bullet drills slowly into the head of the nearest man, already fragmenting, leaving a bloody caste-mark in the very centre of his forehead, the flesh rippling slightly under the pull of an obscene tide. I watch the exact moment when the look of surprise freezes on his face, goes slack, and then the back of his skull swings open slowly like multi-faceted cathedral doors, and the pulsing chunks of white-pink matter float out, carnival-day balloons for a charnel-house Mardi Gras.

Slow it down enough, and everything fascinates. Everything is beautiful.

Little chunks of brain, flying through the air. Scudding like clouds. Floating like jellyfish. I'm casting about for a better simile here because I don't want to admit what they really look like to me.

Tasty little hors d'ouvres. Canapes.

The trouble with being able to slow down time for yourself is that it gives you far too much time to think. And I have better things to do right now than think about that.

I speed things up a little, force myself back on the job as the bullets move faster, one cutting the air next to my left ear, another whispering against the leg of my jeans. My empty hand slaps on the concrete ahead of me and pushes my body up through space, somersaulting until I land on my feet behind a wall of stacked crates. I'm not sure what's in them, but hopefully it's something like dumbbells or lead sinkers or metal sheeting or just big blocks of concrete. Something that'll stop small arms fire. I don't want to patch up any more holes in myself.

There's a sound coming from close by. It's not wind chimes or church bells or a prehistoric monster. It sounds like some kind of guttural moaning, like a monster lost in an ancient dungeon.

I let go of time and it folds back around me like bad origami. The moment passes.

The sound makes some sense now.

It's a child. Sobbing. From inside the crate I'm hiding behind.

That's where they put Katie, then.

At least it wasn't paedophiles. At least it wasn't 'SAY A PRAYER FOR LITTLE KATIE SAYS OUR PAGE 3 STUNNER'. That's something in today's world, isn't it?

It was an old-fashioned kidnap. Scrambled voice mp3 file, two days after she went missing, nestled in amongst the inbox spam with the fake designer watches and the heartfelt pleas from exiled Nigerian royalty. 'Give us the money, Mr. Bellows, or we give you the finger. Do you see what we did there? It's a pun.' Then a time and a place and an amount to leave and no funny business, please.

Mr. Bellows runs a company called Ritenow Educational Solutions. He's the one who prints the certificates when you do the adult courses.

'This is to certify that MARJORIE PHELPS has achieved PASS in the study of INTERMEDIATE POTTERY.'

Marjorie won't get any kind of job with the certificate, even if she achieves DISTINCTION in the study of ADVANCED SHORTHAND. It's worthless, but she'll pay up to a couple of hundred pounds to have it on her wall and point it out to the neighbours.

Mr. Bellows doesn't run any of the courses. He doesn't make the sheets of china blue card with the silvery trim and 'This is to certify has achieved in the study of' written in the middle, with gaps. He just has a list of who's passed and what they got, and he runs that through a computer and then his big printer churns out ten or twenty thousand useless certificates a day. He has a staff of three single mothers and a temp who's just discovered The Specials and thinks that makes him unique, and all they do is collate the list of the gold, silver and bronze medal winners in these Housewife Olympics and then print them onto china blue with silver edging and sell them on for exorbitant amounts of money.

Mr. Bellows runs a company that does essentially nothing to make essentially nothing. He's the middleman for a useless end product. He's living the British Dream.

And now, the British Nightmare.

Doing nothing to make nothing is a profitable line of work. Mr. Bellows has two houses and two cars, neither of which have more than two seats. He also has a flat in Central London which he's working up the courage to install a mistress in. Little Katie Bellows is going to Roedean as soon as she's old enough. If she gets old enough. Mrs Bellows collects antique furniture as a hobby. And Mr. Bellows has my mobile number.

That doesn't come cheap.

"Find them, John," he said.

He had whisky on his breath and his voice came from somewhere deep in his throat, rough and hollow, choked with bile. "Find them and kill them. Bring her back safe." There were tears in his eyes that didn't want to come out. A big, gruff man who could solve things with his fists if he had to, but not this. Standing in the drawing room he'd earned with graft and grift and holding my dead hand and trying not to cry. The echo of his wife's soft sobbing drifting down from an upstairs bedroom. An antique clock on the mantelpiece that hadn't been wound, silent next to a photo turned face down because it couldn't be looked at.

Frank Bellows had my number because he'd used me in the past to do things that weren't strictly legal. He hadn't always had the monopoly on doing nothing to make nothing. He'd needed someone who didn't strictly exist to break into a competitor's office and burn it to the ground. Because if the perpetrator doesn't strictly exist, then it isn't arson, is it? Not strictly.

I smiled gently behind my shades, a non-committal little reassurance. Then I stepped back and nodded gently. He only sagged.

"Get them. Kill them. Get out." His voice was choked as though something was crawling up from inside him, some monster of grief that had made its nest in the pit of his stomach. I felt sorry, but what could I do? They only make promises in films.

But then, they only make this kind of kidnap in films. If they'd been real crooks, well, she'd be vanished still. 'HUNT FOR MISSING KATIE CONTINUES PAGE EIGHT. Saucy Sabrina, 17, holds back the tears as she keeps abreast of the news of Little Katie – and speaking of keeping a breast! MISSING KATIE BINGO IN THE STAR TODAY.'

These weren't 'real' crooks. They were fictional. The script-written ransom note. The suits from Tarantino, the bickering and sniping at each other with perfect quips that they'd spent months thinking up, while I stood on the warehouse skylight, the one they hadn't even bothered to check, picking my moment to crash through the glass and kill them all because the customer is always right. The lack of any covering of tracks, because they were too busy being 'professional' to actually be professional.

There's nothing more dangerous than a man who's seen a film.

The police would have found them eventually, but by that time Katie, age six, probably would have been killed.

They're keeping her in a crate and shooting at her, for God's sake.

It can't be healthy.

Bullets smashing wood, sending splinters and fragments into the air, puffs of shredded paper. The crates are full of catalogues, thick directories of day-glo plastic for schools. 'Teach your child about disabilities. Neon wheelchairs help kids learn.' Most of the bullets thump into those, gouging tunnels and trenches until their energy is spent.

One comes right through the crate I'm hiding behind. Right through, and there's a little yelp. A little girl's half-scream, too frightened to come all the way out.

The silly bastards have hit her.

Instinctively, I grab time and squeeze it until it breaks. Dead stop.

This is the slowest I can go. I look at the bullet, crawling from the hole. Slightly squashed but unfragmented. No blood on it. It missed.

Oh, thank God.

I'd never have managed to explain that.

Time rushes past me like a tube train and my legs hurl me backwards, firing over the top of the crates at them. Follow me. Shoot at the catalogues. No father's going to mourn a listing of expensive fluorescent dolls with only one leg. Shoot the crates over here, you silly bastards, you wannabe film-stars.

And they do.

I squeeze off a couple of shots at them, but they've found their own cover. More crates, more catalogues. Right now they seem to just be blazing away with their guns held sideways like in a music video. When they run out of bullets they'll probably chuck them at me. The trouble is, they're such rubbish shots, because of their crappy sideways gun shooting and their stupid unprofessional Tarantino mindset that thinks all they have to do is blaze away and the bullet will magically find its way into my face if they can only look cool enough doing it, that they're going to blow Katie's head off long before they put a hole in me.

It's time I got a little bit creative.

One of the advantages of being dead is that you can do things that people who aren't dead can't do. Actually, most people who are dead can't do them either, but never mind that for now. The important thing is that I can do them.

For example, my left hand – the one not sporadically pointing the gun over the crates and keeping them busy – is severed. It's held on with surgical wire.

I have no idea when this happened.

I mean, it must have been done after I woke up ten years ago. Surely. Nobody living has their hand chopped off and stuck back on the stump with surgical wire.

I mean, you'd have to be insane.

What sort of person was I?

My memory is a little fuzzy on things like that – whether I'm insane or not. I do kill a lot of people.

And I do eat... occasionally, I do eat people's...

But I have better things to do right now than think about that.

I shoot off three or four rounds to keep them busy, then put the gun to one side and grip my left hand in my right. And I pull. I'm a lot stronger than the average person, even the alive ones. Since I feel no pain and never need to rest, my muscles can work much harder, strain much longer. The wire snaps easily, link by link, and my hand pops right off in a couple of seconds, like a limb off a Ken doll.

Now I'm holding my left hand in my right, feeling the dead weight of it. Only it's not dead. Well, it is, but it's still wriggling. Twitching. Flexing.

I can still move it.

I wiggle the fingers on my severed hand. I snap them, and the sound is like a dry twig snapping. Then I toss it over the wall of crates like a grenade – a hand grenade, ha ha. The fingers hit the floor first and skitter like the legs of a giant beetle. I can feel them tapping the concrete. And then – it's off. Racing across the concrete floor as the wannabe filmstar boys widen their eyes and make little gagging sounds in their throats. They know what kind of film they're in now. Oh yes.

I can feel it moving. I can feel the fingers tapping. I'm reaching to pick up my gun, but I know exactly where my other hand is. Moving quickly across the floor, skittering and dancing, a dead finger ballet. I can see it in my mind's eye. Is it me, drumming my fingers, that's propelling it along? Or is it my hand, moving further away from me now, a separate entity crawling and creeping on its own stumpy little legs?

The further away from me it gets, the more I think it's the latter.

The more it moves on its own.

That's pretty weird, if you think about it.

What sort of person was I?

I can still feel the fingers tapping, but I'm not directing it any more. It's close now. Skittering around the crates as they lower their guns and stare in horrified fascination. I can't help but hum to myself at moments like these.

Their house is a museum... when people come to see 'em... they really are a scree-um... the Addams Fam-i-ly.

Ba da da DUM.

It leaps.

I mentioned how strong I am. And when my hand is this far away from me... there's really no human impulses to hold it back. The fingers flex and push against the concrete and launch it forward like a grasshopper, onto the face of the nearest cinema tough-guy. He's in a film now, all right. He's in *Alien*.

Where's your Tarantino now, you tosser?

Fingers clutch, sinking into cheeks. I can feel his lips against my palm, squashed, pleading desperately, trying to form words. I have no control over my hand, my evil hand. But I still enjoy feeling it squeeze... and squeeze... and squeeze... until the fingers plunge through the flesh and crack the bone, crushing the jaw, the thumb and the forefinger alone mustering enough pressure to punch through the temples, cracking the skull, sending ruptured brain matter seeping out of it.

Brain matter.

I've got better things to do than think about that.

My hand drops away, sticky with blood and juice, as the last one starts blazing away at it, shrieking like a little girl. He misses every shot. It's a hard thing to hit, a scuttling hand, and besides he's probably still holding his gun sideways. I'm trying not to laugh, I really am.

Does that make me a bad person? Does that make me a monster?

What sort of person am I?

Crushing a man's face with my severed hand that crawls around on its own when I let it off the leash, that probably makes me a monster, I'll admit that. But I can be forgiven for the occasional chuckle at the death of a would-be child murderer. *The News Of The World* would canonise me.

His gun clicks out. He's fumbling for ammo now. He's in a whole other world now, the silly bastard. There's nothing so important to him as killing that thing that's come scuttling around the corner of his little school-catalogue fort and broken everything he thinks is real into little pieces. He's forgotten everything else in the world, which is stupid, because I'm in the world.

And I'm coming for him.

Grab time. Slow it down. Gunshots flatten and stretch into whale songs and I'm floating, somersaulting over the crates, converse trainers smacking the ground, propelling me forward as the gun comes round...

And there aren't any bullets in the gun.

How did I miss that? The slide's all the way back.

Do I even have any ammo on me?

How could I possibly miss something like that?

What sort of person am I?

He's seen me. He turns like a cloud formation revolving in a light breeze. The gun lifts like the thermometer in an unsuccessful TV telethon, one atom at a time. So slow. But so am I.

That's the trouble with compressing time. It looks great, but there's no use in slowing time down if you're already too late.

The gun goes off, slow and beautiful as sunrise, and here comes the bullet. Cross-cut head this time. I throw my weight off, but he's too close...

You need a bit of space to dodge bullets.

I don't feel pain, but still, it hurts. It hurts because there's no real way to patch the holes up when I get shot. I've been shot a fair bit, although not as much as I should have with the life I lead. In my arms and legs there are little tunnels and trenches where I've been shot with 9mm ammunition, a couple of nasty exit wounds packed up with clay. In my left breast, there's a big ragged hole from where some crack shot tore my heart open with a well-placed sniper round. I stitched up the hole as best I could, packed it with gauze... but my heart is sitting in my chest, not beating and torn apart. And that does hurt.

Because I do try to know what sort of person I am.

I do try to be normal.

I really do, with my severed hand and my time senses and my strength and my speed. I try and be a normal guy, as much as I can. I drink, I eat, I go to the bathroom, though it's just to sit and think for a while – there's no pressing need for me to be there, if you get my meaning. I go to the cinema and watch the popular films. I get popcorn. I used to watch *Big Brother* but now I've stopped, like everyone else. I buy *The Sun* but I get my actual news from the Internet. I listen to Radio 2. I make up opinions about religion and music and television and political parties and I try to stick to them even if they aren't very logical or intelligent. I want to be like everyone else.

I want to fit in.

I try.

I can feel the bullet press against my gut, then pierce the skin, boring into me, fragmenting, splitting, shrapnel shredding my intestines, cutting and tearing. Slowly and carefully, like surgeons' scalpels in a random operation, the surgery dictated by the roll of dice.

My arm moves forward, pushing against time. It's like I'm underwater. The gun begins to arc slowly through the air, my empty, heavy gun. Rolling and tumbling through space.

Chunks of tattered, bloody meat drift out of the ragged hole in my lower back. My T-shirt has 'The Dude Has Got No Mercy' written across it, and it's brown with kind of seventies lettering in orange and white. It's my favourite shirt and it's ruined. My shirt's ruined. My belly's ruined, because I was stupid and this silly filmstar wannabe bastard got off his lucky shot...

I watch the gun tumble through space, turning over and over, like a space station on a collision course with a nameless, forbidding planet.

I threw it very hard. The sound of his skull fracturing is like a great slab of granite, big as the world, being snapped in half by cosmic giants. It's a good sound. It makes me feel better about my shirt.

Stitch that, bastard.

I let go, and time closes over me like the case for an old pair of spectacles. The moment passes, and I stumble for a couple of steps, feeling more meat slop out of my belly and back, more scraps on the floor. There's a hard thud as a hundred and fifty pounds of flesh that used to be a human being crashes onto the concrete.

I walk gingerly around the stacked crates and have a look. His legs and arms are thrashing, his eyes rolled back in the sockets. His skull is cracked and bleeding. His fragile, fractured eggshell skull.

And the tasty yolk within.

And all of a sudden –
– all of a sudden my head is pounding and there's a hot
metal taste in my mouth and I don't have anything better
to do than think about –

– Brains –

– and now it's later.

How much later? How much time has passed?
It feels like a long time.

Mr Tarantino, the filmstar, the silly bastard, he's still
lying at my feet. His position's changed. Like he's been
shaken about like a rag doll.

His head is... empty.
Hollowed out. The top of it missing, cranium tossed
across the room, and there's something... something is
clinging to my lips. To my tongue.
Something I've been eating.
The taste is still in my mouth.
And it tastes so good.

Time is still slow, still in my grip. I look to the left, and
I see a small, terrified eye staring at me through a bullet
hole in the side of a packing crate. The eye slowly closes,
like a curtain majestically falling, then rising, opening
again. Blinking.

There's a sound in my ears like lowing cattle. It's Katie's
sobbing. I wonder how much she saw?
I try to be normal. I really do. I try so hard.
But I just can't seem to stop eating brains.
And that's the sort of person I am.
I let go.
Time wraps around me like a funeral shroud.
And the moment passes.

For more information on this
and other titles visit...

Abaddon
Books

Price: £6.99 ★ ISBN: 1-905437-13-7

Price: $7.99 ★ ISBN 13: 978-1-905437-13-9

Simon Spurrier

The CULLED

THE AFTERBLIGHT CHRONICLES

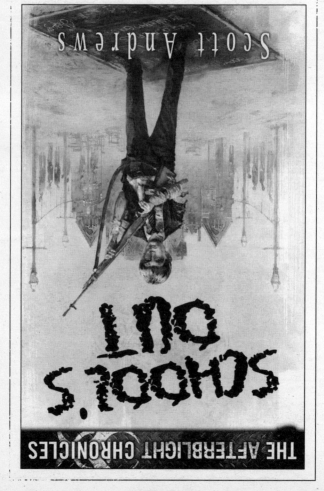

Price: £6.99 ★ ISBN: 1-905437-40-4

Price: $7.99 ★ ISBN 13: 978-1-905437-40-5

SNIPER ELITE

SPEAR OF DESTINY

Jaspre Bark

Price: £6.99 ★ ISBN: 1-905437-04-8

Price: $7.99 ★ ISBN 13: 978-1-905437-04-7

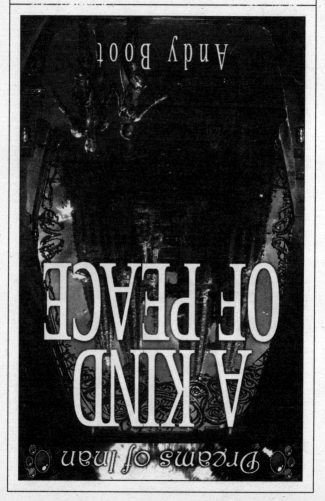

Also Available

Dreams of Inan

STEALING LIFE

Antony Johnston

Price: £6.99 ★ ISBN: 1-905437-12-9

Price: $7.99 ★ ISBN 13: 978-1-905437-12-2

Price: £6.99 ★ ISBN: 1-905437-53-6

Price: $7.99 ★ ISBN 13: 978-1-905437-53-5

Also Available

PAX BRITANNIA

UNNATURAL HISTORY

Jonathan Green

Price: £6.99 ★ ISBN: 1-905437-10-2

Price: $7.99 ★ ISBN 13: 978-1-905437-10-8

Also Available

PAX BRITANNIA

EL SOMBRA

Al Ewing

Price: £6.99 ★ ISBN: 1-905437-34-X

Price: $7.99 ★ ISBN 13: 978-1-905437-34-4

Abaddon Books